Look for Something Good

Robert Drews

Vertū Publishing, 2022

A Component of Vertū Marketing, LLC

VERTŪ PUBLISHING

A Component of Vertū Marketing LLC

Ordering Information:

Quantity sales. Special discounts are available on quantity purchases by corporations, associations, and others. For details, contact the publisher. Orders by U.S. trade bookstores and wholesalers please contact: Tel: (866) 779-0795.

publishing@vertu-marketing.com

Printed in the United States of America

ISBN 979-8-9870674-2-0

Acknowledgements

To Tylie Vaughan Eaves and her team at Vertu Publishing and Marketing, I thank you for your skills, graciousness, and assistance, and for giving me this opportunity. My appreciation to Lindsay and April for your continued encouragement and help, and a special shout-out to Caroline whose editing and keen eye for detail are beyond compare. Most of all, gratitude and love to my Lisa, for wisdom and support and for believing when I don't. I could not do this—or anything—without you. Every day at your side is a blessing.

Chapter 1

A penitent left the confessional and knelt in contemplation, crossed herself with holy water, and disappeared into the twilight. The pews finally empty except for him, J.J. Werth breathed a sigh of relief and checked his watch. It was unlikely anyone else would come in to bare their souls, not with only five minutes remaining in the confessional schedule on another glorious Friday evening in Southern California. Confession may be good for the soul, but here in God's country, clear skies and dinner out were more than enough for most people.

Late sunshine gleamed through a stained-glass window above the altar to create a brilliant mosaic on the aged but immaculate white tile floor of Saints Peter and Paul Catholic Church, like watercolors painted in light. J.J. took no notice. Instead he walked slowly to the booth, knelt inside, and folded his hands in prayer. He caught a breath to collect himself and began to speak. The words came slowly.

"Bless me, Father, for I have sinned. My last confession was a long time ago."

This was the first time in a week J.J. had put on anything other than pajama bottoms and a robe, let alone ventured outside. For days on end, he'd vegetated in bed, and yet, despite the endless hours in a semi-conscious state, he still felt like a dead man walking. His sleep, or attempts at it, were useless and exhausting as he tossed and turned fitfully, bound by wadded sheets and the oppressive weight of his own thoughts. On the rare occasions when he forced himself up, he had stumbled around his comfortable, ranch-style home in a well-kept but overpriced Los Angeles suburb. He'd eaten little beyond a few slices of watermelon and the remnants of a leftover restaurant salad that consisted of a few shredded carrots and more than enough iceberg lettuce browning around the edges. Picking at the sad pieces of salad, he shook his head at the idea of eating something most people, including himself not that long ago, would have tossed out days ago. What did it say about him? Was eating spoiled greens a metaphor for his life and loss of value? Did it—and he—really matter anymore?

When he had finally stopped to look at his image in a hallway mirror, the sight unnerved him—a confident and self-assured man who once took pride in his manicured, styled, and trimmed appearance, workouts at the gym, and neat-as-a-pin wardrobe, now reduced to a mess in sloppy clothes, five o'clock shadow grown into midnight, eyes turned from glowing to glossy. Worse yet, J.J. was disappointed in himself—of what his life had come to, what he had come to—in just the few days since the bolt out of the blue that played over and over in his mind like a movie with the same miserable ending.

The previous Friday felt like a lifetime ago that he walked into his office, whistling and content, ready for a full day and a fuller weekend. There were two appointments in the morning, one in the afternoon, and magnificent pastrami on rye from his favorite deli just around the corner to look forward to in between. Then for Saturday night, he had planned an outing for a Dodgers game and good company with his baseball buddy from church.

As was his custom, J.J. had arrived for work at six a.m., poured the first of his bottomless mugs of caffeine fix with a double dollop of cream from the office kitchen, and settled in at his desktop computer, where the world of finance—his world—was fingertips away. He adored the action of trading in stocks, bonds, commodities, and currencies and could not get enough of a love affair that had sparked the first time he picked up a copy of *The Wall Street Journal* his freshman year in high school. Majoring in business and finance in college, he had started as a stockbroker and, over the decades, moved up the ladder to vice president and financial consultant at a prominent investment house. He took pride in doing well for his clients and took satisfaction in the fact that they were more than names and numbers to him, offering words and tissues during bereavements and breakups and hugs and handshakes at new beginnings and new arrivals.

At seven a.m., his desk phone rang.

"Mr. Werth? This is Ms. Rasmussen. Ms. Wagner would like to see you."

J.J. chuckled at the sudden stilted greeting while not knowing what to make of it. Popular and well-liked, he had always been on a first-name basis with Ruth Wagner, his supervisor, and Jane Rasmussen, the receptionist, and everyone else in the office during their twenty-three years together.

"Hey, Jane, what's with the formality? It's not April first, but is this some kind of joke?"

She forced out the words. "Please, Mr. Werth. Ms. Wagner would like to see you immediately."

"Well, okay, Jane. I mean, Ms. Rasmussen. I'll be right over."

J.J. put his sport coat back on, straightened the bow tie and sweater vest, and poked his head into the boss's office. Ruth Wagner rearranged a pile of papers on her desk and looked up with serious eyes. She arose. "Please close the door behind you."

"What's going on with..." he started, but Ruth held up a hand and didn't let him finish. "I'm sorry, Mr. Werth, but we have to let you go."

J.J. stared at her in disbelief and felt his stomach churn as if the stock market had reprised the crash of 1929. A jumble of words swirled in his brain but only one came out in dry mouth.

"What?" He dropped into a chair.

"This is very hard for me to tell you, but we have to let you go," she repeated. "I fought hard, but you just got caught up in the numbers game after last year's merger. You know as well as I that a person can do all the right things and still end up on the wrong side. I'm so sorry and wish there were another way or something I could do."

As a student of the corporate world, J.J. knew what she was talking about, the flotsam of expendables cast off because of staff cutbacks, bad earnings, or the suits getting a bug and deciding to streamline. But the thought never crossed his mind that one day he might be among those getting the tap on the shoulder. Of course, no one ever expects it.

His eyes moistened, and his stomach felt so upset that he asked Ruth to bring him a cup of water. "When do I have to leave?"

She looked at the *Man of La Mancha* print on her wall, then moved from behind her desk and pulled up a chair next to his. "I'm afraid immediately. You have one hour to clean out your desk, and you will be escorted to your car. This is not my way of doing things, but I have my orders."

J.J. also knew this was how it was when employees were let go. Get them out the door before any shouting matches or mayhem, make the cut clean and quick, no time or occasion for drawn-out melancholy and drama in the hallways by the affected and their colleagues. And certainly no time for pilfering files or reaching out to clients.

"Well, I guess that's it. What about…"

Before he could ask about his compensation and benefits, Ruth spoke. "What about your severance package? Well, you may not be in line for a golden parachute," she said with the hint of a smile appearing, "but I think you will be satisfied, given the circumstances. I've seen to that. You will get a year's salary paid as a lump sum, retain your pension, and medical insurance will be continued until you turn sixty-five. The documentation will be FedExed to you today."

This was at least some consolation. Never one to live ostentatiously, J.J. didn't believe in denying himself either. He enjoyed the fruits of his hard work and earnings, loved to spend almost as much as he loved to save, grooved on financial planning, and at age sixty-one could get Social Security benefits in just a year, if need be, not that he would.

J.J. pushed back his chair, conscientious of the floor, and got up. "Ms. Wagner…Ruth…Thank you for that, and for everything. I know how difficult this must be for you. I have no hard feelings whatsoever and will always treasure my years here. Beyond that, I just don't know what else there is to say."

Ruth embraced him until he broke it off. They both dabbed away tears.

"I'm going to miss you, J.J. More than you'll ever realize. Please keep in touch."

"Count on it."

Jane sobbed at her desk when he walked back and, after a good cry himself, attempted to joke away their shared sadness.

"Look on the bright side," he said. "Now there'll be coffee here for everyone instead of me hogging it all day."

"Oh J.J., don't say that. You mean so much to me, to all of us…" She offered a weak smile, quick hug, and excused herself.

J.J. stood there alone with his thoughts, undecided whether to be mad, distraught, or something in between, until the security guard said it was time to go. He wordlessly returned to his desk, packed up, and went to his car.

An hour passed while he sat in the parking lot staring out the windshield and failing miserably at trying to calm himself now that the centerpiece of the life he had built and cherished was gone. Finally, he drove away, but before turning the corner out of the parking lot, he stole a final glance at the window of his darkened office, in its own way like a death in the family.

The days incarcerating himself at home dragged by in his blur of self-pity and anger until J.J. finally realized he was better than this, and it was time to talk and do some serious thinking. And so, he had arrived at the church at five, sat in the back pew, and closed his eyes, hoping to find some peace—or answers—in this holy place.

Memories drifted in.

Life was sweet, idyllic even, as a young boy on the third-generation ranch known as The Big & Little about thirty miles outside Billings. The "Big" inscribed on the arch over the driveway was for his dad, Alvin, respectfully known in those parts as Big Al. "Little" was for his mom, Evelyn, fondly called Little Evie by all who knew her, the nicknames endearing as much as showing the contrasts between them. Al, a born cattleman, stood all of a sturdy five-foot-five in his boots. Evie was a city girl and willowy with her six-foot-one frame. Their eyes met at a church social one Sunday afternoon in the spring, and after a two-year courtship, they married and happily settled into life on The Big & Little.

Al and Evie were both raised in one-child families, and they vowed it wouldn't be so in theirs. First came Charles Robert. Three miscarriages and nine years later, James Joseph entered the world. Jimmy, never J.J. in those carefree days, idolized his brother. The Werth boys were a fixture all over the countryside, doing chores, hiking, fishing, and horsing around, older and younger brother as close as any siblings could be. In the innocence of youth, J.J. vowed to never leave Charlie's side.

Their inevitable day of separation did not arrive when Charlie happily went off to college or walked down the aisle. Instead, he left the safety of The Big & Little fresh out of high school to enlist in the Army and march off to a war in Southeast Asia, many thousands of miles away. "Vietnam? I never heard of it," J.J. pleaded at the family conference after supper. "You can't go, Charlie. You might get hurt."

"Now, now," Big Al said in attempt at reassurance. "Your brother knows what he's doing."

Charlie looked at his brother. "Jimmy, we recite the Pledge of Allegiance every day at school and raise the Stars and Stripes in our own front yard. How can I do that and not answer when my country calls out for me to serve?"

Dad and Mom accepted his decision. Jimmy didn't, and the day Charlie departed, J.J. did not release the bear hug until Big Al pulled him away. "Please don't go," he yelled through tears as Charlie waved through the bus window.

That was the last time they saw each other. Instead of the usual letter Charlie would mail back home, one day there was a man in uniform at the door to deliver the news that Charlie had been killed, a casualty in the battle of Xa Cam My scarcely a year after the United States first committed troops to a conflict that ultimately left millions dead or wounded and tore America apart. A numb Jimmy saluted for a final farewell as his brother went to eternal rest in the family plot. Jimmy was ten years old.

Things changed after that.

Gradually his love of the ranch seeped away, and in his high school years, he knew life would take him away from there. He gravitated to math and economics and the world of business and became a devoted reader of *The Wall Street Journal*. Now going by J.J. to everyone except his mom and dad, only and always their Jimmy, he earned a bachelor's degree in business and an MBA at the University of Montana. He moved to an apartment in Billings and started work as a stockbroker.

J.J. strayed from the ranch life but not from his parents. Every Sunday he went with them to Mass, followed by one of Little Evie's glorious breakfasts centered around her legendary three-egg omelets. After that, they enjoyed a drive or watched a football or baseball game on TV, maybe going to a church function for fellowship followed by dinner at their favorite buffet, The Happy Rancher.

"Let's go for a walk, son," Big Al offered one morning after church. Evie came up between them and put her arms around both.

"Is something the matter, Dad?"

The awkward silence said there was.

His father spoke plainly. "I heard from the doctor this week that I have pancreatic cancer."

Evie started to weep.

"And it's not good," Big Al continued. "They figure I have four to six months, and I don't want any of that stuff they pump into you."

J.J.'s heart pounded. "Maybe the doctor is wrong."

"I don't think so."

"We'll pray for a miracle, love," Evie said.

J.J. prayed morning, noon, and night for one, but no miracle arrived. Three months later, Big Al was buried beside Charlie. And barely six months after that, Little Evie was there too, dead of a grief-induced heart attack. J.J. was twenty-eight years old.

The time had come to leave this part of his life behind, and so he did. J.J. sold the ranch and headed to the big city, first Chicago, then New York, Boston, and finally Los Angeles. Awakening mornings with giddyap and purpose in his step, his career as a financial adviser blossomed, as did his life outside the office.

He embraced the City of Angels, and it him. After the wintry blasts of Montana, the Midwest, and the East, California's climate was a blessing. Comfortable in his own skin, neither requiring nor rejecting companionship, J.J. loved the ocean and beaches, the hikes along golden hillsides, trips down to San Diego and Mexico, jaunts to Las Vegas. By now he had acquired some culture, loved art shows, museums, and fine restaurants, but he never forgot the simple pleasures of his boyhood home, frolicking with Charlie and playing cards with Big Al and Little Evie.

Mostly, he loved hanging out, kicking back on a park bench with a good book, sitting in the stands at Dodgers ballgames, heading to Hollywood to people watch, catching a movie at Grauman's Chinese Theatre (he refused to call it TCL Chinese Theatre), and grabbing a sausage sandwich from a sidewalk vendor. He regularly took vacation days to sit in the audiences of game shows. And the place he could never get enough of was Disneyland. Every year, J.J. bought an annual pass, and many of the workers knew him by name. Not a week went by that he didn't go there, if for no other reason than to sit on a bench along Main Street and ride the Disneyland Railroad.

Now and then, he felt an undimmed Big Al and Little Evie and Charlie beside him, train chugging, the four of them laughing and talking, a breeze caressing their faces, his imagination not allowing that, like the fantasies in this land of Disney, all things must come to an end.

Once J.J. got over the shock of being let go, a grim reality set in. Always he had had someone or something to fill his heart. Someone was always there to share with and love in times of joy, and they were there to turn to and lean on in times of distress. After Charlie died, he had his parents. After Big Al went, there was Mom. And after her, his career and fun in the big city reached out 24/7. Now there was no one and nothing to help him cross this void. No brothers or sisters, grandparents, aunts, uncles, cousins, wife, girlfriend, or children of his own. Ruth and Jane and other colleagues from the office called with sympathy, and clients— make that *former* clients—sent cards and flowers and filled his voicemail to capacity. But it wasn't the same. Even his favorite haunts gave him no joy. He felt no connection anywhere, with anyone.

For the first time in his life, James Joseph Werth felt totally alone.

Chapter 2

As much as he loved Charlie, J.J. felt some relief that his brother was not alongside him in the church pew. Big Al and Little Evie didn't raise their boys to feel sorry for themselves, and older never let younger get away with being a sore loser in a pickup basketball game or long-faced over a perceived slight. And yet J.J. knew that was exactly how he had been behaving, a grown man acting like a sniveling snot whose favorite toy had been taken away. Were Charlie alive to witness his pathetic pity party of the past week, J.J. could almost feel the whack coming upside the head.

He playfully gave himself one. "That's for you, big bro."

Once again in the world of the living, or at least in orbit around it, J.J. had been brought back to it by advice from beyond the grave. His mom and dad, both devout Christians, told him time and time again to always turn to and trust in the Lord, and they confided that without the comforting words of Scripture and their parish priest, they didn't know how they would have made it through Charlie's death.

J.J. had preceded his visit to church by falling to his knees in contrition at his bedside.

"I'm sorry, Mom and Dad. You raised me better, and I will do better. I promise. You, too, Charlie. I'll be strong, like you." Picking up the Bible his parents gave him when he turned seven, J.J. opened it to the inscription his mom had written in her flowery handwriting.

"I can do all these things in him who strengtheneth me."

Philippians 4:13

If J.J. hadn't heeded the words of Scripture and come to church still a whining basket case, the pastor waiting in the confessional would have given him a dose of respectability in short order. Father Thomas Kearns was a man of great compassion for society's needy, grieving, and broken. But for those who complained of the twenty-first-century pseudo-epidemic of stress, which most times amounted to a bad hair day in the grand scheme of things, he was a man of great conviction. "Jesus Christ wasn't a wimp, and neither should his followers be," he intoned to the young, old, and in-between who made the mistake, in his eyes, of being blessed and not being thankful to God for it.

Father Thomas sensed where and when to draw the line because he had experienced life on both sides of the fence. Born and raised in Cicero, Illinois, his domestic disaster was the product of a father who abandoned him within an hour of conception and a promiscuous mother, whose revolving-door of boyfriends got their kicks pushing him around. Growing up, Father Thomas came to be grateful to his dad, wherever he may be, for one thing. He was a big, powerful man, whose genes were passed from sire to colt. By the time his progeny reached puberty, the pushing stopped, and in high school, young Kearns advanced from punchee to puncher.

The smart-aleck editor of the student newspaper, after watching Thomas from a safe distance thrashing one of his victims, dubbed him "Mr. Charm" in his sophomore year. Later shortened to Mr. C, the nickname stuck, but anyone who wanted to keep his teeth intact or his nose in place never dared utter it within earshot of Thomas. Fueled with anger and armed by brute strength, Kearns was feared and avoided everywhere. He hated Cicero, his mother, her boyfriends, classes, teachers, everyone, life, himself. Somehow, he managed to stay out of jail. That he graduated from high school was a minor miracle, though many believed the district passed him because they didn't want him around any longer.

He showed up on graduation day, trading the traditional cap and gown for jeans, cowboy boots, a Cubs baseball cap, and a T-shirt boasting MR. C, CLASS OF '67 in big red letters. The crowd sat in amused silence as he walked across the stage for his diploma. The principal warmly shook his hand, even gave him a slight pat on the back.

Like Charlie Werth, Kearns heard the siren call of Vietnam but not out of duty and patriotism. Instead, he envisioned the twin opportunities of death and destruction, and he couldn't wait. The day after graduating, he enlisted in the Marines, went home, threw his diploma on the dirty kitchen table, and announced, "Doris, I'm going to Vietnam to kick ass and kill Commies."

"Good for you," she shot back. "And don't you think just once you could call me Mom?"

Kearns glared. "Have a nice life. Doris."

He walked out and slammed the door behind him.

He intended to never see his mother again.

Warfare was nothing like Kearns expected, and it was exactly what he needed. Two tours of inflicting death and agony on a people he knew nothing about and witnessing the same inflicted on his friends and brothers-in-arms, sometimes holding them at their last breath, drove the rage right out of him. In the years to come, he would tell confidantes that the only things keeping him together some days and nights near the end of his time there were praying with the infantry chaplain and humming to himself the Beach Boys' song "Little Deuce Coupe."

Kearns didn't know if it was fact or legend, but a buddy back from patrol with him told of reading about a Japanese fighter pilot in World War II who, after multiple kills of the enemy in the Pacific, returned to civilian life and pledged never to kill another living thing, not even a mosquito, for the rest of his days.

He couldn't vouch for mosquitoes, but Kearns determined to never take another human life, and more than that, he vowed to help save them whenever and wherever he could. This was not always easy for a man who, for most of his life, had let his fists, or worse, do his talking. He fell into fits of depression over the wrongs he had done and, from time to time, looked not above for answers but down into the bottom of a glass. Eventually, however, fortified by veterans' benefits and a growing faith in Jesus Christ, he earned a bachelor's degree in philosophy from the University of Illinois, then enrolled in and graduated from Saint Joseph College Seminary. An ardent student of the Bible and a messenger of its power, he took his vows as Father Thomas Kearns at the age of thirty-eight on September 15, 1987. He called it his day of resurrection.

Father Thomas allowed himself one gift shortly after joining the priesthood. Going into a tattoo parlor in downtown Chicago, he asked for *Semper Fi* in modest letters on his left bicep. "With respect, you're the first priest I've had in here," said the artist, a muscled young man named Adam.

"With respect, I'll bet I'm not your first Marine."

The artist laughed. "Right you are, Father."

The inscription complete, when Father Thomas reached for his wallet to pay, Adam held up a hand. "On the house."

As to his name, Father Thomas owed one debt of gratitude to his mother. He discovered in his Bible readings that the name she picked suited him perfectly. Many in the Catholic community associated the apostle Thomas with the doubt he felt after Jesus rose from the dead, refusing to believe in the Resurrection until he saw and touched the Lord's wounds. Father Thomas chose instead to focus on the zeal and courage described in John 11, when his patron saint declared his willingness to accompany the Lord to the dangerous Judea after Lazarus died. "Let us also go, that we may die with him." Father Thomas could recite the entire passage, verses 1 through 16, by heart, and once, in a moment of lightheartedness during his nightly prayers, looked up and said, "Lord, you would've made one fine Marine."

The priesthood took Father Thomas to people and parishes around the country, where he was always immensely popular. His first assignment out of seminary was down the highway a piece to Springfield, followed by Albany, Lexington, Santa Fe, El Paso, and finally Los Angeles, where he was appointed pastor at Saints Peter and Paul Catholic Church. He was sixty years old when he headed west and knew this would be his final mission.

Father Thomas was filled with the Holy Spirit, loved the priesthood, and thanked God every day for leading him to it. As he looked back, he realized the Almighty had designed every step of his path, that the difficulties in his early years were preparation for him to help and guide people on their earthly journeys. Divine intervention was not some abstract notion but a living, breathing reality that carried him through childhood, high school, and the Marines. He told the hopeless that sometimes God answers prayers even when they aren't prayed and that he did not always answer them as the petitioner wished, no matter how fervent or frequent the appeal.

Blessed with empathy, Father Thomas sensed when to speak

and when not to, knowing that the grieving and hopeless don't always need to hear another voice. Sometimes they just need someone to listen. When led to speak, the priest always concluded with the Our Father. Eyes closed and holding hands with the distressed, he prompted, and they followed. "Our Father, who art in heaven, hallowed be Thy name. Thy kingdom come, Thy will be done, on earth as it is in heaven." Afterward, in the silence of his heart, Father Thomas never failed to thank God that his will prevails and that God makes it known.

The conviction motivated him every day of his priestly life.

But Father Thomas was not only a man of God. He was also a man of God's kingdom on earth, and he greatly enjoyed the pleasures therein—a good cigar, a funny movie, the racetrack, doughnuts, oldies music, playing "Be Thou My Vision" on his violin. At the top of his list of favorites were hot dogs and baseball, preferably together but not a requirement.

It was in the enjoyment of those twin indulgences that the lives of James Joseph Werth and Father Thomas Kearns intersected on a starry Saturday night, their unforeseen roles as confessional penitent and pastor two years in the future.

Chapter 3

J.J. waited in line at a concession stand. It was still an hour until game time, but he always endeavored to be at his seat when the National Anthem played before the first pitch. In all his years attending baseball, he never once missed standing at attention and singing "The Star-Spangled Banner" in memory and honor of his brother.

"Beautiful night for a ballgame, isn't it, my brother?"

He turned to the words from behind him and was momentarily speechless. A man about J.J.'s age stood ramrod straight, a shade under six-foot-five, a shade over 260 pounds, head of black hair accented by a ponytail that stretched three inches below his neckline and touched off with a neatly trimmed goatee. In the heart of Dodgers Country, he wore a weather-beaten Cubs cap. The black shirt and trousers, white collar, and plain wooden cross hanging at his chest from a silver chain quickly identified him as a man of the cloth.

His brown eyes blazed.

"That it is, Father. That it is," J.J. answered amiably. After a pause, he added, "Let's play two."

"I see you followed the Cubs back in the day," the priest said and laughed heartily. "Ernie Banks, my man." His was a happy laugh, the laugh of a man at peace with who he was and where he was. He extended a hand.

"I am Father Thomas Kearns."

"I'm happy to meet you. People call me J.J."

Father Thomas squinched his eyes. "Hm. J.J. I don't recall that name anywhere in the Bible."

"It stands for James Joseph, but I have gone by J.J. for many years."

"If I may, I would prefer to call you James," Father Thomas answered. "A good biblical name. His little book has some of the most instructive readings in Scripture."

James.

J.J. liked the sound of it. No one had ever called him that, not even his mom when he acted up as a boy. And, J.J. figured, who was he to argue with this mountain of humanity, let alone a priest, let alone a man with a voice so melodious, indeed almost angelic, that it seemed to come from the Holy Spirit itself? He surveyed Father Thomas, certain it would be wrong to call him Father Tom.

His intuition was spot on.

Awaiting their turn to be served, they discussed the merits of Dodger Dogs as opposed to the Chicago Vienna, Costco Special, and New York street vendor franks.

Not only did they agree on the superb delicacy of the wieners in question, but they also found themselves in lockstep at the condiments table. Both smiled good-naturedly while slathering their dogs with deli mustard and drowning them in onions and relish.

"Would you like to join me in my suite?" Father Thomas offered.

J.J. saw no harm in it. "Why not?"

Neither J.J. nor Father Thomas had any problem being alone; in fact, they enjoyed it. Yet, when good company presented itself, they were not ones to turn it down, and both quickly sensed a compatibility with the other.

J.J. did a double-take when he arrived at the suite.

"Father Thomas, you have the best seat in the house."

"I'm glad you agree, James. I wouldn't sit anywhere else."

They took their place in the left field bleachers. The wide expanse of gorgeous green opened in front of them. Beauty aside, the seats offered many other pluses. They afforded a bird's-eye view of the action, the possibility of catching a home run ball, joining with brethren who knew and appreciated the nuances of the game, and a good chance for moving somewhere else should an obnoxious lout sit nearby.

The two made a curious pair. If Father Thomas' stature and spirituality could fill a room, J.J.'s blended in like tasteful wallpaper in a finely appointed study. Smoothly dressed as usual, his blue jeans were ironed to a crease. A blue Polo shirt matched his bright LA baseball cap. A touch over six feet and a touch under 180 pounds, he kept his light brown hair cut stylishly short. His face was smooth, his hazel eyes gentle.

The Anthem played. The two stood and sang along, J.J. with his right hand over heart, Father Thomas in a crisp salute.

They clapped at the first pitch and at the last out and liked the two hours and fifty minutes in between. When it was over, the Dodgers prevailing by a score of 4–2, J.J. and Father Thomas shook hands and went their separate ways.

During the remainder of that 2015 season, all of the next one, and the early stages of the one after that, they shared Saturday nights off and on, always by chance. They met at the customary place in line for Dodger Dogs, said the customary grace before taking the first luscious mouthful, and strolled to the customary suite out in left field. In time, theirs blossomed into a breezy, comfortable acquaintanceship. They enjoyed watching baseball together, commenting between innings on a play, hit, pitch, or the goodness of heaven on a bun at the ballpark.

Neither man ever discussed his past or his future and only rarely his present. One of those occasions happened during their second summer together in the eighth inning of a slow, lopsided game against the Atlanta Braves on a night when all but the diehards had left to beat the tedium and the traffic. Without turning his head, Father Thomas said softly, "James, I take it you are a Christian?" Having expected something more along the lines of "Who do you think was better, Henry Aaron or Willie Mays?" J.J. was surprised by the question but not uncomfortable with it. He took a sip of beer before answering. "Yes, Father, I am. My parents were devout Catholics and loved the Bible, and I have faithfully attended Mass on Sundays all of my adult life. I read Scripture daily, or try to."

The priest looked over and smiled. "I'm glad to hear that. All good in life comes from our Heavenly Father's teachings. If I may ask, where do you go to church?"

"I've gone to Saint Justin's ever since moving to Los Angeles about twenty years ago. I always attend the eight a.m. Mass."

"Ah, Saint Justin's. I know the pastor, Father Luke, very well. He is a good man, a holy man."

"Yes, I like him very much."

"In fact, he and I recently co-hosted a Bible study on James 2:17. Do you know it?"

The game plodded on.

The only verse J.J. had committed to memory was the cherished one from Philippians his mom bequeathed in the Bible.

"No, I'm afraid I don't."

"It goes, 'So also faith of itself, if it does not have works, is dead.'"

J.J. wasn't sure if Father Thomas was sermonizing him, which seemed unlikely given the casual nature of their relationship, or making conversation, which seemed more plausible before their talk took a turn.

"The pastor does have one failing," Father Thomas said, J.J. raising an eyebrow at the surprisingly blunt remark about a fellow man of the cloth and a friend at that.

"Oh?"

"He's a Cardinals fan."

The two chuckled together, perhaps at the joke, perhaps at the futility of Dodgers' pitchers this night after collectively issuing their fourth walk of the inning and ninth of the game. Making the notation in his scorecard, Father Thomas spoke again.

"I'm the pastor at Saints Peter and Paul. It's a beautiful church with a wonderful congregation."

"I know right where your church is. I've driven by several times but never went in."

"Well, consider this an open invitation."

"Thank you, Father. I just may join you sometime."

The game mercifully ended for the home team twenty minutes later, the final tally, in the words of broadcaster Vin Scully, "Atlanta a lot, Los Angeles a little."

J.J. and Father Thomas walked to their cars, shook hands, and went their separate ways.

Chapter 4

Fall and football permeated the air. With each passing year, Father Thomas liked the former more and more because it brought relieving cool in the weather, the latter less and less because it brought unhappy realization that baseball season was drawing to a close.

September zoomed by, and soon it was the last Sunday of the month. Four weeks had passed since Father Thomas talked of Scriptures and his parish with J.J., and he worried that perhaps he had been too forward with his baseball brother.

The concern proved to be groundless when the priest took the pulpit to greet the congregation at Saints Peter and Paul Church for the eight a.m. Mass.

Father Thomas smiled when he noticed J.J. and smiled even more broadly at his chosen place—the far-right side of the second-last pew—and made a mental note. In all the years J.J. attended Mass as an adult, he occupied the same spot he occupied as now, always arriving plenty early to guarantee his seat and allowing time to pray, meditate, and shut out the world.

J.J. smiled back and waved a hand in hello. He liked Saints Peter and Paul from the moment he crossed the parking lot, and not just because of his friend up front.

Benches inscribed with benefactors' names reached out along the front walkway. A last planting of daisies fluttered as if greeting the worshippers, and sparrows sang avian hymns from their perches in three fruit trees—one lemon, two apple—that provided shade on hot summer days and steady yields of produce for a nearby homeless shelter.

The serenity outside paled against the understated majesty within. The church's patron saints themselves would have felt at home preaching in this holy place of stained glass, immaculate pews, plain wooden altar, and fourteen ornate Stations of the Cross spaced evenly along brown plaster walls. As the bells pealed a call to worship like a mother beckoning her flock to the supper table, parishioners of all ages and walks poured in, many in their Sunday finest, others in slacks and blouses, some in T-shirts and torn jeans, drawing old-school *tsks tsks*. The church filled to its capacity of over three hundred.

At eight o'clock on the dot, Father Thomas stood at the altar and uplifted his arms.

"The Lord be with you."

"And with your spirit," the parishioners answered.

"Good morning, my dear brothers and sisters. I pray you are

well and happy, loving our Heavenly God on this glorious Sunday.""Amen!" and "Praise the Lord!" rang out.

As Mass proceeded, J.J. joined in praise and song in this happy church, a blessed place of worship filled with love of the Lord and deep affection and respect for the pastor. He sensed the contentment here could be his for a long time. To him, church was a retreat as much as a house of God, a source of comfort as much as one of forgiveness, and he felt no guilt for letting his mind wander in prayer or contemplation during the sermons. Today he thought back to his parents and brother joining in their Sabbath mainstay, "Be Thou My Vision," when Father Thomas moved in front of the altar. Years ago, he had abandoned the podium for celebrating Mass and delivering his Bible message, saying in explanation, "I want to share testimony, not deliver a speech."

An ambulance roared past. Its siren pierced the morning stillness, faded, and dissipated quickly.

"Like the Lord, I love parables. I can't lay claim to creating this one I am about to share, but I do lay claim to repeating it," Father Thomas intoned, drawing a chuckle from the congregants.

"One time, heavy rains caused a river to flood, and residents in a small town were told to evacuate. All left but one, who said upon hearing the warning on TV, 'I trust in the Lord.'

"Water started pouring down streets. A police SUV traveled down the man's street, a voice on loudspeaker announcing, 'Anyone still here come outside and get into the van.' The man opened his door and responded, 'I trust in the Lord.'

"The water rose up to his doorway. Two people in a motorboat went slowly down the street and yelled, 'If anyone is here, come outside and save yourself.' The man opened a second-story window and told them, 'I trust in the Lord.'

"The water poured into his house. The man managed to get to the roof. A police helicopter flew over, an officer calling out, 'We'll lower a ladder and bring you up to safety.' The man called back, 'I trust in the Lord.'

"Floodwaters swamped the house, carrying the man to his death. Arriving in heaven, he said to the Lord, 'I put my trust in you, but you never answered, and I died.'

"The Lord answered, 'What are you talking about? I sent you an SUV, a boat, and a helicopter.'"

The couple next to J.J. applauded, drawing an embarrassed stare from their teenage daughter. J.J. mocked a tip of the hat approvingly toward Father Thomas.

"The message, my dear friends, is that when our Lord extends his loving hand, we must not only accept his refuge but also, as believers, draw on his strength to do our part. Faith and works go hand in hand."

Twenty minutes later, the Mass ended, and Father Thomas stood just outside the entrance, where departing worshippers stopped for thank yous, hugs, and handshakes, like the receiving line after a wedding.

The priest beamed when J.J. walked up.

"James, so good to see you."

"It was wonderful being here. I very much enjoyed it," he answered.

"And I see you like sitting in the outfield at church too."

J.J. paused and then said, "I've never thought of it that way, but you are exactly right, Father."

After a few more pleasantries, the two went their separate ways.

The remaining weeks and months of 2016 passed. By the New Year, J.J. became a regular at the Sunday worship, no offense to Father Luke, Saint Justin's, or Saint Louis. He always received Holy Communion, regularly participated in the responsorial prayers, and even started listening to and reflecting on Father Thomas' testimonials.

But he never did go to confession, preferring to express sins in his own direct audience with the Almighty, until his world tumbled down on that glorious Friday evening the following spring.

Chapter 5

Father Thomas' watch displayed a few minutes to seven after a penitent left the confessional. Awaiting him at the parsonage were a slow cooker of chili and a couple of hours to unwind watching the Dodgers on the road against archrival San Francisco. Over the years, he had decorated and fashioned the cottage a short walk from the church into a reflection of himself, from a modestly appointed living room with an ancient TV console and a plain wooden crucifix mounted above it, to the bedroom, freshened daily with flowers sent over by the parish office. The small study served as go-to retreat with a wall of meditational and murder mystery books and, above his oak rolltop desk, a photo of a donkey lovingly nuzzling her foal. Whenever anyone pointed to it and asked about the photo when joining him for counsel, prayer, or company—and they often did—Father Thomas explained that Jesus entered Jerusalem not majestically as a warrior on a chariot or a prince on a white horse but humbly as a redeemer on a colt, just as we must walk with our God.

Like always, the retreat could wait on this splendid Friday. His mission at the moment was to serve the parishioners, and it was no problem at all if they came to confession until midnight or the crack of dawn. Still, Father Thomas was mildly surprised when the confessional door opened and someone entered and knelt just as he prepared to lock up and leave.

The voice surprised him more when he immediately recognized it as James'. "Bless me, Father, for I have sinned," began the whisper so timid the priest strained to hear. "My last confession was a long time ago."

Father Thomas made the Sign of the Cross and said, "In the name of the Father, and of the Son, and of the Holy Spirit."

J.J. hadn't attended Mass the previous Sunday or the ballgame Saturday even though his beloved Milwaukee Brewers were in town for their only visit of the season. Both absences hadn't gone unnoticed by Father Thomas, but he paid little mind to either one. He just figured J.J. was ill or had somewhere else to go. And in the nearly two years they had known each other, neither one had offered or asked for a phone number or e-mail address.

From the other side of the confessional screen, J.J. resumed, speaking up a little braver. "I don't know where to start, Father."

"Let's try at the beginning."

"Well, it's the beginning that was good. It's the now that has me worried...scared...angry...confused...I don't know." He wrung his hands. "I guess I'm feeling lost."

The two sat in silence. Then, "Please, my friend, talk to me more."

J.J. wrestled with the urge to get up and leave. Maybe this was a bad idea and he should have stayed home and worked things out for himself. On the other, he desperately needed to talk to someone, and what could it hurt to see where this went?

The other hand won out.

"Is…is it a sin to take the good things in life for granted?"

Used to hearing, "I used the Lord's name in vain a hundred and four times" or "I slapped my sister yesterday," the question was not an everyday one, but then again, Father Thomas had heard it all in his time. Grief and self-hatred over abortions, regrets for spousal abuse, admission of crimes. One time, someone tearfully confessed calling in sick at work to attend a Dodgers game. To that penitent, the priest fought the temptation to say, "At least you sinned for a good cause" and instead prescribed five Hail Marys and an equal number of Our Fathers as penance.

He was prepared to stay with J.J. as long as it took to give him peace, and if not that, at least some spiritual guidance. Praying silently for the right words, he started in.

"Certainly, we as Christians and Catholics are taught to follow the Ten Commandments. You shall not kill, commit adultery, steal, take the Lord's name in vain, and so on. But repeat for me, if you will, the First Commandment."

J.J. absently chewed on his lower lip until the long-ago

Catholic school lessons kicked in. "We shouldn't worship false gods."

"Correct, or as worded in Exodus 20:3, 'You shall not have other gods beside me,'" Father Thomas said, and added, "What exactly does that mean to you?"

"I suppose just what it says. That we shouldn't worship gods of other faiths or idols like people did in the Old Testament."

"That's true to a point. But people now worship other gods all the time that have nothing to do with other religions."

"What do you mean?"

"Sex, money, delusions of infallibility, these are the contemporary idols, our versions of the golden calves we read about in the Bible."

J.J. liked to consider himself a thoughtful man but had never included those among the orders on the tablets Moses brought down from the mountain. He was intrigued by the idea and chose to listen more rather than to speak.

"So, since you raised the issue," the priest continued, "let's take a look at taking life's blessings for granted. I prefer to call this by another name. I prefer to call it pride."

J.J.'s kneeler creaked. "Pride?"

"Yes, definitely."

"Well, I don't go around thinking I'm all it, Father." J.J. shifted and looked at his watch. It was past seven-thirty. "Do you have time for this?"

"I have all the time in the world."

J.J. let out a heavy sigh.

"There is nothing wrong with being proud of family, accomplishments, a fulfilling life, or financial success," Father Thomas said. "Nowhere in the Bible does God order Christians to wear hair shirts and eat honey."

"Thank God for that," J.J. retorted.

"But we must realize that all those gifts are from God above. He offers them to us to take hold of, however large or small. When we assume we have reaped earthly benefits solely through our own doing and have not acknowledged that they come from God, that is pride, and that is sinful. Arrogance and smugness are two sides of the same coin."

"I suppose I may have been smug without saying it," J.J. admitted, "but I have never considered myself arrogant. Quite the opposite, in fact."

"Most people don't either. But there is more to it. When we live a life of self-satisfaction, believing these gifts are our own doing or taking them for granted and complacently failing to constantly acknowledge that all blessings flow from a higher being, we also fail to realize that along with those blessings comes responsibility."

"What do you mean by that, Father?" J.J. asked in surprise.

"With our blessings, we have a duty as Christians, as Catholics, as people, to reach out to others, to not stay within ourselves but to share the Lord's goodness."

"Well, I donate to charity all the time, and I try to be a good person," J.J. said, defending himself as if he'd been accused of stealing from the poor box or refusing to help an old lady across the street.

Father Thomas shook his head so strongly J.J. almost felt it. "When was the last time you helped someone who needed charity not from your bank account but from your heart, serving and sharing God's goodness with others rather than being served with them yourself?"

The long silence made J.J. uncomfortable until Father Thomas added, "I'm talking about the gifts of giving your time, of lending compassion and a sympathetic ear, of showing someone who needs it that you care."

"I try to do that when it's needed, certainly at work, and I never refuse a request to help someone. I'm a friendly guy, at least I think so, but wouldn't say I'm particularly outgoing."

Father Thomas fought the urge to remind J.J. that nothing seemed to hold him back when they met at the ballpark the first time. He asked instead, "How well do you know the Bible?"

"I read it, but I'm no scholar."

The sound of the front door of the church opening and closing interrupted them. "Father, you still in here?" a voice called.

Father Thomas stepped out of the confessional to speak to the security guard making his rounds.

"Yes, I have a late appointment. I'll be sure to lock up when I leave."

"Okay, Father. God bless you."

"God be with you," he answered and returned to J.J. "Now, where were we?"

"We were discussing how I don't know the Bible very well."

"Oh, yes. In Genesis 17, we learn of God telling Abraham of great things he had in store for him and Sarah, along with a new son, Isaac. And do you remember Abraham's reaction?"

"Not really."

Father Thomas took the Bible sitting next to him, and J.J. heard him turning the pages until he found the passage. He read under the dim light, "Abraham fell face down and laughed as he said to himself, 'Can a child be born to a man who is an hundred years old? Can Sarah give birth at ninety?'"

J.J. listened, hearing a soft thump as the priest closed the Bible.

"And thus, their child Isaac was born, disbelief turning to joy. Just like with them, all things can change in ways we can't possibly imagine if we put our trust in the Lord. It happened in Genesis, it has happened with me, and it can happen with you."

As he let his message sink in, Father Thomas prayed for the Holy Spirit to guide and inspire him to offer the right words and for the man baring his soul across from him to be open to them. The priest rebuked himself for not sharing more during their times together on Saturday nights and after Sunday Mass. Given the chance, he vowed to correct that, starting immediately.

J.J. said nothing, his chest rising and falling. Finally, "I was doing all the right things, or thought I was, and then something happened recently that pulled everything out from underneath me.

Am I being punished? Maybe. But why? I don't know, and I don't know where to turn."

The priest clasped his hands in prayer.

"Contemplate what God has said to you tonight through me and look to Abraham. He was called by the Lord to break out of his ways, to leave behind what he thought to be an ordained path, and to believe in the Lord for a life he had never imagined."

J.J. laughed. "Okay, Father. I'll wait to be a hundred, find my Sarah, and we'll have a child together."

Father Thomas laughed with him. "Not a bad idea, but in the meantime, try something else."

J.J. listened.

"Share the goodness within you that your brothers and sisters in life need, and by so doing, you will also discover the goodness that lies in so many, many people in this world. What I am saying is that if you are at a point where you don't know where to turn, look for something good. It is all around, waiting for you to find it and for you to provide it."

J.J. asked, "Father, may I sit here a little while?"

"Certainly."

"Will you stay with me?"

"Happy to."

Ten minutes later, J.J. bowed his head. "Thank you very much." He rose to leave.

Father Thomas made the Sign of the Cross over him. "God bless you, my friend. Go in peace and find peace, to serve rather than be served. He who humbles himself shall be exalted."

J.J. faced the altar, dipped two fingers in the Holy Water, crossed himself, and left.

From his car, J.J. watched until the priest walked home and closed the cottage door, relieved Father Thomas was here for him and not in the least embarrassed with the realization that Father Thomas had to know, despite the secrecy of the dim confessional box, that it was he who came to confession that night. In the darkening night outside, life and lives carried on. Engines gunned, and brakes slammed, and horns honked. A boy chased his smiling, runaway Labrador. Bugs ganged up in the flow of streetlights, and J.J. reflected on what Father Thomas said. But as he drove away, one thing ran through his mind.

Now what?

Chapter 6

The usual cast assembled two days later at eight a.m. Mass, minus one. Father Thomas wasn't particularly surprised when he didn't see J.J. but hoped that their talk Friday had shown him the wonders of bringing an alive God more into his own daily life, just as he had experienced after those empty years in Cicero and Vietnam and war's aftermath. With J.J. in mind, he embraced his ritual private meditation before the Sunday services and turned to the words of John 10:10 to have life "more abundantly."

A minute away as the crow flies and thirty as the traffic grinds, J.J. sat in his living room. He thought of Father Thomas and read along in his monthly, at-home Mass subscription, but needed time alone. He was not moping around but busy thinking. He hadn't gone out since returning from Friday's confession, and he determined not to leave again until he put the priest's words into action. The newspaper and internet announced no shortage of opportunities to volunteer. Nursing homes, the Salvation

Army, food kitchens and pantries...a new appeal seemed to pop up every day for willing arms and strong legs to "give back," using the modern catchphrase. Good and worthy causes all, he was confident that he could be of help to them in some way, and maybe someday would, but they just didn't click. No, he needed something more. Instead of begetting Isaac, did Abraham and Sarah join a Boys and Girls Club?

It's not like he admired himself in the mirror and felt a need to make some headliner, grand splash of righteous deeds in the world. He had never been cut from that cloth. Mom, Dad, and Charlie all lived modest lives, and within that modesty was their pride—there came that word again—and strength. Didn't Father Thomas himself preach the virtue of humility?

Finally, after several days of fruitless searching and contemplating, he prayed for help from the words his mom taught him as a young boy.

Now I lay me down to sleep. I pray the Lord my soul to keep.
If I should die before I wake, I pray the Lord my soul to take.
If I should live another day, I pray the Lord to guide my way.
Amen.

Sometimes a person's prayers aren't answered, sometimes they're answered right away, and sometimes they're answered in the unlikeliest of ways. J.J.'s came less than twenty-four hours later.

While eating supper, he tuned in to a financial network for his nightly fix. He may have been ejected from the game, but that didn't mean he couldn't watch it. After highlighting the day's action in the corporate world and financial markets, the newscaster brought in a guest analyst from a major investment house who discussed how an amateur could select what stocks to purchase, what trends to watch, who to listen to, and who not to. "Of course," she said with a grin, "there is always the dart-board theory."

"The dart-board theory?" asked the newscaster.

"Yes. Some believe that even with all the research tools and forecasting models available to us today, investors can outdo the market or at least keep pace with it by taping the newspaper stock listings to the wall, randomly throwing darts at them, and picking the stocks the darts hit."

The newscaster chuckled.

"In fact," the analyst continued, "I have heard of good-natured investment contests in which one team picks baskets of stocks using market analysis and one team picks theirs by throwing darts. Sometimes, the dart-throwers even win!"

"I presume you wouldn't advise this for everyone," the newscaster said, "or you'd be out of a job."

"Without a doubt. But it's still something to try in good fun. And to my clients, don't worry. I don't own any darts."

With that, both laughed and the show ended.

But the end of the show was merely the beginning of the wheels turning in the Werth home. As the idea hit him, he nearly jumped out of his chair. The dart-throwing approach stuck in his mind, and he remembered that he had once jokingly discussed it with his colleagues. Although he'd never seriously entertained trying it out with a client or two, the thought had intrigued him.

Now, in this moment, it intrigued him a great deal more. "You're a genius!" he yelled at the TV. "If it can work for stocks, why can't it work for me?"

He smiled broadly. "Of course, it can."

His mind went to work. At nine o'clock sharp the next morning, the rest of him followed.

First, he went to the AAA office where he got a map of the United States. After that, a sporting goods store for two boxes of darts, followed by an office supply store for a corkboard and pushpins. He hurried home, went into the garage, and shut the blinds, bursting with glee to the point of feeling a bit off. And maybe he was.

J.J. mounted the corkboard on the one empty wall in the garage, pinned the map to it, took a few steps back, and shook his head in amusement. The corkboard lined up a little lower on the left side than on the right, and the map wasn't exactly what one would call straight either. No matter. He recalled Dad's response to his youthful displays of mechanical incompetence.

"Jimmy, I love you dearly, but take my advice and be sure to find a career using your head instead of your hands."

J.J. stood in his garage, pleased, but still yielding to his father's advice. "Point taken, Dad. Again."

After all this heavy lifting, he needed a break and took some java to his Formica kitchen table. Unable to sit still, he walked around in high-strung energy, ending up madly working the flippers at the same retro pinball machine where he used to unwind after hectic days in the office. He was proud of this house, though not in Father Thomas' sense of the word, and would accept no shame for how he had made it in his own image: snug living room with working fireplace and accented by thrift-store paintings, master bedroom decorated with family portraits and pictures, a second wallpapered bedroom serving as his study, the third a spare in inviting shades of pink, but in his two decades living here, it had yet to host an overnight guest.

He had never been away longer than a week but knew that would change now.

Fortified at the thought of what lay ahead, J.J. returned to the garage and fired the darts one by one at the lopsided map on the lopsided corkboard. He pulled up a lawn chair, took a seat, and admired his handiwork.

"There, that's the route I'll travel," he announced proudly. To look for, and find, something good, wherever it may be.

Chapter 7

The more J.J. thought about it, the better the drive sounded. People from every walk of life embarked on road trips for all kinds of reasons, and now that summer was around the corner and kids were out of school, the interstates and their offshoots would burst with travelers. There were educational road trips to monuments and historic sites, the great outdoors road trips to national parks, family road trips to visit relatives. And then there was his, a road trip to accomplish the unknown. And not only that, but a road trip mapped out by throwing darts.

There was much he needed to do before departure. J.J. didn't want to dilly-dally, but he didn't want to feel like he had to get the preparations out of the way either. After decades of work and schedules, he wanted to enjoy planning the trip as well as the trip itself. He had enough money and more than enough time. All the time in the world, in fact.

He set a target departure date of June 15, ten days away. And for good measure, June 15 was his parents' wedding anniversary.

Not able to shed his business frame of mind, the most immediate task was ordering business cards to arrive before he left. Most people would set out on a road trip without even considering such a thing, and although his only "business" would be meeting new people, he wanted a way to quickly offer his name and contact information. Despite living in the smartphone era, J.J. preferred some of the old-school ways. He ordered his cards online with a rush delivery. Black letters on a tan backing, etched with his name, cell number, and e-mail address. As the finishing touch, at the bottom of the card in italics lettering he ordered:

In the beginning, God created the heavens and the earth.

In his desk was a half-empty box of business cards from his days at the firm. With a flourish, J.J. threw them into his recycling bin, then, after a pause, fished one out as a keepsake. He put the sole survivor into the back flap of his wallet and snapped it closed.

Making lists came as natural to the man as breathing, and the only thing better than a scripted day was a really scripted day, to-dos stuck to the refrigerator and written in neat block letters in his bulging planner now keeping the business cards company in the trash. Pen and paper in hand, he started with what clothes to bring on his trip, figuring on packing them the last day before leaving. A week's worth would do. There were plenty of laundromats along the way, which he actually looked forward to visiting as occasions to kick back and people watch.

Food, drinks, and snacks presented another happy duty, and list in hand, he was off to the grocery store. An hour later, he emerged lugging a cardboard box stocked with packaged foods and snack essentials, and one non-essential—though mandatory—Starbucks gift card.

The day's final requirement was equally pleasant. J.J. wasn't exactly the party-hardy type of Greater Los Angeles, but neither was he a recluse who never answered the doorbell. He was especially friendly with the neighbors to the left of his house, a nice Indian family who arrived in the neighborhood shortly after he did. Both of the children, a boy and a girl, were born after the parents moved in, and he had watched them grow up to become respectful, responsible teenage kids, which, sadly, all too often set them apart from their peers in the times in which they lived.

As J.J. walked across the lawn on that cloudy Monday evening to tell his neighbors of his plans and ask for their help while he was gone, the lingering aroma of an Indian supper brought back happy memories of meals they had shared. Over the years, the family joined his backyard feasts of barbecued chicken, corn on the cob, beans, fried potatoes, and lemonade, with homemade apple pie for dessert. Partly out of necessity and more out of enjoyment, J.J. managed to turn himself into a pretty fair cook although his spreads were no match for his neighbors' exquisite preparations.

Sahil answered at the first knock, his wife, Nandu, beside him, their son, Sai, and daughter, Suneetha, behind them clearing the table. The smell of tandoori chicken wafted out the door, and J.J.'s stomach growled. While leftovers were too much to ask for, he could always hope.

"J.J., my friend, how good to see you. Please come in," said Sahil, gracious as always, extending his right hand.

"Children, leave some of that food out for Mr. Werth."

Yes, there is a God, he thought to himself, wondering if Father Thomas would consider the remark flippant, then realized his fellow foodie would likely say the same thing, and probably even out loud.

J. J. hugged Nandu, waved to Sai and Suneetha, and seated himself at the nearly cleared dining room table.

"If you insist," he said with a smile. The tandoori chicken and brown rice were scrumptious.

"J.J., we hadn't seen you in a bit and were becoming concerned," Sahil remarked.

J.J. realized that perhaps he could have brought his problem to them, but it hadn't felt right. Still, he needed to give them at least some details if he was going to request that they be his house guardians for what would undoubtedly be many weeks.

"The truth is, I got laid off from my job recently." He wanted to talk more but had to stop to collect himself, not yet past the recent days' wrenching emotions. Before he could continue, Sahil was at his side followed by the others.

"We are so sad to hear this, my friend," Sahil said and exchanged a glance with his wife. "You could have come over to talk. Our door is always open to you."

"Thank you for that, but I didn't want to burden you with my own problem."

"A burden? How could you possibly be a burden?"

Nandu turned to the children. "Please now, bring us some tea."

A grandfather clock chimed on the hour and pair of parakeets chirped away in a sunny corner while the adults sipped from steaming mugs and the children sat respectfully, seen but not heard.

"This tea is delicious," J.J. said. "Thank you."

"We're glad you like it."

Sai and Suneetha asked to be excused and on the way to their rooms went to J.J. "We hope you feel better soon, Mr. Werth," the boy said.

"Yes," his sister added. And he distinctly noted that he barely heard their bedroom doors click shut.

"They're good kids. You can be proud of them," J.J. said. He cleared his throat. "Now, if you don't mind my asking, there is something you can do for me."

"Anything," Sahil and Nandu said.

He spent the better part of the next hour telling of his trip, describing how he was looking forward to it, and asking if they wouldn't mind keeping an eye on his house. Not only did they clap their hands at his plans and graciously agree to cut his lawn, water his flowers, and take in his mail, but they also refused to accept the $300 he offered them for their time and effort.

"We absolutely will not hear of it, J.J.," said Sahil. Nandu added, "God puts friends in our lives for just such moments of need."

"You are wonderful people. I am so happy and fortunate to have you nearby," J.J. said and put one of his business cards on the coffee table. In a tight circle they held hands in farewell.

"Don't worry about a thing," Sahil beamed. "And have a wonderful trip." J.J. looked back over his shoulder one last time before making his way home.

As he was getting ready to turn in for the night, a thought occurred to him. Could it be that he had already found, mere footsteps away, something good to reach out for like the man in the flood that Father Thomas talked of on J.J.'s first visit to church? And for that matter, hadn't Father Thomas also been there all along, waiting?

When his alarm rang the next morning, J.J. bounced out of bed for the final step of his preparation. Coffee and bagel to the side, he sat at a card table in the garage, the map of the US spread out before him and a blue highlighter in hand. Eight red pushpins marked where the darts had landed. He had added to them three green ones for pre-determined stops he intended to make along the way. The two yellows were his favorite part of the plan, another tip of the cap to his dad.

Never one to excel at the occasional bar game of darts, J.J.'s very first throw the day before had punctured Tijuana, undoubtedly a fine place to visit but not exactly what he had in mind. The other mocked him two inches off the coast of California somewhere in the Pacific. His two-year-old sedan, Ruby, could do many things, but driving on water wasn't among them. J.J. made it a habit, some called it strange but he didn't care, of naming his cars after their color or model. Not particularly creative on his part but endearing. To him, a car was not something you drove until the wheels fell off or a better one came along. It was a pal that took you places, made you feel comfortable, waited patiently no matter your mood, the weather, or time of day. Even stranger, and again he didn't care, was that he talked to his car from time to time, particularly when it beat talking to himself. And it certainly felt less strange than saying to himself, "I'm glad we stopped here for the night, J.J."

Sitting back, hands behind his head, he couldn't have been happier with the trip that stared out at him. He had never been to the places marked red, there were plenty of cities near and between them to offer interest, and the three destinations poked by green held a special place in his heart. To be sure, he hadn't winged the darts totally at random, instead shooting in a west-to-east pattern, then south, then east-to-west, so the result would be a true road trip rather than stops clustered in Iowa or Nebraska or the Great Salt Lake Desert. And when one had landed in a mountain, river, or presumably a pasture or cornfield, he pinned the nearest urban dot on the map. It was, after all, his trip, and within limits, he could arrange it as he liked.

In the following days, he researched online each of his new towns and cities so he wouldn't just arrive, shrug his shoulders, and wander the streets looking for people to talk to and places to go. Twice he woke up in the dead of night and went into the garage to admire his dartboard handiwork with a feeling of accomplishment that equaled—and in a strange way surpassed—the highs during his years of career focus.

And then, finally, the big day arrived.

He polished off a hearty breakfast before sunup, did a final walk through the house, and circled Thursday, June 15 on the calendar pegged to his kitchen cabinet. The car was already loaded and ready when he climbed in, Bible open to Philippians 4:13 in the passenger seat. With one last look at his beloved house, J.J. drove off and proudly announced to the morning, "Abraham! Here's to you, my brother!"

Chapter 8

Car window down halfway and sun in his face, J.J. sang along with "California Dreamin'" on the radio. He had always loved The Mamas and the Papas' hit, from the time when he was a boy of ten with pillow fantasies of life in Shangri-la out West to when he was a grown man sustained with visions of blue skies and warm weather during the bitter winters spent in the Plains, Midwest, and East. To this day, the vinyl record J.J. unwrapped fifty-one years ago under the Christmas tree lived among the treasures in the pine trunk at the foot of his bed. Every time it played, he joined in, whether singing silently to himself in line at a bank or on an elevator or bellowing out loud as he did now, driving north tuned to an oldies station. Never had it occurred to him during his California dreamin' that he might actually end up in LA. But then a lot of things he never imagined had turned out real, for better or worse, including the idea of driving weeks or months to towns and cities he had never visited and sitting down to talk with people he had never met.

Finally putting Los Angeles traffic behind, there was at least a semblance of open highway. Unless you were out in the boondocks, California roads at any time of day or night congealed with cars, trucks, motorcycles, and RVs, but at least today he moved steadily at the speed limit. In the big city, when he was still a member of the working class, he tried not to let clogged streets and freeways get to him. Interludes of radio music relieved the tedium at times, but it was the rosary draped over Ruby's rear-view mirror that served him during the daily motorist slog by providing a reminder to light a candle rather than curse the darkness.

When traffic was moving at a snail's pace or not at all, this meant taking the opportunity to pray rather than to seethe. Over the years, he prayed countless times for clients who were sick, on hard times, going through divorce, or dealing with the death of a loved one. At times he prayed for world peace and an end to hunger. Sometimes he prayed for a homeless man or woman he happened to see on the street or for a motorist contending with a flat tire or engine trouble.

But now, going for a drive on a temperate summer's day, he wondered why he never prayed for himself. People in the Bible did. "The great King David often asked God for help, even wrote a bunch of psalms doing it," he said to the open window as he passed a truck. The man in the big rig gave him a flippant wave, cigarette in hand. J.J. raised his hand in return and thought some more. Maybe if he had prayed after the layoff, he would've dealt with it better, but then he might not have gone to Father Thomas, wouldn't be here starting out on a drive across America.

"All things happen for a reason," Mom told him so many years ago. He daydreamed of her as he drove north along the spine of California, and of Big Al and Charlie too. Surely they were happy in heaven, but he still missed them mightily here on earth.

J.J. shut off the radio to soak in the sounds of the traffic, Ruby's reliable motor, and his own thoughts. His office crowd had talked over the years about how the pleasure of music had a time and a place, but these days it seemed to blare all the time at every place without relief, at restaurants, stores, groceries, and banks, from cars idling in parking lots or at red lights, the volume jacked up to nuclear. Maybe, J.J. and his coworkers surmised, we're just getting old and crabby. Or maybe, and more likely, people feared or couldn't stand the melody of their own voices and thoughts anymore and needed constant distraction. One thing was for certain, they agreed. People in this age of entitlement didn't care if their racket bothered those around them, possibly reveled in it, and maybe even saw it as an in-your-face challenge. One time, J.J. asked a waiter to turn down the country and western blast, and all he got was a snotty "no."

He never dared request the same consideration from someone sitting in a car unless he wanted some nut job to follow him home and slash his tires, or worse.

But all that was far away as he sailed along on the open road. The hours passed by gently, and in early afternoon, he reached the first dart on his map.

J.J. had never been to Salinas, never bothered stopping for lunch or a bathroom break or to look around during his few trips to the Bay Area to visit San Francisco and Oakland for the sights, nightlife, and a baseball game. But here he was, eager to see what the day and his first adventure would bring.

Driving past a pretty park, he figured it was as good a place as any to stop and dig into his provisions for lunch. He made a U-turn, parked, and walked up the path. A bunch of kids played on the swings and monkey bars, but he thought better of approaching them and their hovering moms, who likely eyed any stranger within shouting distance, especially male, as a threat. A distant picnic bench beckoned instead, maternal stares fixed on his every step. Tuna on rye washed down by lime Gatorade and accompanied by entertainment from songbirds in stately trees put him in a more relaxed mood.

He set off to explore the city and its people.

Either the opportunity to make contact with people never presented itself or he never presented himself for the opportunity, but by early evening, his hopes landed nowhere. The sights around town were fine. The museum dedicated to author John Steinbeck, the zoo, an art gallery, and a couple of historical sites amused and interested him, but he felt no connection with anyone, no comfort in striking up a conversation, not even a simple, "Hi, how are you?" from him or to him. He didn't blame the people of Salinas, who seemed a decent sort, but only himself for stepping up to the plate and then just standing there with the bat on his shoulder and not taking a single swing.

J.J. returned to the park and calculated what to do. It didn't take long. Acknowledging that road trips aren't built in a day and refusing to be discouraged that the reality was more difficult than when he laid out the plans on paper in his garage, he poured on the coal out of town.

Driving in what passed for the slow lane gave him time to think. At this hour of the day, his next scheduled destination was too far to contemplate reaching before nightfall. Nor did he particularly feel like making a random overnight stop in the Bay Area, where he had already visited often in times past, and then have to battle the monstrous commuter traffic in the morning. Monterey presented a nearby possibility, or maybe there'd be a motel off the highway to eat, sleep, and regroup in the morning.

Then, a mileage marker just ahead caught his fancy. The place probably wasn't even on his map, but the biblical name sounded intriguing. At the very least, it had to offer a decent meal and suitable lodging for the night.

After momentary hesitation, he decided to go for it. J.J. exited right and headed for San Juan Bautista.

Chapter 9

Sunset was two hours away when J.J. arrived, and the town center seemed tranquil. A young couple leisurely pushed a stroller, their little one looking out and about. An elderly man and woman held hands sitting on a bench. Two Boomer bikers parked their Harleys and ambled into a tavern on the corner.

"I'm glad we stopped here for the night, Ruby," he said and pulled up beside the two lovebirds on the bench.

"Excuse me, is there a hotel nearby?" he asked amiably.

"As a matter of fact, young man," the man answered, equally amiably, "there's a nice place two blocks up and one block over."

The two waved as J.J. drove off. He waved back.

The hotel proved better than nice, and the bountiful buffet the next morning nicer still. Fortified with food and coffee, he set out on foot.

Because this stop was unplanned, J.J. had done no homework. All he knew thus far was that the people seemed comfortable with themselves and that San Juan Bautista was a world apart from Los

Angeles. The town woke slowly and proceeded into the day even slower, a pace he welcomed from the nonstop action of his adoptive hometown. He discovered San Juan Bautista had a Spanish mission dated to the days of Father Junipero Serra and featured in the movie *Vertigo*. J.J. walked leisurely through it, stopped to pray at the church, and took in an early lunch at a Mexican restaurant. Then he was off to check out the antique stores recommended by the nice lady at the Chamber of Commerce. After that, he figured he would probably have dinner, watch a pay-per-view movie in his hotel room, and depart first thing Saturday morning.

He was about to enter the last shop on the block when a very senior citizen hefted a small wooden box up the front step. The afternoon sun didn't stop her from wearing a red sweater over a white muumuu decorated with purple and white flowers.

"May I help you, ma'am?"

"That would be very kind of you, *señor,*" she answered. "I thought I could make it all the way from up the street, but this step may be the end of me."

"Happy to help." J.J. brought the box inside the shop and set it on a counter surrounded by shelves packed with treasures of someone somewhere sometime but now lonely, abandoned, and longing for a new home to love and be loved in. In a once-over, he spotted salt and pepper shakers shaped like a hen and a rooster, teacups and plates, old family photos, well-used cookbooks, and shot glasses and refrigerator magnets from Pigeon Forge, Wall,

Philadelphia, and other places across the landscape of America.

"I gather you work here?" J.J. inquired.

"Yes, I do. In fact, I'm the owner, bringing in some goodies I found at a garage sale this very morning." She followed his eyes around the store. "I figure ninety-one isn't too old to be running an antique shop."

"Not at all."

They exchanged smiles.

"My name is Juanita Martinez." J.J. took her offered hand in his. "And you are?"

"I am J.J. Werth. A pleasure to meet you, *señora*."

"You speak Spanish?" she asked, lifting her eyebrows hopefully.

"Five words, maybe, and I just used one of them."

Her laugh brought to mind bells tinkling. "J.J., like the blue jay?" Juanita asked.

"No, those are my initials. My first name is James." He thought of Father Thomas. Would he be at the ballpark Saturday?

"Ah, James…Jaime."

"*Jaime* is James in Spanish?"

"*Si.*"

"HI-meh. I like the way it sounds."

Juanita's shop wasn't desolate, but it wasn't Grand Central Station either.

No music played.

Two middle-age women held up a lamp and remarked how it

reminded them of their childhood, and a young couple headed to the sofa on display in the window. A young boy stopped in to help himself to the candy dish. J.J. and Juanita used the time between inquiries and customers to talk, and when the couple called her over to ask the price of the furniture, J.J. took the opportunity to browse through the books and observe Juanita herself. Her skin was deeply wrinkled, white hair drawn back in a bun, brown eyes dulled by the years, and yet she moved with an age-defying grace. Her smile lit up the room and seemed so perpetual that J.J. was convinced she wore it in her sleep.

The two of them alone again, Juanita beckoned. "Perhaps I can treat you to dinner for your kindness in helping me today?"

Sensing and seizing an opportunity to accomplish what he set out to do on the trip, he responded immediately. "I would be happy to join you." His answer felt as natural as two long-time friends deciding to get together for pizza.

At five o'clock, she locked the door on her way out. He was waiting on a bench nearby, and the two set off for her favorite restaurant. They walked comfortably together, along the way passing the Harleys parked outside the tavern. Juanita's pace was slow but firm, aided by a fine hardwood cane.

She used the cane to point to the restaurant just ahead, the same restaurant where J.J. had lunch, and remarked, "I got this nice cane from my sister Veronica for Christmas one year. She and her husband live just up the street, spring chickens both of them. She's eighty-six, and he's eighty. I like to tease that she found a young one."

The two laughed.

"Back again, *señor*. And *Señora* Juanita! Lovely to see you," the hostess proclaimed when they walked in. She looked at J.J. and said, "Juanita is one of our best and longest customers. We all love her so."

Everything on the menu called his name, but he settled for the plate of beef burrito, rice, and beans, Juanita content with a bowl of menudo. "Do you mind if I say grace?" she asked him when the food arrived. "Not at all," he answered. "In fact, I will join you if it's okay."

Talking leisurely during their meal, her peace and the simplicity of her nature fascinated him.

Born and raised in San Juan Bautista, Juanita started waitressing as a teenager, joined the antiques store in her fifties, and bought it when she was seventy-four. "I live just around the corner from here," she explained at one point. "It's the house I grew up in."

Her eyes looked far away as she went on. "In fact, aside from a few months in a small apartment, I have resided in that house all of my years."

When she took a drink of iced tea, J.J. noticed for the first time the gold wedding band snug on her ring finger, but he felt it would be wrong to ask.

"Enough about me," she said with a dismissive hand. "Please talk about yourself, Jaime."

He did, to a degree, telling of his mom and dad and Charlie, days back on the ranch and jobs around the country. Although he had been many places and seen many things and she had never been out of California, in listening to his story and telling hers, Juanita never expressed or displayed disappointment or a feeling that the world had passed her by. In fact, quite the contrary.

"My life here is all I ever wanted, and I thank the Lord for that," she said, and added with a laugh, "*The National Geographic* takes me on my travels."

"I like reading it myself. What's your favorite place you've read about?"

She looked out the window and waved to a passerby.

"I think the Holy Land."

"Yes, the Holy Land. It's on my bucket list."

"What's a bucket list?"

Before they knew the time had passed, it was seven o'clock.

"Oh my," announced Juanita. "We'd best be going. And I insist on paying."

He knew better than to argue. "When are you leaving?" she asked as he walked her home.

"Probably tomorrow."

"Well, Sunday is Father's Day, and later after Mass there is a fiesta. I've been going for many years, and it is always so wonderful. Perhaps you'll decide to join us."

"Perhaps I will."

On the way back to his hotel, he decided to do just that.

The next morning, he skipped the hotel breakfast, checked out the bakery recommended by Juanita, and came out with a large coffee and bear claw that was actually the size of a bear claw. The hours passed, this day another in his life and in Juanita's, in the languorous pace of San Juan Bautista and in the frenetic pace of Los Angeles, all headed to the same eventual end by way of unknown paths.

J.J. hadn't been able to go inside the mission church on Saturday, so when he took his place Sunday for the nine a.m. Mass in his habitual spot on the far-right side, he found it every bit as beautiful as Saints Peter and Paul. The church filled, and he waved to Juanita when she walked in with perhaps ten other people, who reverently arranged her in the middle of their pew.

The fiesta on the mission grounds got rolling just after noon. Mariachis played, and barbecues sent up blue smoke and filled the air with frying aroma. Families and people from the very young to the very old poured in, eating, talking, laughing, dancing, and enjoying the day. J.J. spotted the parish priest and introduced himself.

"Hello, Father. My name is J.J. Werth. I'm visiting here and very much enjoyed your message at Mass about Jesus as Father and father."

The priest put his plate of hot dog, macaroni salad, and potato chips down onto a picnic table. "Thank you, J.J., and welcome to our town and fiesta." He gestured to the crowd, then turned his attention back to his guest. "People usually think of the Lord as our

Father in heaven, as the prayer says. But when he was on earth, he served much as a father to his apostles and to those who loved and followed him, caring for their needs, comforting them, providing for them. These are all duties of Christians. We must worship our Lord, and we must also emulate him every day of our lives."

Parishioners approached, vying for the pastor's attention, Juanita among them. J.J. excused himself and wandered around, happy he decided to stay and hopefully talk a bit more with her. After a time, she sat down at a picnic table, and he came over.

"What a lovely day, Jaime," she said. "I have been at more of these Father's Day fiestas than I can count but never tire of them. I am happy you joined us."

"It is very nice, yes," J.J. said. "May I treat you to lunch tomorrow, Juanita?"

"Thank you, but I won't be here. Our shop is closed Mondays, and I'm going to Capitola with my sister and her daughter to spend a day near the ocean. I love it there. But perhaps you'd like to have supper with me again tonight?"

"I'd enjoy that very much. Same restaurant?"

"No. Some *deliciosas* enchiladas are baking at home in my oven right now, and I'd love for you to join me. Is five o'clock again okay?"

"Perfect."

J.J. thought a bit. "May I ask you a question?"

"Certainly."

"You knew nothing of me before I came to town. And yet you

invited me to the restaurant and now have invited me into your house. How do you know I am trustworthy? I could be many things, a lot of them bad."

Juanita put her soft hand on his.

"Jaime, I have lived long enough to know people. And any man who says grace before a meal and talks so lovingly about his parents is a good person. Your mother and father taught you well, and that is good enough for me."

After a siesta from the fiesta, he walked to her address and thought of his parents and how they would have so enjoyed meeting and talking with Juanita. She stood waiting at the front door.

"Welcome to my home." Her house and its furnishings were trim, neat, and nondescript, the type found with slight variation in neighborhoods, towns, cities, and states everywhere but one of a kind and very special in the eyes of a little lady who had lived all but a few of her 1,095 months within these walls in an obscure corner of the world.

Juanita guided him to an armchair that lacked style but made up for it in comfort and was so soft it felt like an oversized feather pillow. The dining room table for two was tastefully set, and after twenty minutes, a timer went off, and they sat down to eat, passing the evening pleasantly over the enchiladas and flan. As they settled on the sofa for coffee afterward, J.J. noticed a framed photograph on the mantel above her small fireplace. He pointed to it.

"Who is that?"

She brought the picture over and, with her right index finger, traced the face. It was that of a young man, full of confidence and life, in military uniform. "This is my Armando."

J.J. feared he had spoken out of turn and quickly apologized.

She shushed him. "We were sweethearts already in grade school, my Armando and me. He would carry my books, and I would bring him treats for lunch. We shared our first kiss on my sixteenth birthday. And in our last year of high school, we married." Juanita touched her wedding ring. "My goodness, that was seventy-four years ago, back in 1943, both of us seventeen and so much in love." She sighed and swallowed. "We still are."

From the edge of the sofa, J.J. looked intently at her.

"We went to Santa Cruz for our honeymoon," she continued. "Oh, what a time we had! After that, we moved into a small apartment and talked of the family and the good life we would have here in San Juan Bautista. But my Armando said, 'First things first.' We were at war, and he knew it was his duty to serve. I knew it too."

J.J. thought about telling her of Charlie and Vietnam but decided against it, allowing her to continue.

"He enlisted just after turning eighteen, and we thought it best that I live with my parents again until he came back. We shared a farewell kiss at the train depot in San Jose when he went off for his basic training, and he went from there to the Pacific. We wrote to each other, sharing our love and dreams of the future together."

She picked up the picture and held it close to her chest.

"His last letter to me was February 16, 1945. Ten days later, he was killed in a place they call Iwo Jima."

She traced the youthful face again. "My Armando, I love you so."

"Juanita, I am so very sorry," J.J. said in a choked voice.

Juanita walked to the window and pulled back the curtain. The moon and stars performed a brilliant light show. "My Armando is up there waiting for me," she pointed. "And one day we will be together again. Until then, my sorrow will remain deep inside as I live on for the both of us and thank the Lord for blessing me with friends like you to ask about him. Whenever I tell our story, it is like he is alive and sitting beside me here in this house."

"Thank you for telling me about him, Juanita." His voice, filled with emotion, was little more than a whisper.

She smiled. "My Armando would have liked you."

Juanita returned the photograph to its place on the mantel, and soon J.J. rose and reluctantly told her it was getting late and time for him to leave. He offered one of his calling cards, and she accepted it.

"I'd be honored if you want to keep in touch," he said, but as soon as the sentence left his mouth, both of them knew they would not meet or speak again after tonight. Some good things are meant to be heard and not seen, and even then for but a moment, like words of a love that lives on long after the loved one has departed.

At the door he held her left hand and lightly kissed it.

"God bless you, Juanita. I will remember you and this night

and our time together."

J.J. lay in his hotel bed later, reflecting on Juanita's sweet and pure manner and how he would be content if his trip ended today, although there was no way it would. Determined to resist the pull of posting his every move on social media, he made a notation in the small daily calendar he brought to record events and thoughts on his trip.

San Juan Bautista

Juanita

A wonderful lady with a loved and loving heart.

I am richer for our time together.

He didn't leave his hotel on Monday, choosing instead to kick back poolside, read a dusty Western novel left in the lobby, take a nap, and watch a night baseball game on TV. He wondered what Juanita and Veronica were doing in Capitola and hoped they had a good time. The next morning, he drove out of town while it was still dark and the streets were empty.

Chapter 10

The road trip shifted eastward at mid-morning. Puttering along in the high desert countryside, J.J. thought of Juanita as the day unfolded sunny and bright. It felt good to travel leisurely, his next destination within easy reach.

Reno's skyline intervened.

The Biggest Little City in the World was a special place to the Werth family. Big Al and Little Evie honeymooned there, and in the days after Mom passed away, J.J. had tearfully paged through the happy album of their trip. Over his adult years, he had spent memorable vacations in Reno himself, but it had been a while, and he quickly decided his schedule could wait while he indulged in the games of chance and merry-go-round of casino buffets.

Twenty-four hours later, J.J. had his fill of both, breaking even at the card tables and coming out substantially ahead at the food tables. "Thank God every day for his abundant blessings," Mom always admonished her two boys, and at feasts like these, it was abundantly clear what she meant. He toyed with staying longer but, following his third hearty meal, decided it wasn't in the cards or his waistline.

J.J. had become familiar, either in name or visitation, with many cities during his life out West. Lovelock wasn't one of them. As determined by the second red pin on his map, however, that is where he landed ninety minutes after hitting the asphalt.

According to his internet research, the population of Lovelock was 1,894. J.J. saw exactly two people as he drove the highway through town to its eastern edge, then made his way back in to the heart of the town and liked what he saw. A working town, a ranch town, a family town. He parked his car and walked into a hotel lobby, which led into a casino—where he dropped a ten in a bank of quarter machines—which led into a restaurant, where he picked up a cup of his constitutional.

On his grand tour, he noticed the motels scattered along the roadway for people coming from somewhere, stopping for the night, and leaving for somewhere once the cock crowed. One place stood out. It was a brick building, twenty rooms in a handsome single story in the shape of a U. The No Vacancy sign glowed red, but the parking lot stood empty.

J.J. was interested, or nosy, depending on how you look at it. He stopped, not knowing what to expect but still was surprised when the door opened to his pull. A man looked up from behind the office desk. "May I help you?"

"I was passing by and am just curious why there isn't a single car in the parking lot even though the sign says the place is full."

The proprietor preceded his answer with bellied laughter. "You know, you're the first person other than the townsfolk to come in here and ask. I think most strangers are afraid this is a Bates Motel."

It was J.J.'s turn to laugh. "Is it?"

"Not hardly." The man walked around to the front of the desk and extended his hand, a twinkle in his blue eyes. "My name's Chester Adams. I run this motel with my wife Lily."

"I'm J.J. Werth. Pleased to meet you."

Chester had graying hair and was of medium height, medium build, medium everything, save one. He carried himself as a man who didn't let burdens weigh him down, no matter how heavy.

J.J. liked him.

"So, what brings you to town?"

"Passing through, sir."

"Ah, like most people."

A boy J.J. guessed to be eight or nine peeked around the corner, then hurried up to hide behind Chester. Skinny arms stuck out of a plaid T-shirt, skinny legs out of olive-green shorts. Freckles dotted his nose. He wore sandals and a sports cap backwards, representation unknown.

"Bobby, say hello to Mr. Werth."

"Hi," the boy said, fixed like a statue and anxiety in his voice. "Are you here about my mom?"

J.J. shot a questioning look at Chester, who shook his head as a cue.

"Your mom? No, Bobby, I was driving through town and stopped by to look at your motel."

"Bobby's a good boy," Chester said, tousling the boy's hair. "Aren't you?"

The child nodded.

"Are you back from school with your grandma?"

"Yes, Grandpa."

"Why don't you go see if she needs help making lunch?"

He ran out through a side door.

"Nice boy," J.J. offered.

"Yes, he is." Chester went to a small table and poured himself a cup of coffee. "Join me?"

J.J. remembered his cooling cup of Joe in the car but was never one to refuse an extra. "Sure."

Chester seemed more than willing to quell J.J.'s curiosity and began chatting like a man who spent too much time sitting alone at the front desk of an empty motel. After long-time servitude as engineers in Silicon Valley, Chester and Lily had fled the rat race and corporate jungle a decade ago moving to laid-back Lovelock, where they replanted themselves, bought the motel, spruced it up, and did a nice business, anticipating living the good life until retirement.

Chester's face turned solemn as he said, "But when our daughter made a foolish mistake and descended into drugs, we pivoted and brought Bobby here to live with us."

He left most of the blanks unfilled while nursing his coffee, but J.J. could see the pain and weariness in his face.

"That's wonderful of you," J.J. said.

"We're happy to do it and want to help the boy in any way we can, especially with his condition. He has autism."

Only someone who fell off the turnip truck would be unaware of how autism was sweeping through American kids, and J.J. was acquainted with it on a personal level as well. Two of his favorite former clients parented an autistic boy, whom he had grown very fond of and who called him "Uncle J" at family birthday and holiday parties.

"You seem to be doing very well with Bobby. I know from some friends of mine how difficult an autistic child can be."

"They call it a labor of love," Chester said. "Even before Bobby came to us, we made sure he got all the intervention and help he needed, and being here for him all the time, we can do even better. We are so proud of the boy. He is doing extraordinarily well."

Chester rubbed his eyes and smoothed his hair. "But it gets complicated, not that either of us mind in the littlest bit. We just feel that my wife or I need to be there for him before, during, and after class. That works okay when things are slow, but now with him in summer school and business, as always, really increasing, a person can't take care of this place alone. We obviously can't take a break from Bobby, so the break has got to be from the motel."

The light bulb went off inside J.J.'s head. "So, you have no guests now?"

"Yup."

"Must be hard. I figure your business is good this time of year."

"Excellent, actually. We've even had to turn away regulars, but what can we do? We can't be in two places and take care of two responsibilities at the same time, and our place now is with our grandson."

Bobby's voice called through the side door. "Grandpa, time to eat."

"I'd better be going. It was nice meeting you and hearing your story, sir," J.J. said. Chester walked him to the door.

"Thank you for listening, J.J. I didn't mean to take up your time. It helps to talk sometimes."

"I'm glad you did."

"Have a pleasant trip the rest of your way, wherever it is you are going."

Not that he minded, but J.J. realized he hadn't said more than a few words about himself while Chester unwound.

He drove back to the restaurant, which led to the casino—where he won fifteen bucks at a bank of nickel keno machines—which led to the lobby of the hotel, where he booked a room for the night.

He turned in early, but sleep didn't come easily as he thought of Chester and Lily and their predicament. J.J. went back to the motel in the morning. For the first time he took note of its name: Yours, Mine, and Ours. The office door was locked.

"May I help you?" came a female voice from inside.

The law of probability ordered that it belonged to Mrs. Adams.

She opened the door a crack. "Yes?"

"Hi, I'm J.J. Werth. I was here yesterday."

"Ah, Chester told me about you. I'm his wife, Lily."

Lily mirrored her husband in affability and appearance in every way except one. Her eyes were green.

"I was wondering if I may have a word with you and Chester."

"Why?" she tensed up.

"Nothing bad, I assure you. Really. Hopefully, it's very good, in fact."

She thought a moment. "Let me talk to my husband about it. I'm leaving soon to join him at school with Bobby. Come back later, say around four?"

"Okay."

J.J. meandered around town, taking in the small museum, driving through the outskirts, checking out the shops and hangouts, eating lunch, enjoying the renewed sunshine.

At four o'clock, he returned to the motel office. Chester and Lily were there, keeping an eye on Bobby, who was singing and riding a scooter just outside the window in the parking lot.

"What's this all about?" Chester asked, voice controlled but firm.

J.J. thought about how to start, wanting to be sincerely helpful but not overstep. "I lay in bed much of last night thinking about what you said yesterday."

"What do you mean?"

"About your not being able to divide your time between Bobby and your motel."

Chester raised a hand. "Hold on right there. I never meant to suggest that we minded."

"I know. Please hear me out. I would like to help, if I may."

Lily looked at her husband, then at J.J. "And how could you do that?" She frowned.

"I want to offer you my time. You don't know a thing about me as a stranger passing through, and I appreciate that. But I can give you phone numbers of former coworkers and neighbors who can vouch for me."

"What exactly could you do?" Chester challenged.

"I could go to Bobby's school and leave you two here to take care of your business. I'm sure I'd be able to help in the classroom, and the teacher and other aides would be with me. I'd certainly be of more use there than trying to run a motel by myself."

"How could we possibly leave Bobby alone with you?"

"Fair enough. I'm willing to do some chores at the motel to start with so, hopefully, Bobby will get to feel comfortable around me."

Chester interrupted. "J.J., you're right about one thing. We know absolutely nothing about you, your background, where you're from, or where you're going. And Bobby? He's seen you only once, and that very briefly. You being here would be highly irregular to his routine." He and his wife looked at each other. "Others in town have offered to help," Chester continued, "and we've decided to do this the way we had planned." He paused. Lily shook her head. "But I'll tell you what," Chester continued. "It was kind of you to stop by, and there can be no harm for us to at least think about it, though I caution you not to get your hopes up. Can you come back at six-thirty?"

Lily shot him a look. "Chester."

He put a hand on her shoulder, keeping his eyes on J.J, "That's all I ask. We'll see you then."

As J.J. walked away, the blinds of the motel office were pulled shut, and Chester and Lily talked loudly enough for him to catch that the discussion was heated. J.J. wondered if maybe he had overstepped but dismissed the thought of going back and telling Chester and Lily to forget his offer. He had taken it this far and wanted to see this through, wherever it might lead, if anywhere.

He killed time over a supper of vegetable soup, shepherd's pie, and Apfelkuchen for dessert at one of the four window tables in a diner across the street. The teenage waitress topped his coffee and waved to someone whom J.J. assumed was her boyfriend when he pulled up on his motorcycle.

Reading from one of the twelve paperbacks he had brought along on the trip helped pass the time gently and without interruption, for which J.J. was thankful. Over the decades, he had been out by himself a great deal in restaurants, movie houses, and ballparks and noticed that people alone in public got profiled as weird, wretched, lonely, perverted, or desperate for conversation. But if you were alone in public reading a book, people just profiled you as, well, wanting to be alone. And the last thing J.J. wanted as a strange face in a town of 1,894 was to be profiled as weird, wretched, lonely, perverted, or desperate for conversation.

The waitress stopped for his third coffee refill, smiled, dropped off the bill, and said a quick "Thank you" when J.J. told her to keep the seven bucks and change from the twenty.

He knocked on the motel office door at half past six on the dot.

Chester brought him a cup a coffee without asking and looked over at his wife. Lily raised her hand. "You know that I was opposed to this from the start and wanted to send you away. As I told Chester, we've turned down offers from our friends in town, and yet here we ready to invite into our house someone we've known for a whole hour?"

Chester held up two fingers.

"Okay, two hours." She patted her husband's hand. "But he's the soft-hearted one in our marriage and said he liked you and could tell you really wanted to do this. So, I relented and decided to call the phone numbers you left us. They all sang your praises, and Ruth Wagner, my goodness, she made you sound like a saint."

"But the best endorsement," Chester added, "came from our grandson. We asked Bobby if he liked you. He's usually pretty shy and maybe even mistrustful around new people, but he said yes, he did."

A skateboard scraping on the empty parking lot caught J.J.'s attention. Bobby whizzed around in circles and waved.

"He is such a wonderful boy," Lily said. "We can't let anything happen to him." She teared and looked away.

"Nothing will, you have my word, Lily, both of you, all three of you."

Chester put an arm around his wife. "With that, J.J., we've decided to accept your offer, mind you, initially, only to help around here, and on one condition."

"What's that?"

"As long as you're helping, you will be our guest, including meals, free of charge."

"That's really not necessary."

"It is necessary if you want to do this."

"Okay then. Deal."

Bobby stuck his head inside out of breath. "Grandma and Grandpa, can I play a little longer?"

"Yes, but stay where we can see you," Chester said.

The boy glanced over. "Hi, Mr. Werth."

"Hi, Bobby. Have fun out there."

Chester said, "Mr. Werth will be staying with us for a little while."

"Epic."

"I guess that takes care of that," J.J. said. The three laughed, relief filling the room. "I'll check out of the hotel tomorrow morning and come over."

They talked excitedly about the days to come and the responsibilities J.J. would have at the motel.

Chester was with Bobby at school the next morning when J.J. arrived.

"We've put you in Number 5, our favorite room," Lily said as they walked over to the unit. It was pleasant and clean, providing a small desk, love seat, fresh flowers on the coffee table, a twin bed, a modest TV, and a dinette, upon which, five minutes later, Lily placed a coffee pot, a plate of hot breakfast, a bowl of cold cereal, a carton of milk, and the day's newspaper. Later she showed him around the motel grounds.

"Chester and I usually do the bookkeeping and reception ourselves and clean the rooms as well. That's why we're closed right now. We've never found anyone who gives it the home touch we like. The only employee we have is a local lady who does the laundry."

"I suppose I can start by helping you clean once guests start coming in again?" J.J. offered.

"I guess you can."

That afternoon J.J. went to school with Lily. Chester stayed behind, smiling as he switched the glowing red sign to *Vacancy*. Six vehicles sat in parking spaces outside rooms when J.J., Lily, and Bobby returned to Yours, Mine, and Ours.

"Wow!" Lily proclaimed. She and Chester beamed. "We can't thank you enough for this."

"Here am I; send me," J.J. answered.

All nineteen rooms filled by the weekend, and J.J. got his wish to help clean the rooms, plus take out the garbage, sweep the parking lot of careless debris, bring the guests extra towels, and water the flowers. He'd taken pride in the aching muscles from working by the sweat of his brow while in high school and college to earn extra money, but it had been a long time ago, and he found this a refreshing return after the years of sitting behind a desk. He also took turns keeping an eye on Bobby when he skateboarded and scootered, even rode along with him in the parking lot on a bicycle abandoned by a customer. By the next week, they had grown comfortable enough together that J.J. stayed with him in class while Chester and Lily remained back at the motel. Even with the times he felt completely helpless when Bobby acted out, J.J. loved working with the boy to the point that the teacher half-jokingly offered that if he wanted to move to Lovelock, she would happily recommend him as an aide in her classroom during the regular school year.

What J.J. had expected to be a stop of one or two days turned into an enjoyable ten and counting. On Saturday when the day's work was done, the four of them sat around a fire pit in a garden area hidden away behind the motel, ate barbecued hamburgers, ribs, or chicken, and savored life and one another's company.

Looking up to the heavens, Bobby announced, "I'd like to be an astronaut and see what life is like in outer space. Maybe you could come with me, Grandma and Grandpa. And Mom, and you Mr. Werth."

"We'll be there," J.J. said quickly. "And if we're too old, just bring us back an alien."

"One for each of you," said Bobby.

After the boy went to bed, Chester turned to J.J. "We are so thankful that you came into our lives. It has meant so much to Bobby. And it's nice that we've been able to keep Yours, Mine, and Ours open. We have some regular customers who come the week of the Fourth, and now we won't have to turn them away."

"The pleasure is all mine," J.J. responded and continued, "I was thinking of heading out shortly after that, early Friday morning since Thursday is Bobby's last day of summer school and you'll be able to stay here with him all the time and won't need me anymore."

Chester and Lily exchanged glances. "You've gone above and beyond for us."

He stopped them. "There's no place I'd rather have been."

On the way home from school Monday, J.J. told Bobby of his plans to leave.

"I wish you didn't have to go." The boy looked sadly out the car window. "My mom said she had to go too. But she promised to come back to me, and I believe her. Will you come back, Mr. Werth?"

"Of course, Bobby. We'll always be friends, and I'll return to see you, I promise. You can visit me in Los Angeles too. We'll go to Disneyland."

"Really, Mr. Werth? Can I?"

"Certainly. And your grandma and grandpa, and your mom too."

America's birthday came, was celebrated, and went, and Friday arrived. J.J. was up with the sunrise. He had a huge drive ahead, nearly nine hundred miles, but was determined to get to his next destination. The goodbyes would be difficult.

Chester, Lily, and Bobby walked beside him when he loaded his car.

"We'll miss you and think of you," Lily said. Bobby wrapped his arms around him. "Please come back soon."

Chester stepped forward. "We have something for you."

J.J. unwrapped the small package to find a framed photograph of Chester, Lily, and Bobby standing in front of Yours, Mine, and Ours. He choked up, unable to find the words. Lily came to his rescue. "You've changed our lives, J.J., and we'll forever think of you as one of the family."

"It's you..." J.J. started and looked affectionately at the photograph. "Thank you so much for everything." He handed Chester his calling card. "Get in touch anytime. Who knows? Maybe you'll need me to come back and help clean."

Chester chuckled. "You have a date."

"Can I have a card too?" Bobby asked

Chester nodded. "Sure thing, son." J.J. gave him one, and it was time to go.

The three waved as they watched him leave.

The No Vacancy sign glowed red, and the parking lot was full.

Chapter 11

"We've all heard that the Lord works in mysterious ways. But how about meaningful ways? Of course. Magnificent? Most definitely. And miraculous ways? Today is living testimony."

Father Thomas spoke to a small gathering around the baptismal font at Saints Peter and Paul Church on a brilliant summer's day in late June. A baby slept in his arms. In the assembly surrounding him were mother Bridgitte Pierce, beaming grandparents Paula and Bryan Pierce, godparents Ethel and Ray Hogan, and three family friends. Like J.J., who on this very same day basked amazingly in his own joy working in Lovelock, Father Thomas just a few months ago could scarcely have envisioned such a scene.

Over the course of their nine years at the church, Paula and Bryan managed to build a reputation among the congregation as being aloof at best and insufferable at worst. Self-absorbed and excessive, they graced the church with their attendance as if they were attending a party at the governor's mansion. They pranced in to the eleven a.m. Mass, coiffed and cocky, to the middle of the front pew, oblivious to those they passed who masked contempt and pinched themselves to "be Christlike." Father Thomas himself had to rein in his ill will. Even men of the cloth have their limits.

Their "match made in wherever" traced its genesis to the early '90s when Bryan dropped out of UCLA after excelling in his twin majors of partying and living off of his parents' largesse. His mom and dad were rock solid and owned a tire business that, in time, expanded to a chain of six outlets in the Greater Los Angeles area. When they were killed in a car accident, Bryan, as the only child, inherited a mint, left college, and brought his dissipation to even greater heights. But at least he exhibited some good sense for the first time in his life by letting his managers run the family business while he did nothing except live handsomely off the profits.

Perhaps even more galling, Bryan was a glib know-it-all on any social, moral, and political quandary of the day, even though he had never lived beyond a fifty-mile radius from the house where he grew up. As far as anyone knew, he had never confronted a serious issue head-on and was ill-read to the point where he believed that one of the Marx Brothers was named Karl. He blew off the death of his parents with a flippant, "Everyone has to die sometime."

Then there was Paula. While Bryan used textbooks as door stoppers, paid friends to write his term papers, and made the Prodigal Son seem like an altar boy, Paula spent endless hours in love with the mirror, primping her hair, dousing herself with enough perfume to throw off the scent of a bloodhound, and picking out which clothes to wear for nightly clubbing escapades. She didn't even bother with the charade of college or employment. Instead, after high school, she went husband hunting, aiming for the twin trophies of looks and money, and her four-year safari scored its prey when she and Bryan hooked up at a Rolling Stones concert in Oakland in 1994.

Where Bryan had a ready answer for everything even though he had been nowhere, Paula always had opinion on how people should run their lives even though her own universe was closed to the point that whether to put her jet-black hair up or down presented a bona fide dilemma. Both of her parents lived in a nursing home that she visited a total of one time.

"It's their own fault for not taking better care of themselves when they were young," she told her brother, John, after that first and only visit. "And besides," she added, "it smells in there."

As far as Father Thomas knew, the Pierce pair had no friends or acquaintances in the congregation, refused to exchange handshakes or smiles during the fellowship greetings, and hadn't participated in a church event since showing up to assist at an ice cream social and stalking out when told they had to wear aprons. He often wondered why they bothered to attend Mass other than to show off their latest outfits.

One particular December morning stood out. While Father Thomas passionately gave testimony on how the world more than ever was in need of Christian compassion and mercy, Paula openly texted and Bryan dozed. It was all the priest could do to not hurdle the Communion rail and throttle them.

Whether they realized it, or more likely took it for granted like they did everything else, the Pierces had one very special blessing. Respectful and fiercely loyal to her parents, their daughter, Bridgitte, was everything they were not, and despite their worst efforts, she developed into a humble, kind, sharing, and, yes, compassionate and merciful teenager who regularly attended Bible studies and served at interdenominational soup suppers for the homeless, hungry, and hopeless.

Praying constantly that the girl's example would shine through to the Pierces, Father Thomas knew he would do anything for her.

He got his chance.

After finishing off one last mound of pumpkin pie the day after Thanksgiving, he dressed for bed and half-listened to some TV talking head drone on about Donald Trump when the phone rang. It was not unusual for him to get late-night calls from parishioners in need, a duty he embraced and welcomed.

He picked up and answered without hesitation. "Hello?"

"Father?" a woman asked.

"Yes, this is Father Thomas." He thought he recognized the voice but was sure it couldn't be.

It was.

"This is Paula Pierce, Father." Her voice trembled. "I'm sorry to bother you at home so late at night."

"It's no bother at all, Paula. What can I do for you?"

"I was wondering if you could come over to our house?"

"Certainly. I'd be happy to. How does next Wednesday sound?"

"I mean like right now."

The urgency was unmistakable and even more so unbelievable. Neither of the Pierces had turned to him a single time in their years at the church, their contacts nothing more than a cursory, "Nice sermon, Father," when they felt like saying it as they walked out at the conclusion of Mass. But the past was of no matter now.

"I'll be right over."

He pulled up at the house within twenty minutes after plugging the address into his car's GPS system. Paula opened the front door before he could knock, and two more surprises greeted him. She was not slathered in makeup. And she was crying.

"Please, come in."

She escorted him to a lavishly furnished living room where Bridgitte sat on the couch, looking down. Her arms squeezed a throw pillow so tightly it looked ready to explode in a blur of polyester.

Bryan paced, in a lather. "Pregnant!" he screamed. "Pregnant at sixteen!"

Paula flopped onto the floor and bawled, "Look at her, Father," then turned to Bridgitte. "How could you do this to us?"

Father Thomas slowly absorbed the scene, went to Bridgitte, and took her hands in his. He looked at the parents and knew that quickly restoring calm and eliminating the blame game were about as likely as the Cubs winning the World Series. But wait—they just had! Well, okay, as likely as them winning it again.

"Perhaps you could leave Bridgitte and me alone for a while so she and I can talk."

"No way," Bryan snarled.

The priest's eyes pierced him. "Let me rephrase that. Leave us alone for a while."

Without another word, Bryan stomped up the stairs. Paula turned toward Bridgitte, stopped, narrowed her eyes, and followed her husband.

Father Thomas put an arm around the girl and waited until she was ready to talk. After a short time, she dabbed her eyes and said softly, "I'm so sorry, Father." Rain pattered on the windows. A cat meowed and jumped onto her lap. "I thought he loved me."

The priest looked into her eyes, waited, and listened.

"I'd been dating this boy in high school—his name is Matt— last year when I was a freshman and he a senior. Just before he went off to college in August, well, it just happened."

"You mean sex happened?"

Her cheeks turned red. "Yes. Just one time. And of course I got pregnant. I just told my parents."

Father Thomas sighed deeply, sad but accepting that anyone, even the sweet Bridgittes of the world, fall victim to temptation and pay the price. "I'm here to help you, not to judge."

She leaned onto his shoulder. "Thank you, Father. My mom

and dad, they've been awful, threatening to kick me out, to sue Matt's parents, other things I can't repeat." Her voice caught, and she started to cough. "I'm so thirsty," she said, standing, allowing the cat to slide off her lap onto the couch. "Can I bring you anything?"

He accepted a bottle of water when she returned from the kitchen, and she cracked open a can of soda. The conversation resumed.

"When I told Matt, he was all, 'I've got a future to think of and how could you not be more careful?'" She started to cry again. "What a jerk."

The priest nodded and gave her his white handkerchief.

"I held off telling my parents and hid it as long as I could, but last night, well, we had a really good time at Thanksgiving, and I figured they would be accepting and open-minded. Silly me." She petted the cat, who resumed its place on her lap. "My baby is due six months from now, in late May. And you know, Father, I may be only sixteen, but I really want this baby and am sure I can take care of it. Not that he wants to anyway, but I don't want Matt's help or to have anything more to do with him."

"Have you talked since you told him?"

"No. And I don't intend to talk to him again."

Father Thomas knew all about turning your back on someone and going it alone. He took a Bible from his satchel, put her hand on it, and his hand atop hers. "You can count on me to help any way I can."

"Father, thank you, thank you. You don't know how much this means to me."

"Maybe it's time to bring your mom and dad down here," he suggested.

"I guess." She rolled her eyes.

Before either could speak when the parents returned, Bryan announced, "Your mother and I have decided you're gonna get an abortion."

Bridgitte was speechless. Father Thomas was not. "There will be no abortion!" he thundered.

"I don't think that's a decision for you to make," Bryan shot back.

Father Thomas was familiar with the path of trouble, both as a witness and traveler, and knew that love, not despair, was the only proper step to take. Neither Bryan nor his belligerent attitude daunted the priest.

"Nor is it a decision for you two to make," he retorted. "Abortion brings serious consequences, and for a young mother, unimaginable ones. It is not the answer, not now and not ever."

"Easy for you to say, preacher," Bryan sneered.

Father Thomas ignored the comment. He said, "But there's more."

"Which is?" Bryan bellowed.

"Bridgitte wants to keep her baby."

They stared at her, dumbfounded.

She walked over to them. "Mom and Dad, what if you had

decided you didn't want me or couldn't take care of me? What if I had never been born because you aborted me?"

"But we did want you," Paula pleaded.

"Just like I want this baby myself."

Wife stared at husband. "My God, what will people say? What will they think of us?"

"Is that all you care about, what the neighbors will think?" Bridgette cried. "Maybe I should just leave home, find someplace else to live."

Her words startled Paula like a slap in the face and for the first time her tone softened. "Honey, it's not that easy. You're young. You have no husband. The baby won't have a father around."

"But we'll have you two," Bridgette said. "Won't we?"

Paula and Bryan exchanged glances, sat on the loveseat, and lowered their heads.

Father Thomas couldn't tell if the girl's heartfelt appeal had made an impression on them or they just ran out of answers and opinions, but for whichever reason, he was thankful that they appeared to ease up on their angst and anger if ever so slightly.

"I told Bridgitte she can count on my help and that I will be there for her. That goes for you as well."

The two said nothing and didn't move. Knowing he could do no more this night, Father Thomas got up to leave. "Paula, you are right. This won't be easy, for her, the baby, for you. But I encourage you and Bryan to listen to your daughter and to help her as loving and compassionate parents. If you need to talk, my door is open any time."

He saw himself out and walked around the block, sidestepping puddles.

Later, he unwound in his study, humming along with the hymn "I Will Sing Praise" while playing his violin. "Lord, let me be your instrument of peace in this household and help me to help them," he prayed.

God obliged, eventually.

Weeks and months passed without word from the Pierces or their appearance at Mass. There's a fine line between inquiry and intrusion, and Father Thomas always treaded it lightly lest he mean the former but commit the latter and force unintended consequences. More than once, more than twice, he picked up the telephone but replaced it without calling. He beseeched the Almighty and waited.

One Sunday in May, when the daisies in front of the church were in full bloom, Father Thomas was about to say the opening prayer when a noticeably pregnant Bridgitte walked in along with Paula and Bryan. They sat together in a pew toward the back. Bridgitte gave a little wave, and Father Thomas returned a little smile.

The service opened with the priest's "The Lord be with you."

"And with your spirit," the congregation responded, the three Pierces joining in unison. From time to time, Bridgitte sat back and rubbed her tummy. After church, they sat and waited on one of the benches along the walkway. Father Thomas approached, arms outstretched.

"What a delightful surprise," he announced. Bridgitte walked up, her parents close behind holding hands.

"There's a lot to talk about," Bryan said. "Do you have time to sit out here with us?"

"Of course. It's a lovely day."

For the next hour they marveled at how things can change.

"After you left us back in November, we did something we hadn't done in years, if ever," Bryan started. "We talked, or at least Paula and I did, about ourselves, what we had become or never were. That night was a real wake-up call."

He reached over and touched his daughter's hand.

"We realized that when we first heard about the baby, neither of us cared about Bridgitte. We cared about ourselves, what people would say, how it would disrupt our self-centered little lives," he continued, "and we didn't begin to consider how our daughter felt."

Paula spoke. "Since that night, Bryan and I have tried to put Bridgitte and the baby first and put aside our own selfishness."

Father Thomas' face lit up with a smile. "From where I'm sitting, it looks like you're doing just fine."

"Well, let me tell you. It isn't easy to stop being a diva," Paula laughed.

"Or a jerk," Bryan chimed in and pointed a trigger finger at his head.

"But," Paula went on, "by turning to and not away from each

other, good things started happening and then happened over and over."

She kissed Bridgitte on the cheek. "You tell him."

"Well, the three of us went to my high school where we talked to the principal and my guidance counselor about how I could make everything work with my studies and having a baby to take care of. I definitely want to get my diploma and after that, go to college."

Standing on its hind legs, a squirrel stared at them from the other side of the walkway. A light breeze tousled the fruit trees.

"When I went in to talk to the principal about being pregnant, she was super understanding and said that the teachers and counselors would help me as much as they could. That night, Mom, Dad, and I talked and thought, wouldn't it be great if there were a support group at the school for pregnant girls and teenage mothers and fathers and their parents, people to talk to, people to help with your studies, people to take you to doctor's appointments. I mean, the school staff can only do so much."

Father Thomas looked from one to the other, awed by what he was hearing.

"So," Bridgitte went on, "the three of us went to the principal a couple of days after that and told her about our idea. Not only did she love it, she said we were the perfect ones to start it. And so, we did."

"We've immersed ourselves in this," Paula said, "and helping Bridgitte these past months." Bryan added, "But yesterday we all decided it was time to rejoin the world, or maybe for the two of us, Paula and me, to join it for the first time. And here we are."

Bridgitte opened her purse and handed Father Thomas a brochure. "We have six girls already, along with nine of their parents, and even three of the fathers," she said. "Do you like the name?"

He traced the bold letters on the front.

LABOR OF LOVE

A Support Group

For Teen Parenthood

"I love it."

Father Thomas smiled broadly at the girl. "I'm so proud of you, of all of you. When is your baby due?"

"Any day now," she giggled.

"We'll call you from the hospital when he is born," Bryan said.

"He?"

"Yes, we know it's a boy. And we are hoping you'll do us the honor of baptizing him."

"It will be my privilege."

He walked them to their car. "Have you picked a name?" Father Thomas asked.

Bridgette smiled brightly. "We're naming him Thomas for the one who believes in miracles and Lazarus for the one who is proof of them. Thomas Lazarus Pierce has such a wonderful sound, don't you think, Father?"

Five weeks later after everyone had left Saints Peter and Paul following the baptism on that brilliant summer's day, Father Thomas knelt at the altar, head bowed in prayer. "Lord, to you be all the glory for your grace in the lives of Bridgitte, Paula, and Bryan and in giving them this precious little boy."

Sunlight poured through the stained-glass window.

Father Thomas wept.

Chapter 12

Lovelock receded in his rear-view mirror, and for a fleeting moment, J.J. considered turning around and returning to the familiar happy faces at Yours, Mine, and Ours. But this trip was about going forward, not backward, and especially to the destination half a day ahead.

"Maybe I can't go home again," he told himself, "but I can at least return for a visit."

Driving along, J.J. became so lost in his thoughts that he almost missed the turnoff to the highway that would take him north to where it all began. Where the heart is, or was, and, for those who are lucky, will never be too far away whether they're going by car, plane, boat, or thumb. He would have it no other way than Billings being first of the three stops that he alone determined rather than a projectile on his garage wall. On the map at his side, the city was circled in green to match the pin on the garage wall. Color coordinated and borderline anal, as always.

He managed to leave Lovelock at just after six in the morning, a good thing considering the long day ahead. He estimated his arrival time in Billings at ten that night. This allowed thirteen hours for driving, the loss of an hour switching from Pacific to Mountain Time, and two hours of stops for one of his favorite indulgences—even an acknowledged obsession—that traced back to one of Big Al's nuggets about the open road.

"Son, never be in so much of a hurry that you can't enjoy the rest areas along the way."

In all his adult years of country driving, J.J. disregarded that advice only once, when his girlfriend at the time, Alice (...or was it Emily?), whined so much at every stop after the first that he finally gave in to her and passed them by. He'd made two promises to himself afterward. Never again to disregard rest areas and never again to make a long trip with someone unless he'd cleared in advance that she was of like mind. To this point in his life, he'd made good on both and over the years managed to see rest stops in all shapes, sizes, and conditions, expansive, postage-stamp, good, bad, and indifferent.

Notwithstanding his three must-see pit stops in the middle of nowhere, the hours and hours and hundreds and hundreds of miles driving on this long stretch could have been nothing more than a seemingly endless ribbon of concrete and asphalt for someone who was unimaginative and found no joy in simply looking out the window and enjoying the American landscape in all its forms and beauty. J.J. had not been not cut from that cloth of boredom, however, and enjoyed the wide open, cruising at seventy miles per hour in the summer's heat. The front windows were open, the radio off, and he was content. Ruby barely missed hitting a jackrabbit that, for some reason, just had to cross the road to get to the other side.

Other than the lure of the rest areas, nothing along the way really compelled him to stop. Yellowstone sounded nice but not that nice since hiking never appealed to him. The only thing he cared about buffalo was when they were processed into burgers, and by the time he saw directional signs to the national park, it was nearing nightfall. After going north then east once again, he arrived at 10:15 p.m. on the western fringe of Billings, where he booked a motel for that night and the following three.

The next morning, he dozed in bed for half an hour after his alarm went off and mentally mapped the long-anticipated day, then got himself together and set out. The first destination couldn't wait. He took the long way, hoping to immerse himself in familiar places, but instead met only disappointment. The high-rises downtown looked strange as did the new restaurants where patrons dined *al fresco,* and none of the residential areas seemed even vaguely familiar. Had the city changed that much in the decade since he was last here, or had he simply forgotten?

Feeling out of place in his own hometown bothered him, and it showed when a man waiting at a bus stop shouted, "Be grateful, buddy!" which brought a sheepish smile from J.J. that the man did not return. When the stranger started walking toward J.J.'s car, he sped off. Maybe this wasn't turning out to be such a good idea after all.

A shopping center up ahead re-focused his bearings with a deli that offered comfort food, the day's lunch special of footlong baloney and ham sandwich and a bag of chips. A thrift shop next door fulfilled his seating needs, and he purchased a rusted but usable lawn chair, whittled down to a price of two bucks.

Arriving in an old section of town, J.J. was relieved to see that the Church of the Ascension and graveled driveway hadn't changed a bit. Nor had the cemetery behind. There, beneath a sycamore tree providing shade and comfort for the Werth family and three adjoining plots, rested for eternity the three most important people of his life, then, now, and forever. Hollyhocks, columbine, and daisies decorated everywhere, courtesy of a dedicated and caring church staff who believed that death, like life, requires beauty.

He knelt in front of the headstones, placing has hands on the names one by one.

Alvin Henry

Evelyn Margaret

Charles Robert

His was there, waiting, next to Charlie's.

James Joseph

Hopefully, the absent year after "*1956*—" was a ways off.

"Hi Mom, Dad, and Charlie. I'm here."

He set up the chair, unwrapped the sandwich, and breathed in, filling up his lungs like a balloon just short of bursting. There was not a sound, no well-wishers or mourners, no birds or squirrels, not even a breeze to disturb the stillness. It was as if God himself ordained this Saturday afternoon for the family to be together.

Over the next couple of hours, J.J. lived in the moment. The layoff from his job felt as if it had happened to someone else, and in a way, it had. He did not lament the past or worry about the future, and, in fact, didn't think about anything at all. He couldn't remember ever feeling so far away.

A voice broke the trance.

"Jimmy?"

He jumped up.

"It's you, isn't it? Jimmy Werth. My gosh, after all these years. It's me, Father Timothy."

J.J. recognized him. "Father Timothy, of course. Great to see you again."

It had been ten years since J.J. saw Father Timothy Warner, but he looked as if it had been thirty. Once-flowing black hair had changed to sparse and white, a steady posture and gait reduced to hunched shoulders and a shuffle assisted by a cane. And yet, the man's spirit and love of life were unmistakably as youthful as ever.

"What brings you to town?" he asked after the men shared a warm embrace.

"I'm driving cross-country, Father, and wanted to stop to visit my parents and see the old church."

"Well, they're still here, it's still here, and, praise God, I'm still here," he laughed.

"I hope you'll stay for Mass tomorrow."

"Of course. You still have the eleven a.m. service?"

"Never changes. Oh, and something else hasn't changed. Do you remember those monthly all-you-can-eat spaghetti suppers?"

"How can I forget them? Charlie and I almost put you out of business, we ate so much."

"Not hardly. And you'll be happy to know we are having this month's tomorrow."

"Really?"

"Really. Starting at three, as usual."

The spaghetti suppers were a tradition for the church and the Werths since before Charlie was nothing more than a gleam in Big Al's eye. The two, then three, then four seldom missed. Bittersweet though it may be to go for the first time by himself, J.J. couldn't wait.

The feast on the lawn just outside the rectory turned out to be a step back in time, and he hadn't realized how much he missed it. Many faces, like his parents', were gone, but they gave way to those of kids now grown with kids of their own, some even grandkids, all of which allowed for an afternoon of memories kindled and rekindled, lubricated by food and conversation. Bored adolescents hung out with long faces, and babies cried. Dogs romped free of their leashes. Some things never do change, after all. J.J. stayed with Father Timothy and the parishioners well past the posted six o'clock ending time. Many asked the same question, "Have you been back to the ranch?" and often gave the same warning: "It's not the same, Jimmy."

The next day he found out for himself how right they were.

Its state of disrepair shocked him. The new owners' pledge that they would love and care for it as his parents had proved to be empty words. The Big & Little arch was no more, lying on the ground in pieces covered in dirt and weeds. A metal fence and barrier blocked the driveway and entrance to the property. J.J. climbed over and walked up to the house, now a boarded-up, ramshackle ghost of the place where he, Charlie, Big Al, and Little Evie spent those years living and loving. Faded foreclosure signs taunted him from the front door.

He wouldn't have looked inside if he could.

"I can't take this," he finally announced to the morning air, returned to his car, and drove away. J.J. wouldn't let himself look back and, in hopes of steadying his nerves, set out for the little store where he and Charlie bought nickel Popsicles and candy bars as kids. J.J. hoped against hope that Mr. and Mrs. Hayn would be on duty, that they hadn't slipped away along with so much of the city he once knew. Besides, his road provisions were running low, and he could give them some business.

They weren't there. The store wasn't either, replaced by a parking lot with six spaces.

Deep in disappointment, J.J. took the long way back to his motel. He realized for certain that the Billings he had known as a boy was not the one he now saw as a man decades later, the city he once loved was now just another place in Montana, USA. He couldn't decide if that was bad or good and figured maybe it was neither, that change doesn't always need a judgment attached. Layoffs, death, loss, all happen for many reasons or no reason at all, and it is not ours to decide but rather to go on and make the best of things. He had done so after his family went by one by one, knew more with each passing day that he must do so now given the loss of his job and, in a way, his identity, and surely would have to do so again in an unknown future. Back in his motel room, he fell asleep thanking Big Al and Little Evie for being a good mom and dad.

On Tuesday he checked out, intending to find a place closer to downtown. Not knowing when, or if, he would ever return, J.J. figured he might just as well see the city that had grown into a stranger and take the opportunity to connect more with Father Timothy and some of the folks he had met at the church dinner.

Just off the main drag, he stopped at a place with a sign in the window, *We Speak German.* For a short time, he had dated a woman from Düsseldorf who was on assignment at an American bank, and one of their pastimes had been her teaching him some of the language. J.J. decided to try out his skills.

No one manned the desk when he stepped in. He ticked the bell on the counter, and a rumpled twenty-something jumped from the back.

"*Guten Morgen, mein Herr. Wie geht's?*" J.J. began, smiling broadly at the boy.

"Huh?"

"*Guten Morgen,*" he repeated.

"Don't you speak English?" the clerk demanded.

"Of course, I speak English, but your sign said *We Speak German*, so I did."

The clerk rolled his eyes. "Oh that. No one here speaks German, at least not anymore. The former owners did, but they died, and the new ones never bothered to take down the sign."

"Right," J.J. responded. "Just curious. Has anyone ever come in here like I just did, speaking German?"

"You're the first, pal."

J.J. turned to leave.

"Hey!" the clerk shouted.

"*Ja?* I mean, yes?"

"Just what did you say when you walked in?"

A number of answers sprang to mind, but J.J. figured he might as well play it straight.

"I said, 'Good morning, sir. How are you?'"

"I'll remember that."

"*Auf wiedersehen,*" J.J. muttered and hurried to his car.

He ended up spending the rest of his days in an upscale hotel not as a hometown boy but as a tourist. He did some of the *al fresco* routine himself and checked out new sights and sounds. Father Timothy joined him for lunch one day and then afterward at the Yellowstone Art Museum.

Their talked turned to a schoolmate of J.J.'s.

"Do you remember Eddie Covington?" Father Timothy asked.

"I sure do. One of my best friends starting in first grade and a real go-getter in high school. Voted 'Most Likely to Succeed,' wasn't he?"

"That he was."

"For a minute there at the spaghetti supper," J.J. admitted, "I thought and hoped he might show up."

"Sadly, he moved away. He doesn't live around here any longer."

"What?"

"Eddie hit some really hard times. After college, he came back to Billings, settled down, had three kids, was highly successful, then everything fell apart."

"What happened?"

"He got laid off from his job as an advertising executive at the firm where he worked, and he never recovered."

"I can certainly sympathize."

"You've been laid off, Jimmy?"

"As a matter of fact, yes, and recently."

"I'm sorry to hear that." He studied J.J. "It looks to me like you're doing okay."

"I'm getting there, but it can be a struggle."

"Unfortunately, the struggle was more than Eddie could bear. He found no other suitable position around here, and his wife pleaded with him to relocate. He refused and became embarrassed and withdrawn and finally degenerated into anger and despair to the point that his wife finally left him and took their kids. They, the house, everything Eddie had worked for was gone.''

"I wish I could find him and we could talk."

The priest shook his head.

"The last I heard, he was somewhere out of state bouncing around homeless shelters and finding meals where he could."

"It can be hard to cope when you're hit out of the blue like that, Father. Take it from me."

"Cope, yes. But give in, refuse to try again? No. That is not the human way, and dare I say, it is not God's way. How I tried helping Eddie, talking to him, but he wouldn't listen, not to his wife, not to me, not to anyone."

J.J. told him about Father Thomas. "I believe the two of you would get along famously."

"I'm sure we would." The priest patted J.J. on the back. "You're a good boy, Jimmy. Your parents would be proud of you. So would your brother."

"I try, Father."

"No matter what, never fall into such despair that you turn your back on everyone, including yourself."

"I won't, and thank you."

"Thank me for what?"

"For being here."

He dropped off Father Timothy in front of his church and waited while the priest slowly moved up the sidewalk. J.J. turned the corner, and Father Timothy waggled his cane in farewell.

Chapter 13

J.J. left Billings two days later, the city no longer belonging to him. And he was okay with that. The magical boyhood days would remain in his heart, but boyhood and its magic end, maybe sooner, maybe later, not a matter or if but of when. Onward and upward, they say, but who exactly are they, and where does onward and upward lead to? *Those are thoughts for greater minds*, J.J. mused and took off to his new destination.

The day's drive would be far shorter than the last, and that alone relaxed him. Between enjoying the Great Plains through his windshield and the mandatory stops at rest areas, he amused himself with how the finagling factor directed him now to one of America's most famous sites, one of Hollywood's most recognizable movie scenes, and a place that had been on his bucket list for years.

Mount Rushmore lured him partly because of its reputation but mostly because of the sequence at the end of *North by Northwest*, where Cary Grant and Eva Marie Saint elude their evil pursuers on the staring faces carved in granite. J.J. watched the movie for the first time, but not the last, on a lazy Friday night in college but never created the opportunity to visit there in person. The dart in his hand in the garage changed that. When one landed in the middle of nowhere in a state he couldn't quite make out from the distance, he harkened back to his high school physics class. In Mr. Alf's room, when an experiment yielded something undefined and unrecognizable, he and his study partner finagled the numbers to come within a range of the intended results. Presto! When the dart landed in undefined territory, he figured *why not* and finagled it to the southwest corner of South Dakota, where the colossal carvings of Washington, Jefferson, Roosevelt, and Lincoln awaited thousands upon thousands of visitors. Finally, J.J. would be among them. And, besides, he had heard good things about the cafe at the park.

Neither the park nor eatery disappointed.

A Sunday in the heart of summer, tourists from all over the country and the globe hankered like J.J. to see the iconic monument. The parking lot jammed bumper to bumper with cars, pickup trucks, minivans, RVs, motorcycles, new and gleaming, pre-owned, and pre-pre held together by spit and promise. But all made it, and that's all that mattered to them and their cargo alike.

An idiosyncrasy to some, a happy habit to him, J.J. never intended for a visit to a shrine like this to be a one-and-done event. He had no problem going back a second day or even a third to catch something he missed on the first go-round, to see something again, or to soak in the atmosphere. After spending the afternoon for his initial sightsee of the park and its grand monument and a lovely time over a plate of pot roast, mashed potatoes, and peas at Carver's Cafe, J.J. headed to Rapid City, where he booked a three-night stay at a rustic lodge.

His second and third days in the Black Hills were even better. He hit the park when it opened at eight in the morning and stayed until it closed at ten at night, spent hours in the museum looking over the exhibits, and watched the film about the history of the memorial until he practically knew the dialog by heart. Over and over, he walked along the Presidential Trail to look at the sculpture, participated in activities conducted by park rangers, and breathed in the glorious forestry. From time to time, he looked up at the granite faces and imagined himself instead of Cary Grant in the climactic scene, rescuing the beautiful costar.

Both days he treated himself to the delightful buffalo stew at the cafe, and it was there on Tuesday that he met the Nelson family.

They stood in line about half a dozen people behind him, the mom, dad, and three young children, wide-eyed at the desserts and happy with their adventure. After paying for his meal, he leaned over to the cashier and handed her a hundred-dollar bill.

"You see that family of five in line behind me?" he asked.

She squinted. "What about them?"

"Not so loud, please. I'd like to anonymously pay for their meal."

"Why?"

"I just would. They look like a nice family, and I believe in paying forward, helping someone when they don't expect it and maybe don't even need it."

"Well, I guess it's okay as long as you're not some freak."

He winced. "I assure you I'm not, miss." He lightened the mood. "Are you a college student working here for the summer?"

She brightened. "Yes, I'm a junior at South Dakota State."

"Enjoy college. I surely did. What are you studying?"

"Criminal justice. I want to go into law enforcement or be a D.A."

J.J. wanted to say, "Well, your suspicious nature has you on the right track" but instead signed off, "All the best to you."

Her face softened. "This is nice of you to pay for their meal. First time it's happened since I started working here."

She placed the bill on the cash register. "Hey, what should I do with the change?"

"Give it to them. Say a friend says to have a good time eating and to buy a souvenir and some ice cream. They have three kids, and everything's expensive these days."

"That's for sure. Thanks again for doing this."

J.J. nodded, took his tray of food, and found a table in the corner.

A man strode over twenty minutes later and cleared his throat. J.J. looked up from his book.

"Sir?"

"Yes?" J.J. answered.

"Are you the gentleman who paid for our lunch?"

The cashier shrugged her shoulders and grinned sheepishly.

"I had hoped the young lady would keep it between us, but yes, I am."

"May I ask why?" he demanded. "Do we look destitute to you?" He plunked down the change. "And we certainly don't need charity to buy our own trinkets."

J.J. stood and held up both hands.

"No offense intended. I just wanted to do something nice for what looked like a nice family."

The man mulled over J.J.'s response. "I do thank you then," he said and motioned to the four others, who joined him and together formed a semi-circle in front of J.J.'s table.

"My name is Benjamin Nelson, this is my wife Bonnie, and these are our children Austin, Scarlett, and Sterling." Without prompting, "I'm ten," the older boy announced, "and my sister is eight."

J.J. pointed to the tot. Scarlett held up three fingers.

"It's nice meeting a family like yours," J.J. said.

"Thank you," Benjamin said. "Please forgive me if I seemed rude before."

"Quite all right." He extended his hand to Benjamin. "J.J. Werth."

Bonnie said, "You know, Mr. Werth, I always tell our children that there is decency all around us, often when you least expect it.

And you showed that today." The two older kids offered gapped grins, and Bonnie wiped smears of ketchup from Sterling's chubby cheeks.

Bonnie made a crooked face at her husband. "Benjamin is more suspicious than me, and I keep telling him he has to look for the good in other people and not always assume the bad."

The two men exchanged a knowing look.

"Well, I'm happy to have done it and hope you are all having a wonderful time."

"We are. And you have made it more so," Benjamin answered. "We're off for some ice cream. May I bring you a cone or something?"

J.J. held up a hand. "Quite alright, but thank you just the same."

He offered the change to Benjamin. "On me, okay?"

Bonnie nodded to her husband, who smiled and said quietly, "Okay."

J.J. nursed a third cup of coffee. He admired and respected wholesome, loving families like the one he grew up in. That he hadn't a family of his own did not cause anger or regret. It was just the way things worked out. The one time he was deeply in love and entertained grand plans to marry, the relationship didn't take. Sitting alone, many hundreds of miles from home, with families all around in the expansive café and feeling the hurt over what might have been, he warmed at the memory of the long-gone romance and more at his plan, some days hence, to visit where it all took place.

The rest of the day passed quickly, and on his way back to the motel, he restocked his provisions with a loaf of potato bread, a two-pound bag of almonds, a pound of baloney, a case of Lime Gatorade, five cans of Spanish rice, and five of chili.

J.J. didn't consider himself superstitious but didn't believe in tempting fate either. On driving trips, it was his wont to never congratulate himself and Ruby, or whoever was his four-wheeled companion at the time, for not encountering car trouble along the way. Heading east from Rapid City on a quiet two-lane state road, the only thing on his mind was checking out the local scenery before rejoining the humming interstate.

Whether bad luck, drama, or an inopportune nail, he had gone but a few miles when Ruby thumped and wobbled onto the shoulder. J.J. opened the door and anxiously glanced back. Sure enough, the driver's side rear tire was flat.

Granted clumsy at all things mechanical, he was positively useless at all things automotive. He looked around. No one and nothing in sight. Desperate to locate an AAA service, he returned to the car and began to punch in the numbers into his cell when an 18-wheeler approached in his rearview mirror. While never one to profile, still he couldn't mask his astonishment at the person who hopped out of the rig and walked up to his car. Weighing maybe 110 pounds on a five-foot-four frame, she wore polished black boots, a black Bullhide hat, and casual jeans, her auburn hair arranged in a braid tied off with a ribbon of bright red that matched her blouse

"I get a lot of that," she said in cheery voice as he wound down the window.

"Shocked looks?"

"You got it, cowboy."

J.J. admired the lightly tanned face featuring nary a blemish, prominent nose, and glittering green eyes, but mostly her demeanor. The woman radiated joy.

"Name's Alice Stephens. And you are?"

"J.J. Werth, ma'am," he said, stepping out of the car. "Thank you for stopping."

"My mom is ma'am. You can call me Alice. So, what's the problem here?"

"I have a flat, and you might call me tire challenged."

Her laughter was contagious. "Keys?"

Alice popped the trunk and, no more than ten minutes later, managed to change the flat tire for the spare without removing her hat or breaking a sweat.

J.J. walked over. "I can't thank you enough for all of your help," he said and reached for his wallet.

Alice held up a hand. "I hope you're taking out a handkerchief," she said. "Just happy to do someone a favor." He smiled at the irony of how the tables turned from just a few miles back and his encounter with the Nelson family, he now the shy recipient of goodwill instead of the gracious donor.

"May I ask you something?"

"Sure," she said, tipping her head courteously.

"I thought truckers always traveled on the interstates to make better time. What in the world brought you to this lonely road?"

"I just like to get off the beaten path once in a while and enjoy the countryside. You can't always just blast through life at seventy miles per hour." She pointed to her truck. "But I do have to make some time."

"Of course! Thank you again!" He waited until her truck pulled away before getting back into Ruby and driving on.

Whether it was Alice's statement about blasting through life or the idea of some divine intervention he could bounce off Father Thomas when they got together again in the left field bleachers, J.J. went happily on his way, and half an hour later, he spotted a truck stop with all the trappings of gas, food, and repairs. Along with rest areas, J.J. loved truck stops. He was pretty certain their reality didn't match his romantic expectations, but still, the idea of the open road, sleeping in the back of a truck cab, and eating chicken fried steak and eggs every morning was a nice office daydream when the action on the financial markets lulled.

He pulled into the service station and, while waiting for a new tire, headed over to the diner to satisfy his culinary craving. He noticed Alice in a booth, sipping from a large tumbler of orange juice.

He walked up to her. "Hello stranger."

She laughed. "No more car trouble, I hope?"

"No, just getting a new tire. Hey, can I buy you lunch?"

"No need, but I never turn down free food," she said. "Thanks."

"Chicken fried steak and eggs over easy, hash browns, rye toast," Alice told the husky waitress.

"You're kidding," J.J. joked.

"What's so unusual about chicken fried steak and eggs?"

"Nothing, really. Just a private thought of mine."

The waitress jabbed her pad and pencil in his direction. "This mutt bothering you?"

Alice smiled. "No, he's fine."

"He'd better be. Whaddya want?"

"Make it two."

"Two what?" she snarled.

"I'll have the same as she's having."

The waitress walked away. "Don't try anything funny, buster."

"Yes, ma'am"

Alice removed her hat and laughed. The auburn braid flopped across her shoulder like a third hand. She flicked it back. "I see you make friends all over the place."

"That's me."

The restaurant and environs hopped with truckers for a meal or shower, tourists for refills of gasoline and snacks, unfortunates for car repairs, hitchhikers for a pit stop and maybe a ride to anywhere.

The two got to know each over their mutual meals, Alice doing most of the talking and J.J. most of the listening. J.J. was happy to share a sentence or two, maybe even a chapter from his life, but pouring out his life story to others was as palatable to him as blueberry pie, and he hated blueberry pie. That did not work both ways, however. He liked hearing the stories of others, and Alice was glad to oblige, telling about her life as trucker, a wife, and a resident of Milwaukee.

After a decade of driving for several long-haul companies, she and her husband saved enough for Alice to strike out on her own, and the opportunity arrived on a Sunday afternoon while they headed back to Wisconsin from a driving trip to California. Cruising on a highway outside of Colusa, they spotted a Peterbilt truck lot and agreed, "Why not?" Ever since, Alice steered that king of the road around the country, up, down, and sideways as joint proprietor and sole master of A&R Trucking. She was about to explain the meaning behind the name when a bruiser approached, the perfect match for J.J.'s once-upon-a-time mental image of big rig drivers.

"Hiya, Moth," he barked.

"Hiya yourself, Johnny D," she shot back and gave him a fist bump. Obviously a man of few words, Johnny D walked away.

"Moth?" J.J. inquired

"That's me."

Alice could tell he wanted to know more, and she spilled.

"One night when I was taking country dance lessons back in the day, one of the instructors came over and said, 'Why, you're just as cute and light as a moth.' I'd heard my share of pickup lines, but that was a first."

J.J. signaled for a coffee refill. The waitress ignored him.

"What could I do but say thank you? And, well, the rest is history. The name stuck, and he turned out to be a kind and righteous man, and a good dance instructor to boot. Three years later we had a small wedding in a country chapel ten miles west of Milwaukee. It was September fifteenth, eleven years ago, and a perfect day. We have been happy together ever since."

"That's a great story, Alice. Or may I call you Moth?"

"Why not? I hardly hear Alice anymore anyway."

"May I ask your husband's name?"

"Rudolph, the R in A&R Trucking."

"Is he a driver too?"

Alice good-naturedly shook her head and straightened the unruly braid. "Hardly. He was a Navy pilot, then after the military wanted something with his feet on the ground, so he went to college and got a degree in accounting. Funny couple, huh? The man's the office worker and the woman the trucker."

"Whatever works. And it seems so for you two."

Alice looked at her watch. "Gotta fly. I'm bound for Racine with a load of machine tool parts, and they want it yesterday. Happy trails to wherever."

J.J. left an overly generous tip. "Be good," the waitress said. She winked at Alice.

At the door, Alice turned back to him. "Hey, if you get near Milwaukee, gimme a call." She handed him her card. "You'd like Rudolph, and we always enjoy company."

"I may just do that."

She geared up her way into the distance, and he into his, which, thanks to the day's delay, turned out to take him on a detour to Pierre, where he stumbled on an American Legion baseball game against visiting Watertown, followed by a nightcap of chili dog, fries, and a chocolate shake at a nearby drive-in.

Serenaded by owls, J.J. slept peacefully at a countryside motel bathed in moonlight.

Chapter 14

Traffic whizzed by on the interstate. J.J. thought he spotted Alice's 18-wheeler from his perch on a rest area picnic bench but quickly corrected himself, realizing she was long gone on her mission to Racine. A family poured out of a minivan for a potty break, and J.J. felt extremely grateful to be part of the audience and not a member of the cast.

He opened his daily calendar and wrote:

Alice Stephens, aka Moth. A fine lady.

Fixed flat tire, dined over chicken fried steak and eggs at truck stop.

King, or should I say Queen, of the Road.

Who knows, maybe I'll meet up with her and husband in Milwaukee

Ah, Milwaukee. Another family memory. He peeled back in the calendar to his notations after Billings and added in the margin:

Mom, Dad, Charlie

To the good times

The persistence of a begging sparrow got the better of him, and he threw it the remnants of his sandwich, packed up, and joined the freeway frenzy, glad he had somewhere to go without the constriction of the hour-by-hour templates that dictated his moves as a working man. Being knocked off kilter by the great flat tire incident, as he would refer to it in the retellings back home, did him a second service in addition to meeting Moth. It showed him there was no hurry to get anywhere, no meetings to attend, calls to make, nothing to answer to but his own inklings of when to get up and where to go.

Eventually, the fourth red destination tugged after taking him through the forestry and dairy land of the Upper Midwest, a region he frequented for R&R when he worked in Chicago. It felt great to be back and, as a bonus, to a city where he had never been before.

Wisconsin Dells hummed. At the height of summer on a muggy Thursday, tourists swarmed like ants around candy. Young and old, newlyweds and oldlyweds, geezers and grandkids, happy singles and weary parents, flirtatious teens and energetic kids. Shops pitched souvenirs, trinkets, clothing, day trips, and night trips by merchants eager for dollars to sustain them through the Wisconsin winter when snowdrifts replaced crowds on these same sidewalks.

A street over from him, laughter and screams at a water park added an exclamation point to the spectacle. J.J. didn't know where to start. Supper seemed a fine idea.

Again, no beginning and no end. Buffets and all-day

breakfasts, delis and diners, chains and mom-and-pops. Japanese, Chinese, Italian, Indian, American, whatever. J.J. settled on a place specializing in chicken and waffles and wasn't disappointed. In his motel, he turned in for the night to the sound of young feet pounding in the room above his.

Endeavoring the next morning to acquire gifts for his good friends keeping watch over the *hacienda* back home, he finished shopping by lunchtime and, pleased with his choices, celebrated with a monster plate of shrimp curry washed down by a bottomless tumbler of mango juice. A thought presented itself. *Let's ditch the human tsunami and explore the undisturbed neighborhood streets to rub elbows with the locals.* He had come out here to look for something good, not to buy an *I Love the Dells* hoodie or plastic skull.

He set off.

J.J. strolled and strolled some more and was about to cross a tree-lined avenue to head back to his room for a nap when a female voice boomed. "Well, hello!" He turned to see a woman occupying the better part of a two-person swing on the porch of a cute, red stone house. A teeny dog of pedigree charitably described as "mixed" stood on hind legs and barked excitedly.

"Hello!" She called out again. The dog barked louder. "Oh, Hello, be nice to strangers."

J.J. stopped, feeling a bit confused. "Excuse me?"

"Hello and I like to sit on the porch and observe, and I can't help but let out a greeting when someone passes by. It always works her up." She kissed the dog's nose.

"Your dog's name is Hello?"

"Sure is. Not such a good choice, eh? Maybe I should sing out 'hi' instead."

"Actually, I think it's pretty funny."

"I like that in a man."

"What's that?"

"A sense of humor."

A car passed by, and she waved. "Wonder who that was."

"You don't know?"

"Nah, never saw the person in my life. I'm just neighborly is all."

He approached the front step.

"My name is J.J. Werth, ma'am. And you?

"Marie. Marie Cartwright. Pleased to meet you, J.J."

"And I you, Marie."

J.J. walked up onto the porch. Hello settled onto her lap. "Are you visiting for some fun and sun?" Marie asked

J.J. didn't get into details of how the Dells came to be part of his itinerary by the throw of a dart, but he did explain his visit as part of a cross-country trip to see the US of A and to meet people.

Marie listened, nodded, and stroked Hello. "A non-tourist in town. That's a rarity. And there I thought you came for the ambiance. Different strokes and all that."

They surveyed each other, J.J. wondering where this conversation would lead, Marie seemingly just glad for the company.

"Say, J.J., can I interest you in some lemonade? A freshly made pitcherful is in the fridge just aching to be enjoyed."

"I never turn down a glass of lemonade and the company of a nice lady and a dog named Hello."

"You *do* have a sense of humor. Pull up a chair, *kemosabe*."

J.J. sat in a wicker rocker alongside the swing. Shortly, Marie returned with a tray containing two large glasses along with a box of mint Girl Scout cookies and a dish of milk. Hello trotted along behind her.

"Can't have lemonade without cookies, now can we?" Marie winked. "Or milk for my favorite."

"Sure can't." He winked back.

She bent slowly and placed the milk on the floor. Hello lapped up her treat, jumped back onto Marie, and snoozed.

J.J. quickly learned that Marie Cartwright could teach eccentricity to an eccentric. Her name alone was a giveaway. Not content with the conventional first, middle, and last, she adopted as her own any that struck her fancy, and to date she went by Marie Beatrice Claire Elizabeth Ruth Julietta Paulina. At first meeting she offered only the first and surname, but to those lucky to become her friend, and J.J. fell into that category almost at her first sight of him, it was always the seven names in proper order, and the second to the last started not with a *jay* as in *JAS-per* but with a *hoo* as in *hoo-lee-ETT-uh*.

"I've thought of legally changing my name to include all of

them, but chances are I'll find an eighth, ninth, tenth, who knows," she offered while chewing a mouthful of cookie.

"Sounds good to me, Marie Claire..."

"No, it's Marie Beatrice Claire..." she corrected.

"I'll get it right, I promise."

"Isn't he a nice man," she told Hello. The dog looked up at her and smiled.

At some point in their conversation, J.J. noticed Marie's choice of apparel, which only served to underline her unconventionality. A set of bib overalls hung over a light green T-shirt, accented by black high-top tennis shoes, and a New York Yankees baseball cap pulled back to reveal blonde hair in spikes. A touch of perfume completed the arrangement. Its scent tickled J.J.'s nose.

What he didn't know was that she wore the identical outfit Sunday through Saturday and, being clean and meticulous, insisted on changing clothes every day. In the closet hung seven corduroy bib overalls accompanied by seven light green T-shirts neatly stacked on a nearby shelf, seven sets of high-tops lined up precisely heel to heel at the back, and seven sets of white socks atop them. Unnoticed except by her, each item was labeled by day of the week so that, horror of horrors, she wouldn't accidently wear Wednesday's when it was Tuesday or, double horror of horrors, put on the same ensemble two days in a row.

Only the single Yankees cap was a mainstay.

"Why the Yankees?" J.J. inquired at one point.

"Navy blue completes my outfit, don't you think?"

Ho-kay.

Afternoon turned to evening as the two sat comfortably on the shady porch.

"How about some supper?" she ventured.

J.J. hesitated, but only slightly, figuring the food spectacle on the main drag wasn't going anywhere. "Hey, why not? I'm enjoying this immensely."

"Hot dogs okay?" Marie beamed.

"Love 'em," J.J. answered.

"Good, so do I. Hello does too." She rose from her seat. "You just wait out here. I'll call when it's ready."

She went inside, woman's best friend at her heels.

If he told about no one else, J.J. knew that once back home, he had to relate this meeting to Father Thomas, of this person with seven names and a dog called Hello and, he sensed, of an undeniable decency and good heart. He wanted to know what brought, or drove, her to this neverland in south-central Wisconsin, and given time, he was pretty sure she'd be happy to tell and very sure he'd be happy to hear.

Thirty minutes later, Marie came to the screen door and announced, "Food's on."

J.J. followed her to the small kitchen, stopped at the entranceway, and gaped. On the table glittered place settings for two of China and silver. The countertop behind practically groaned under the weight of a platter of six half-pound hot dogs and oversize buns along with plates, bowls, and containers of relish, diced onions, dill pickles, three flavors of mustard, chopped tomatoes, grated cheese, potato chips, baked beans, and slices of watermelon. The aroma of freshly brewed coffee filled the room.

"You certainly are a woman of surprises," he exclaimed.

"I believe in eating well," Marie said.

Lowering her head and looking to J.J., who bowed likewise, she prayed modestly, then they dug in to the feast, all the while trading tales about their childhoods, he in Billings, she in South Bend, with one major difference. J.J.'s stories were fact, and Marie's were fiction.

While she described her life as the only child of a prosperous and well-suited couple, J.J. could not have guessed that her grim reality instead was an abusive father, a compliant mother, one sibling who committed suicide, and another who ran away never to be heard from again. Blessed with an inner strength, Marie sought solace and redemption in academia, ranked second scholastically in her high school senior class, graduated with honors in economics at the University of Wisconsin, and followed that with a Juris Doctor degree. After a decade of practicing highly successful corporate law in St. Louis, she took her savings and moved to Wisconsin Dells, where she bought this modest house, started her own business, and remained ever since, never telling a single person, not even her dinner guest, the details of her path.

"I'd love to hear more about your trip," Marie suggested later in the comfort of her unpretentious living room. While doing so, J.J. casually looked around and was surprised to see not a single family picture or portrait, paintings or artwork, treasures or personal effects, which seemed to belie her story of happy family life growing up. It was hers to tell, he decided, not his ask to ask, but without realizing, he did stare at the one decoration in the room. In the exact center on the middle shelf of a built-in otherwise-empty bookcase was a small porcelain Santa Claus. Marie caught him staring.

"It's from my store."

"Oh?"

"Yep, that's how I pay the bills. I own a store called My Christmas Corner. Stop by if you're going to be in town another day or two and maybe something will strike your fancy. Hey, you've only got 159 shopping days left."

"Thanks for the invitation. I may just do that."

Rather than another day or two, J.J. ended up spending another six in the Dells and enjoyed every minute of them. Thanks to his internet research before embarking, he came to town with a long list of things to do and places to visit. He enjoyed a couple of boat rides on the Wisconsin River, took in attractions, including the Circus World Museum in Baraboo, hiked a forested nature trail, and for one afternoon at a water park, sat dry and comfortable over cake and ice cream watching everyone else get drenched.

He enjoyed time with Marie too. It passed languidly for them at the shop, on the porch, and in her food-runneth-over kitchen. Often, they did not speak at all or got a good chuckle when Marie called out "Hello!" to a passerby and the dog did her usual routine.

Customers came and went for early holiday shopping at My Christmas Corner. But whether business boomed or lagged, Marie remained bright and cheerful like the string of lights she kept lit 24/7.

"I always loved Christmas growing up," she told J.J. in a well-disguised lie one day just before closing. In fact, Marie despised the season and its festivity because her parents refused to celebrate, not even to buy a tree. Only after being on her own and attending an office Christmas party did she begin to appreciate the joy of the holiday, so much so that when she spotted the availability of the Christmas store on the internet, she snapped it up and began her new life.

Sitting in her shop the afternoon before he was due to leave town, Marie asked if he wanted to do anything special.

"What do you have in mind?"

"Do you like to dance?"

Six months of lessons in his forties had cured J.J. of the dreaded Two Left Feet disease specific to males, and in the intervening years, he was known to cut a rug or three.

"As a matter of fact, I do," he admitted.

Marie sat up straight. "I'm not talking about the jiggling around that supposed adults do these days at stores, in restaurants and cars, even on the sidewalk, whenever they hear anything resembling music. I mean, there are a time and a place and a level of creativity."

"Agreed."

Marie continued. "I'm talking about dancing with style and technique, something you have to learn and practice."

"Okay, you're on," J.J. announced.

"I am?" Marie was pleasantly surprised. "Meet you at my place at eight?"

"I'll be ready."

He was not prepared for who greeted him at the door that night. No bibs, T-shirt, high-tops, or Yankees cap. In their place, she wore a navy blue, pleated skirt, white silk blouse, silver ballroom shoes, black pearl necklace, and handmade barrette noir. Out were the spikes, in was a perm wave.

She twirled a 360. "Like it?"

"You look lovely, Marie Beatrice Claire Elizabeth Ruth Julietta Paulina. Really."

The woman may have tipped the scale somewhere this side of large, but on the ballroom floor, she moved like a butterfly. For three hours, they danced the night away, foxtrots, rumbas, two-steps, cha-chas, even a salsa J.J. had never tried but picked up quickly, thanks to Marie's patient tutelage. J.J. couldn't remember the last time he'd spent such an enjoyable evening, and neither could she.

Later, they hugged goodbye at her front door to the tune of frogs singing from yards and fields all around. "Promise you'll keep in touch," he said after handing her his calling card.

"I will, and you do the same," she said. When J.J. lifted a questioning eyebrow she added, "I'm in the phone book under

Cartwright, Marie, you'll be happy to know. They'd never get all my names on one line, or even three."

Hello kept up when they walked arm in arm to his car, where Marie held out a small box. "Something to remember the Dells by," she said. "Open it later."

"Marie…" he started.

"Shh," she finished for him and brushed her lips on his cheek. "Safe travels."

J.J. drove away deep in thought, and back at the motel made a quick point of writing in his calendar about the unforgettable days in Wisconsin Dells. Then, remembering Marie's gift, he sat on the bed, opened the box, and smiled brightly.

The porcelain Santa Claus looked back at him from the nightstand when his eyes closed to end the day.

Chapter 15

Trains cleansed Father Thomas.

Night after night he tossed in bed yearning for the hark of a horn in the darkness and distance and the sensation of fleeing his boyhood purgatory. A first escape on the rails arrived when he went off to the Marine Corps and visions of grandeur, a second when he returned scarred from war and found sanctuary in the anonymity of seats to anywhere.

Searching for his destination in life and then arriving at it, he took to trains often, traveling north, south, east, west, and variations therein. Whenever and wherever on these trips, he liked to believe he wasn't crossing the fine line between avoiding his past and running away from it. Yet in the stillness of the night, when doubts crowd in, the goblins paid him visits.

Since leaving the military, Father Thomas had kept in touch with his comrades in arms. During annual get-togethers and occasional times over coffee, the phone, or the internet, the men talked, amid the bold and the bawdy, about their emotional visits to the war memorial in Washington, DC. All except one. Father Thomas had never been and vowed to never go. It was in discussions with his best friend from over there, Dexter Jones, that he spoke most passionately.

"Dex, my brother," he would begin and then posit in words one way or another, "I can't comprehend memorials to war any more than I can understand Civil War reenactments. Violence, fear, and death are harsh realities to forget, not to remember. I'm not saying war isn't necessary at times, but do we really have to celebrate it?"

Dexter would listen respectfully, rub his chin, and smile whether face-to-face or place to place. Equally in words one way or another, he would say, "Kearns," never Tom or Thomas or Father, "you're coming at this the wrong way. Our Vietnam piece, like all memorials, is not to the war; it's to the men and women who fought in it, to their duty and sacrifice, whether they went willingly or were ordered to. I don't glorify what went down any more than you do, but going there, to our Wall, is like covering with a soft blanket. I go away comforted by that sacred ground. Just think about it."

"I won't think about it," would come the reply, followed at some point by Father Thomas' standard sign-off, no matter when or where, words and handshake, real or virtual.

"*Semper Fi.*"

Then one spring, Dexter confided in him of late-stage lung cancer and issued a last request that, on behalf of his dying friend, Father Thomas visit their memorial. A few weeks later followed an invitation of a totally different sort, one Father Thomas had received in the mail and plunked into the garbage can for going on twenty years. This time, however, he didn't discard it, reasoning it was time to practice what he preached. There was no longer a question of avoiding or running away from battles. Like his former self, he needed to confront them head on.

Round one rang on a July morning, overcast on the cusp of sweltering. And from the moment Father Thomas beheld the Vietnam Veterans Memorial, he realized his compatriot was right. Visitors spoke in hushed tones if at all. Men and women, young, aging, old, in jeans, shorts, slacks, suits and ties, in ribbons and medals, in fatigues and uniforms of wars before and since, stood, paced, saluted, hugged, traced, touched, bowed, wept.

The priest paid his respects at the Three Servicemen Memorial and the Vietnam Women's Memorial before slowly approaching the Wall. He moved along the panels year by year from beginning to end and back again, and stopped at men he went into battle with, destined here to be a name, not a visitor. His right hand followed the etched remains of those he knew and those he didn't know, feeling proud that he had gone and humbled that God had graced him to come home alive to life renewed and rediscovered.

Father Thomas knelt in front of 1968 and gazed at his reflection in the black granite, lifted the Bible gifted by the chaplain long ago and far away, and opened it at a laminated bookmark.

"Not that I say this because of need, for I have learned, in whatever situation I find myself, to be self-sufficient. I know indeed how to live in humble circumstances; I know also how to live with abundance. In every circumstance and in all things I have learned…" Some joined him wordlessly on their knees, others familiar with the verses in Philippians 4 followed along.

"…the secret of being well fed and of going hungry, of living in abundance and of being in need. I have the strength for everything through him who empowers me."

Paul's words from the time of Christ echoed as much to Father Thomas and to the living beside him as they did to the 58,318 whose names he faced to his left, front, and right. All was quiet. "Peace, my brothers and sisters," he whispered, made the Sign of the Cross, rose to murmurs of "Thank you, Father" and "God bless you," and drifted away.

After his solemn moments at the Wall, Father Thomas needed to exhale, so he took in the city's sights, of which there always seemed to be one more. Seeing for the first time Washington's museums, monuments, and halls of the powerful filled his sense of appreciation, but it was the places of the powerless that fueled his sense of purpose.

There was no better venue, he quickly discovered, than the soup kitchens, faceless amid the fine restaurants and cuisines. His favorite dining experience and fellowship happened at a Bible church food van in the shadow of the Capitol building.

The evening repast served up a hearty helping of lasagna, dinner roll on the side, coffee, and juice, with ice or without. If anyone was unhappy or ungrateful, they didn't show it. Plastic spoons scraped hungrily along paper plates, Styrofoam cups emptied and refilled. Christian music hummed from a boom box. Children laughed, played, and chased. Adults chatted pleasantly. The minister said grace and moved around to shake everyone's hand.

Six people joined Father Thomas afterward on a cement step in the parking lot behind the van. No names were asked, none were offered. All told their story in a sentence.

The thirty-something, living in his car: "I'm working on passing my high school equivalency exam, thanks to a guy at work who helps me afterward and on our lunch breaks."

The teen couple, runaways: "We found each other on the New York subway and are in love."

The graying woman, two adolescents in tow: "My daughter had these two angels and is in jail for armed robbery, so God favored me with caring for them."

The burly priest, who arrived on Amtrak at the best of a military buddy: "I'm praying for and visiting old friends."

Hands held in a circle, the group proclaimed "Praise the Lord!" and went their separate ways.

Three days in Washington of such joyous encounters along with hours and hours of splendid alone time left Father Thomas refreshed, encouraged, and at closure with this part of his life, grateful that the Spirit nudged him to listen to his friend and come here. He knew he would need all that and more for the mission ahead. Sitting back and closing his eyes in the taxi taking him to Union Station for the next leg of his adventure, he beseeched the Lord for fortitude to carry him to and through round two.

Next stop: home.

Chapter 16

"Dex, looks like the joke's been on me all along."

Father Thomas' friend laughed weakly into the phone. "Not at all, Kearns. Despite all those protests of yours, I knew you'd see the light. And I'm grateful you called."

"I should've listened to you before, but now that I finally visited the Wall, I have to admit it was something special and want to tell…"

Dexter interrupted. "Sorry, Kearns, gotta go. The doc just arrived. *Semper Fi.*"

"Okay, Dex. God be with you. *Semper Fi*, my brother."

Father Thomas wasn't one to obsess about the past or get uptight about the future, content to let the present take care of itself in the Lord's capable hands. But just as he had been wrong about the healing he experienced at the Vietnam Memorial, maybe, he wondered, there was something more to be found in the past, perhaps forgiveness, and in the future, perhaps a better heart.

There was plenty of time to think on these things as the train rolled toward his boyhood home, five elapsed decades down to a ticking eighteen hours and dwindling minute by minute, mile by mile. Whatever anxiety might go through his mind on the journey ahead, at least he would confront it in comfort. Even Jesus enjoyed and preached the virtues of life's pleasantries, and booking a private lower-berth Amtrak Roomette that afforded a picture window and two comfortable seats to spread his bulk by day and uncurl in a converted bed by night did not seem ostentatious in the least.

Nor did a good meal in the dining car.

The Black Angus steak special called his name, and he responded, inviting a glass of Merlot along for the ride. Greetings and brief anonymous exchanges with other passengers added a cheery touch, followed by retirement to his click-clacking corner of the world, from where he luxuriated in solitude on this moonless night.

The Bible, opened to Romans, sat on his lap, a prayer card counseled in its inscription.

Show me

Thy ways,

O Lord;

teach me

Thy paths.

But this wasn't a time for Scripture study. Instead, Father Thomas took from his pocket and studied the black-on-beige parchment invitation yet again, having lost track of how many times he had read, re-read, and re-re-read it.

50 Years!

Your Class of 1967 cordially invites you

to share old times and new at our reunion.

When: Saturday, July 29

6 to 10 p.m.

Where: The school gymnasium

Food and refreshments on the house

On the side, a note handwritten in a neat script appealed.

Please attend, Father Thomas!

When the invitation arrived in April, he may not have discarded it but neither did he light up a cigar and rejoice. Instead, he let it sit in a dresser drawer for three weeks until finally one night, after his evening prayers, something told him he had to do this. He marked "X" in the *Accept* box, wrote "1" in the *Number Attending*, and sent it off in the next day's snail mail before he could ruminate and change his mind.

Three questions—a why, a who, and a where, with a corollary of how—nagged him over the following weeks, whispered at first in his parish womb and now screamed louder and louder in his speeding locomotive.

Why the invitation, and with a personal plea no less, after I threw away the last ones without bothering to respond?

Who cared enough to send them?

Where did whoever get his address?

How in the world did he/she/they know he was a priest?

Including his own class reunions, Father Thomas always held the general idea of reunions in mild contempt as occasions for youths grown older and old to boast to classmates they never liked and no longer recognized about adventures and accomplishments that, more often than not, stretched the truth like a limp rubber band. Maybe, he reasoned when he decided to accept the invitation, and again now while savoring the memory of supper in his Roomette on the way back, this was a time not to lord over people but to show them what the Lord can do in a person's life.

He was fully aware that the last time these classmates saw him, he was the school brute and, even with the personable note added to his invitation, hadn't the faintest idea of why they would reach out. "I could always wear the shirt," he laughed to himself after the conductor stopped by for good night and a handshake.

The infamous T-shirt.

MR. C CLASS OF '67 lay neatly folded and packed in his suitcase, out from its hiding place in a cardboard box squirreled away on the top shelf of a corner closet. There it joined one other remnant of his past, a mahogany box safeguarding his Marine Service medals. Father Thomas didn't know if the shirt mocked or amused when he decided to dig it out and bring it along but decided after some thought that, aside from the hopeless task of squeezing into the thing, there was a matter of good taste—to say nothing of letting the past be bygones—for him to want to be remembered silently and unseen. There would be enough on his hands on reunion night without this reminder that he once slugged many of these folks just for the heck of it.

Rested and ready, the following afternoon he bid farewell to his overnighter Capitol Limited and headed for the cavernous, bustling avenues of downtown Chicago. They didn't feel all that familiar but weren't foreign to him either, just streets in the long string of streets he had walked over the course of a lifetime. Only one address held any fascination. Uber answered the call.

Father Thomas double checked the address when the driver announced, "Here you are, buddy," but sure enough, his *Semper Fi* tattoo parlor was no more, replaced by a Vietnamese restaurant. Disappointed that the priest wanted information rather than a table, the proprietor delivered a curt, "No idea," and slammed the door in his face after his question of where the artist might have moved.

The Uber man had told him he'd wait and was true to his word, dialing in directions for the next eight miles that would transport him to the high school in Cicero. It might as well have been eight million for how close Father Thomas felt to the place. When he mapped out this trip, Father Thomas purposely planned to arrive here on reunion Saturday and leave the following morning. Settling into the backseat of the Uber, he was more convinced than ever that it was the right thing to do. Chicago had his tattoo parlor, or at least the memory of it. Nothing in Cicero, not thoughts of home or hallways or hangouts, yielded the slightest tug of nostalgia or remorse. Even worse, and defying his own advice to J.J. to get out and look for the good, Father Thomas questioned whether he should be here at all to maybe expose himself as pariah instead of priest, to ridicule instead of recollection.

"Everything okay back there?" the driver interrupted after a few miles.

"Sorry?"

"Just asking if everything's alright. You're pretty quiet. Most passengers talk my ear off."

The priest managed a laugh. "Sure, I'm fine. Busy thinking."

"No sweat, *padre*."

The car dropped him off.

With the reunion an hour away and a coffee shop standing tall across the street, Father Thomas settled in with a grande extra cream and let his thoughts scatter. One of them landed on J.J., wondering where his pathway was leading this summer and not having the faintest idea that his friend was less than a hundred miles due north in Wisconsin. Next thought was of Dexter Jones and how he was holding up to his new pain and anguish, as if what they had shared back in the jungles and hills of Southeast Asia was not enough for one man's lifetime. Braced with a refill, Father Thomas prayed for his friend with verses from memory in James and Isaiah and concluded with Psalm 25, one of their favorites.

He looked at his watch. Three minutes to six.

Time to lock and load.

From the moment he signed in and pasted on the nametag, his jitters proved to be unfounded even with one early incident when two wise guys approached, arms crossed over their faces, and exclaimed in mock horror, "Please don't hit us, Kearns!"

Feigning amusement, he complied, but in a moment of weakness, he was tempted.

Other than that, it was all good. Father Thomas found himself just one of a crowd with no one vying to be the center of attention and no one-upmanship of ambitions fulfilled or boasting about who had advanced further or traveled farther. The evening glided along in pleasant conversation, handshakes, and kindness of people glad to see each other again after all the years gone by.

Needing a timeout after a few hours, Father Thomas prayed in the silence of his heart while walking along the gym's perimeter. *Lord, I humble myself to you. Forgive my anxiety and fear and thank you for leading me to meet with these good people. To you be all the glory.* He looked around at the banners and trophies celebrating the school's athletic milestones and, at a far wall, stopped at a recognition plaque, its names engraved in bronze below a red inscription.

All Who Served 1965–1973

Between the names *Hahn, Dustin* and *McDonnell, Adam* appeared *Kearns, Thomas.*

He stood there lost in thought, finally stepping back and saluting, them and him. He had just turned to walk back toward the festivities when a man approached.

"Father Thomas, maybe you don't remember me, I'm Russell Bigelow."

The priest did remember him. "Of course, Russell, the editor of the student newspaper, right?"

"Yes, that was me, and I…"

"And you were the one who anointed me Mr. C as I recall."

Russell blushed. "Yes, that's me alright. I'm so glad you finally came. I wanted to apologize to you for doing that and…" pointing to the plaque, "to thank you for your service to our country. I see you've certainly led an active and productive life since leaving these halls."

Father Thomas clapped him on the shoulder. "No need at all for the apology, and I thank you for finding me. I was…am…proud to have answered the call of duty, first to my country and now to those in my parish."

"I must say, none of us ever figured you to become a priest."

Father Thomas shook his head. "Frankly, neither did I."

The two men shared a laugh.

"I'm wondering, Russell, how did the people from our class know where and who I was?"

"The internet is a wonderful thing, Father."

"Ah. Yes it is, I suppose. But I do wonder something else. There was a handwritten note on my invitation asking me to attend. Are you responsible for that, or do you have any idea who is?"

"The answers to those two questions are no and yes." On cue, he turned and motioned toward the opposite wall. "Do you see the person over there looking our way? He wrote the note and has been waiting to meet you."

Father Thomas observed a man he estimated to be in his mid-forties, small in stature, neatly maintained with manicured pepper-

and-salt beard, new suit and tie, and gleaming shoes. Father Thomas was certain he didn't know nor had he seen him during the course of the night. And yet, center dent felt hat in hand, the stranger walked up to them with an air of humble familiarity. Russell gave the two a wide smile, said "I'll leave you alone," and returned to the crowd.

With glistening eyes, the man took the priest's hands in his.

"I've been waiting a long time for this and am overjoyed to meet you at last. My name is Peter Kearns Williamson."

The name did not immediately register, and by the time "Kearns" clicked in Father Thomas' brain, the man had already spoken again.

"I'm your brother."

Chapter 17

Not ready to leave Wisconsin behind, J.J. looked for an excuse to linger. He found one when his stomach growled and another when Moth's open-ended invitation popped into his head.

His trip through America's Dairyland rekindled memories of joyous times here, a favorite of which was when he, Charlie, and Mom and Dad drove through on a road trip to Springfield. One summer, Big Al, a devotee of Abraham Lincoln, packed the family into the car to visit the sixteenth president's final resting place. Dad and Mom planned a leisurely trip for them and their boys and made a point to take in the charms of Wisconsin along the way. Included was a Thursday afternoon game in the left field bleachers at County Stadium where, nourished by hot dogs, cotton candy, and sodas, they watched the Milwaukee Braves blank the Pittsburgh Pirates by a score of 6–0. What followed the next night, at least for J.J., was the *pièce de résistance* of the trip: a Friday fish fry that was and is such a staple among those who call Wisconsin home that it deserves an emblem on the state flag. He still held in his heart and savored on his taste buds that hour spent with the three people he loved most in the world, enjoying their plates of three deep-fried perch, piles of golden French fries, mounds of coleslaw, and slices of rye bread, washed down by iced tea with lemon.

As chance or blessings had it, J.J. departed the Dells these decades later on a Friday. Having made the decision to remain in Wisconsin a day or two longer, he endeavored to arrange a sumptuous reprise in the company of his 18-wheeler friend and her sweetheart. He dug out Moth's phone number from his wallet, Ruby idling alongside an endless field of tussling corn.

Moth picked up on the third ring. "We'd be delighted to join you," she answered his invitation and rattled off road-by-road, block-by-block directions to her house. Whistling in contentment and glancing from time to time at Marie's Santa Claus tucked in the passenger seat, J.J. tooled along, the yap of roaming farm hounds the only violation of his blissful quietude.

Two hours later he turned onto Moth's street, where, among the neat and tidy one-story homes with manicured lawns and blooming flower beds, J.J. recognized what could only be hers. At the driveway commanded by a gleaming yellow Harley with sidecar, he parked Ruby and knocked on the front door without bothering to check the address.

"J.J., how wonderful to see you!" beamed Moth, looking as fresh and happy as a violets fluttering in a light breeze. She hooked his arm and brought him inside to what he instantly knew to be a home of love, warmth, and sharing. Tasteful furnishings and décor in beiges, greens, and blues spoke comfort. Photographs of all sizes, venues, and faces—young, old, and in between—graced living room walls.

"Welcome to our nest, J.J." Moth sand and moved to the side. "And this is my Fly Boy."

Her husband stepped forward. "A pleasure to meet you, J.J."

"And you, sir."

"Please call me Rudolph. I can tell my lovely wife took a fast liking to you. Not just anyone gets to call her Moth right off the bat."

"The man did buy me breakfast," she smiled.

Rudolph stood an inch taller than the woman beside him, looked onto the world from soft amber eyes, meticulously maintained a mostly pepper crew cut atop his athletic frame, and shook hands with a firmness that portrayed unstated poise and confidence of a man who, prior to domesticity, served his country landing airplanes on boats at turbulent seas.

After the introductions and dime tour of the Stephens homestead, they got down to business.

"So, J.J., we know a nice restaurant in Port Washington, not terribly far from here, that has a great fish fry. You game?" Moth inquired.

"Lead the way." Tempting though it was to ask if he could ride in the sidecar out front, J.J. yielded to his better angels that three would be a crowd and bit his tongue. They piled into the get-around Jeep.

"Ever been to Port, J.J?" Rudolph asked as they merrily drove, seemingly without a care in the world.

"Once, to a harvest festival when I came up from the weekend while I worked in Chicago."

"You'll love this place we're going to," Moth chimed in.

She was right. A packed house celebrated the workweek's end with food, drink, and cheer. Country music played. Waiters hustled to and fro. Dishes clattered. A Brewers game played on a large screen over the bar.

J.J. pointed to the overhead TV. "Still can't get used to the Braves not being here."

"You'd love them. We've got this slugger Braunie…"

The hostess approached.

"Welcome back you two. I see you brought a friend."

"A future convert to your terrific fish fry," Moth returned.

While waiting for their food, J.J. glanced up to catch what was happening in the ballgame, the sound drowned out by good-natured conversation. He had enjoyed end-of-the-week festivities in loud bars and waiting-line restaurants over the years, but the companionship in this laid-back, convivial crowd made him think that maybe he hadn't done enough kicking back in enough places with enough people and that there was always room for more.

Moth broke in. "Earth to J.J.? You seem lost in thought."

"Just enjoying myself and soaking in the atmosphere."

The fish and accompaniments proved to be as good as

advertised, and the budding friendship even better. In the ebb and flow of the meal and the trio getting more and more comfortable each other, J.J. looked over and asked, "If you don't mind me asking, how did you come to be a truck driver?"

Moth and Rudolph exchanged glances. He gave her his last piece of perch.

"Well, it all began…" she then gleefully talked without pause or interruption over the course of the next twenty-five minutes.

A passion for vehicles of all manner was ignited in Alice Murphy when her Uncle Ned presented her with a Mighty Tonka at a party celebrating her second birthday. "Girl's gotta learn some time," Ned told his startled brother George and *Frau* Dorothy.

Mimicking the sound, little Alice pushed that Tonka around the house day and night, pretending she was behind the wheel. In the ensuing years, Dad and Mom scoured garage sales to score for their beloved and beloving Alice a three-wheeler, bicycle, roller skates, roller blades, scooter, and skateboard. On the day Alice turned sixteen, mother, father, and daughter went to the DMV to get her temporary driving permit. Six months later, she passed the road test with a perfect score on the first try, and two days after that, financed by a loan from her parents, a pre-beaten red pickup truck she named Ruff 'n Reddy joined the household.

Moth and Ruff quickly became a fixture in her neighborhood, and she repaid her parents' loan plus 1 percent interest in eleven months. Nothing's free in this world. No job was too small, whether delivering groceries after school and on weekends or transporting elderly customers to doctors' appointments and the drugstore. During the summers between her high school years, she hauled bales of hay, once offering to do it free for a week in exchange for taking the tractor out for a spin. The farmer knew a good deal when he saw one and obliged.

One man listened in growing amusement, the other in loving affection, but neither said a word as Moth told her story right up to buying the Peterbilt.

"No matter how many times you tell this, I always love hearing it," Rudolph said when she came up for air.

"I know, love. Now, why don't you tell him about my latest birthday present?"

"Nah."

"Please?"

"You tell him."

"Alright then, here goes." She kissed her husband on the cheek. "My hubby takes me to breakfast and afterward says, 'Let's go for a drive.' We head out of the city and turn onto this back road, and he tells me to cover my eyes. Hey, why not? I'll go along with it. I trust the guy. A little while later he tells me, 'You can open them now.'"

Rudolph waggled his head toward J.J.

"Listen, this is the best part," Alice said. "There in front of me is a dump truck heaped with dirt, a big yellow bow on the hood, and Happy Birthday balloons tied to the bumper. The big guy arranged with one of his clients in the construction business to borrow the truck from a building site so that I could bomb around in it for an hour. And what a trip it was, throwing up dust on that country road!"

Rudolph smiled shyly. When Moth excused herself to go to the restroom, he leaned over. "Next year I'm finding her a bulldozer."

"You two are quite the couple," J.J. said when she returned.

They clinked glasses of the beverage that made Milwaukee famous. "Just curious. Whatever happened to Ruff?"

"The engine finally gave out," Moth replied, "but my mom, dad, and I couldn't bear to part with her, so we parked her in the vacant spot in their three-car garage, where she remains to this day. Every time I stop over to visit, I sit in her, and once or twice a year, she gets a good polishing."

Later, their plates cleaned and the crowd thinning, J.J. was genuinely sad it was time to go and insisted on picking up the tab. "I'm leaving first thing in the morning. Can you recommend a motel nearby?"

The Stephens refused on both counts. "A motel? We won't hear of it," Moth said in a tone that'd scare away the Johnny Ds of the world. "We have a cozy spare bedroom and love having guests."

Rudolph picked up the ball. "And we want you to stay at least another night so we can treat you to a game at Miller Park. The Brewers are playing Cincinnati tomorrow evening."

Knowing there was nothing wrong with wanting his own space, J.J. consistently chose relaxing in front of the TV in a motel room padding around in whatever as preferable to staying overnight at someone's house. But since the trip was about extending himself and this couldn't provide better company than if he sketched characters and abracadabra'd them to the table, there could be no other answer.

"Well, I guess then I am happy to say yes to the room and yes to the game."

"Delightful!"

The guest room proved comfortable and homey and greeted its visitor with a crocheted panel, reading *As for me and my house, we will serve the Lord.* After sleeping like a log, singing to himself during a hot shower, and having seconds at breakfast, J.J. figured that, while he wouldn't make a habit of it, spending the night in someone else's house wasn't so bad after all with hosts who made you feel right at home. Their hospitality extended everywhere, from the house to the yard to the ride along Lake Michigan to arrival at the ballpark—his beloved County Stadium long demolished and mostly covered with parking. Rudolph knew how to fry a mean bratwurst, and Moth arranged a fine tailgate party that left none of them, or those they invited to come on over, thirsty or hungry.

"Bleachers okay with you, J.J.?" Rudolph inquired when they walked up to the ticket booths.

"Best seats in the house," came J.J.'s answer.

"Good to see you folks," an usher said when they walked toward their place in the stands. "No pile of kids tonight, I see."

J.J. asked, "Pile of kids?"

"Moth and I take some kids to a ballgame once in a while."

"Don't be modest," the usher said. "These fine people bring a dozen or so kids from orphanages and foster homes throughout the season."

"We're happy to share God's blessings," Moth said at their seats. "The children have no one. They're like a family to us." When she brushed away a tear, Rudolph squeezed her hand and mouthed, "I love you."

The game moved slowly, allowing opportunity for chit-chat and indulgence in Johnsonvilles and a cold one. J.J. told of attending his first ballgame seeing the Milwaukee Braves and how its memory stayed with him and would to his last breath.

"That's a wonderful story," Rudolph said. "It's nice we're here together to perhaps create a new memory for you."

"I have a friend back in LA who meets me at Dodgers games," J.J. said. "We're a mighty peculiar pair, the two of us, me with my Brewers cap and he with his Cubs. You see a lot of other Chicago hats around, but Milwaukee? Not too many."

"Don't lose that allegiance to Milwaukee baseball," Moth smiled.

"Always had it, always will."

The scoreboard read Cincinnati Reds 8, Brewers 1 when they filed out with the rest of the never-say-die hangers-on. Whether to stay over another night never arose as an issue. Back in the guest room once again, J.J. listened to the sounds of the night, pen in hand, and made a note in his calendar about the three hours and nineteen minutes at the ballpark with his new friends.

The calendar lay open on his chest when J.J. woke to the aroma of sizzling Sunday breakfast and percolating coffee. "I'm hoping you'll join us for our Bible service after we eat," Moth said when J.J. joined her and Rudolph for breakfast.

"Happy to." Born, raised, and still a staunch Catholic, never mind his aversion to the confessional, J.J. had no issue with other faiths or attending other churches. "God is God, no matter where or how you believe," he answered when Rudolph queried about his belief on their drive to worship.

"As it should be," husband and wife agreed.

Moth and Rudolph held hands on the way into church, and afterward, the trio enjoyed coffee and Danish in the fellowship hall and paid six quarters for half a dozen gently used paperbacks at a garage sale around the corner.

"Are your Sundays always this wonderful?" J.J. asked once they were back at the couple's home.

"Yes, they are," said Moth. "It's the Lord's Day, a day of worship, celebration, and rest."

Against the backdrop of setting sun in a glorious pink and turquoise sky, J.J. sat outside alone with his thoughts about the day's "nothing special" that made it so very special indeed. One time, Father Thomas delivered his Sunday message quoting Paul's exhortation in Thessalonians, "to aspire to live quietly, and to mind your own affairs." The priest and his long-ago predecessor were right.

As it had to be, Monday took them back to the world. Rudolph headed out the door at daybreak but, before leaving, gave J.J. a hearty handshake and an invitation to return anytime. Moth told of her next trip, bound for Omaha later in the day to deliver a load of steel foundry parts.

She motioned with a finger and reached behind her. "Something to sustain you." She held up a Styrofoam chest lined with ice packs and stocked with a dozen crisp hard rolls, three summer sausages, a pound of cheddar cheese, a container of butter, and a jar of dill pickles, all neatly sliced with utensils taped to the lid.

J.J. was touched by the thoughtful gesture. "You and Rudolph are two of the finest people I've ever met," he said at the door.

"I hope we meet again sometime," Moth said, "speaking for both Rudolph and myself."

"Me too, with or without a flat tire."

His sojourn in Wisconsin concluded, J.J. savored two slices of the sausage when, half an hour later, he smiled broadly at the thought of Moth and Rudolph and directed Ruby onto the freeway frenzy speeding south.

He stuck to the slow lane.

Chapter 18

The day turned heavy and humid and teased rain, building a setting ripe for reflection. J.J. didn't waste the opportunity.

Second thoughts had arisen within hours of the second green pin puncturing the map on his garage wall back home, and third thoughts arose with the Chicago skyline looming ever closer outside his windshield on the late July day. His trip was going wonderfully. Why come back here of all places to ruin things?

Back in the summer of 1983, he had arrived in this city full of energy. Tempted by possibility, excitement, and the opportunity to prove that James Joseph Werth, son of Al and Evie and brother of Charlie, could grow and prosper away from the familiar and comfortable confines of home, he wanted to make his mark in the financial world. Nothing monumental, just something modest, footprints in the sand. But his desire to make a difference was met with indifference to him by his colleagues and absolute surliness from his manager that he could never quite get his head around. Was he at fault? Were they? After a while, he finally stopped trying to find the answer and went along, another face in the faceless office crowd of white collars and starched faces. Many a weekend afternoon in those early weeks and months, he spent at Union Station fantasizing about jumping aboard to Billings, ditching possessions and job and futility, thoughts maybe not realistic, after all he had worked for, but definitely therapeutic, if fleetingly so.

Returning home one desultory Saturday in late winter or early spring, depending on where one measured on life's barometer, J.J. took the mail from his box in the apartment building lobby and had a flashback. He took the stairs to his flat two at a time and rummaged through the closet until he found the letter Big Al gave him the day he graduated from high school. A lot had happened since he last held the yellowing, handwritten note on *From the Desk of Al and Evie Werth* stationery, but sitting at his tiny kitchen table and watching the snow fall, the words resonated from beyond as if his dad were sitting beside and reading them to him.

Dear Son,

Your path begins now, and I humbly offer some loving words as you make your way.

The people who think life is always bad are as delusional as the ones who think it is always good. Both good and bad are apportioned by the Good Lord, and it is not up to us to decide the breakdown or the when and where. You, me, all of us will face trials from without when the world is a mess and from within when our mind is one. Forget mind over matter. Oftentimes, the solution is putting one foot in front of the other and making it to the next day. Never let yourself succumb to the bad or ridicule the Pollyannas. Anger and hatred and unrighteousness will always be out there. Don't deny them; deal with them. Ride out the hard times and revel in the good ones; neither last forever. Be happy and grateful and strong and always do your best. Heed the biblical wisdom of your namesake, Saint James, to persevere and be patient. Above all, remember that whenever we struggle, God is there to help and to guide.

My dear Jimmy, I will always be with you and always love you.

J.J. read and re-read.

It snowed harder.

His dad's beautiful words didn't make the sunrises and sunsets and time in between pass any easier or move any faster, but they did put them in perspective. He ended up making it through four years on these shores, braced by that love letter, joined afterward by a renewed determination to expand boundaries and the soothing sermons and God's love that washed over him when he found refuge at Ascension Catholic Church, a mile walk from home.

After closing his apartment door for the last time and creating renewed life in a promotion to New York, he had never once felt even the hint of a tug to go back to a city that gave him nothing and meant even less to him. Yet somehow, here he was in the mosh pit of Chicago traffic.

Lake Michigan popped into view, waves lapping onto shore. A

seagull flew by, joined another, and the two sailed off together.

Rain started and invited thunder and lightning along for the party. J.J. tapped the steering wheel. Decision time. To go or not to go. That is the question—or is it even one?

Mom always told him the Lord hates a coward, and with that thought, he exited and at the first red light, touched the rosary hanging from the rear-view mirror. Winding his way in, the streets retained a familiar look despite his years away and efforts to banish the experience. He elected to stay at a modest hotel in Evanston, home to Northwestern University, where, to improve his skills and fill the nights his second and third years working in Chicago, he had taken several classes on finance, accompanied one semester by a history course on the post-Civil War economy in hopes of squiring—unrequited, as it turned out—the professor's perky graduate assistant.

Neither the university nor the lady were on his mind while he checked in, but the subway was. This northern suburb afforded easy access to the L, as the purists constantly corrected him when this was home. Their smugness aside, he learned to love the subway, taking it to points far and near on his days off, observing the hodgepodge of passengers when below ground and taking in the sights when above. One Monday at work, he shared that over the weekend, he rode the subway for two hours just for the joy of doing it, but after ridicule from several of his coworkers, he never raised the subject again.

After picking up a subway map from the hotel's kiosk, he

found his room, settled in, ordered a large, deep-dish, pepperoni pizza, and looked over his to-do list. He had nary a friend, colleague, or treasured memory from here to revisit, so his list was pretty short. Go to Wrigley Field, where the Cubs were to play an afternoon game against the Giants; wander among the exhibits at the Chicago History Museum; and locate a Chicago Vienna, whose charms he had described, lips smacking, to Father Thomas on the night they met in Los Angeles.

The next morning, a warming sunshine replaced the gloom of the day before, and his own disposition responded in kind. He obeyed the Good Book's admonition that the last shall be first, and within not too many minutes of walking into the sunlight from the subway, marched up to a street vendor for a two-hander on a poppy seed bun and adorned with yellow mustard, chopped onions, sweet pickle relish, dill pickle spear, tomato slices, pickled peppers, and sprinkling of celery salt. Every taste bud tweaked, he started along Michigan Avenue to kill time before the ballgame.

A block ahead, pedestrians hurried up and down alone, in conversation with a person or persons, faces fixed on cell phones, eye contact avoided as if it spread the plague. No one noticed, or cared to, a grizzled resident of the streets who looked out on the world through milky, sunken eyes above hollow cheeks. His wardrobe registered as eclectic in SOX cap, washed-out Bears football jersey, threadbare blue gabardine jacket, trousers to mid-ankle, and tennis shoes of undefined color sans laces or socks. He stood erect at a shopping cart piled with old newspapers, older clothing, and neatly folded paper bags. At his feet was a lidless cigar box with a smattering of coins and a bill or two, and beside him, a boxer puppy lay on makeshift bedding fashioned from a pea coat.

J.J. stopped. "How are you today?" he inquired pleasantly.

"Trying."

The dog perked up.

"Sweetie likes you," the man said.

"I'm sorry?"

"I was saying my dog, Sweetie, likes you."

"How can you tell?"

"I know things."

J.J. took a look around. "Be right back," he said to the man, and walked back to the wiener merchant.

"Two more, please," he ordered, "one with everything, the other with nothing."

"Not even the bun?"

"Nope."

"Also, a large drink, and milk if you have it."

The vendor looked up the street to the homeless man then back at J.J. "Need that milk in a dish? I think I have one around here."

"That'd be great."

J.J. handed him some cash.

"Blessings for your kindness," the vendor said.

Drinks secured, food wrapped in tissue paper, and three twenties buried under a pile of napkins in the cardboard container,

J.J. returned and handed over the delights.

"God bless you, sir."

"And you, sir."

Sweetie wagged her stump of a tail.

After a ways, he looked back. Man and companion chewed and drank gleefully, once pausing from their feast to exchange wide grins with each other. J.J. started to wave but thought better of it and walked on, needing no further recognition.

The sunshiny afternoon presented a perfect setting for America's pastime. J.J. took his position in the left field bleachers and soaked in the good feeling that never failed him at this or any ballpark. Big League, Little League, who cares. Beer and hot dog beside him, J.J. noticed that the Wrigley experience had changed some over the many seasons since he was here last. The place looked spiffier, prices of seats and refreshments were substantially spiffier, the beloved Cubbies were more likely to win than to lose. Beyond that, baseball was baseball was baseball.

His evenings at Dodger Stadium with Father Thomas notwithstanding, J.J. was not one to banter with fans, preferring to soak in the smells and sounds of the ballyard and minutiae of the game and free his mind to think its thoughts when play slowed. Today was no exception. What if, he mused during the seventh-inning stretch, he had remained mired in his misery back then or retreated to familiar turf instead of getting up off the mat and dealing with things and staying on the lookout for something better. Lesson learned then and brought home again now. He joined the crowd singing, "Go, Cubs, Go!" after the hometown team triumphed by a final of 9 to 4.

The afternoon's glow faded but not the experience. Ninety minutes later, J.J. bounded down the Evanston subway stairs humming, "Take Me Out to the Ballgame." His mind elsewhere, he nearly ran over an elderly man blocking the way at the bottom and muttering, "Well wouldn't that frost you."

J. J. moved alongside and quickly spotted the reason for his chagrin, a folding personal grocery cart that had slipped from the man's grasp and lay sideways at the foot of the stairs, its packages of meat, cans of vegetables, bags of snacks, containers of beverages, and assorted odds and ends thrown every which way. The men surveyed each other and the mess. Others hustled by, one kicking a can of peas out of the way.

"Let me help you," J.J. said, and they got to work without further conversation. After a cool efficiency restocking the cart, J.J. took a chance and invited, "I'm going for supper. Would you care to join me?"

After looking as his watch, seemingly stalling while he considered the unexpected offer, the man accepted. "I'd be delighted."

Salutations followed.

"J.J. Werth at your service."

"A pleasure to meet you, J.J. I am grateful for your assistance and your generosity. My name is Anthony."

J.J. pegged Anthony to be in his mid-seventies when, in fact, he was eighty-two. His black fedora covered a shock of white hair, and his manner of dress, neither extravagant nor tacky, befit his forty-plus years as a banker. His build was trim, features feline, eyes inviting.

Shopping cart in tow, he maintained a steady pace.

Aside from their acquaintanceship budding into friendship, J.J. and Anthony shared a liking for the day's special—turkey and the trimmings—at a diner up the street. Over their platefuls of bird and its accompaniments, the older shared his story with the younger. They talked for the better part of two hours.

Anthony and his wife Helena met on a blind date their senior year in high school and were inseparable since. After graduating from the University of Illinois—he in business, she in journalism—they returned to their native Evanston, settled down, went to work faithfully, bought a house, and raised two children, one now in Colorado, the other in Florida. He and his Helena enjoyed a full life of happiness and sadness, ups and downs, the hunky-dory and the not so hunky-dory. Three years ago, Helena developed rheumatoid arthritis that confined her to a nursing home three blocks from their marital home, where Anthony continued to live.

"I stay with her every day, help her eat, take her out front to catch some sun, read to her, watch TV together. After all these years, I still can't get enough of her company." On this day, Anthony's shopping cart took its spill on his way home from a run to the grocery on the Chicago side of the street that delineated it from Evanston.

"I'm glad circumstance brought us together, J.J.," he interjected before a last forkful of turkey.

"As am I, Anthony."

Scooping up his last bite of pumpkin pie, Anthony grinned uncertainly at J.J.

"Say, would you like to meet my Helena tomorrow and perhaps spend some time with the two of us?"

"I'd be delighted," J.J. declared.

They settled on ten a.m. to get together and walked into the warm night where Anthony offered a left handshake in farewell. "It's closer to the heart."

Helena proved to be as charming as her husband, with a ready smile and cheery disposition despite being bedridden. Her blue eyes sparkled when she talked of their lives together and blew Anthony a kiss, which he caught and planted on his right cheek. "My Romeo," she giggled.

To J.J.'s delight, both enjoyed intelligent conversation, eschewed blather, and possessed the admirable quality of knowing and enforcing the difference. Sitting idly in their pleasant company brought to mind more of his mother's wisdom when, as a teenager, he complained of having nothing to do. "Doing nothing is doing something, and sometimes it's better than something."

The nothing and something with Anthony and Helena proved so satisfying that J.J. returned to the nursing home early the next day for more talking, eating, snoozing, watching, reading, sitting, and observing. He skipped his visit to the History Museum, which was no small thing to a checklist freak.

The rain returned.

"I love the rain," Helena chirped. "It rained on our wedding day." She smiled at Anthony.

"A good omen, it turned out," he answered and smiled back.

Friday came along and, with it, a need for J.J. to get going, August on the march, but that didn't stand in J.J.'s way of his sitting with Anthony and Helena at the monthly TGIF party, where, along with unlimited popcorn and punch, a local accordion musician had residents tapping fragile toes and fingers and humming faint voices to "Oh! Susanna," "I Don't Know Why I Love You like I Do," "Young at Heart," and other favorites of yore. Eyes misted in the dining room's audience of wheelchairs and white hair and hearing aids and breathing tubes and rolling beds and looks faraway of lives and loves gone but not forgotten. J.J. felt almost among family.

When he stood to depart from Anthony and Helena after supper, one voice chimed, "Till we meet again."

"Don't be a stranger," chimed the other.

They exchanged addresses and phone numbers and bid one another farewell.

Back at the hotel, calendar in hand, J.J. sipped from a can of Coke and wrote in his daily calendar:

Chicago

Anthony and Helena—a love story

P.S. Find Dad's letter!!!

He smiled to himself. As lousy as it had been living here, maybe its purpose was so that he could come back, stronger and wiser and happier. You never know. An idea came to mind and became so irresistible after googling a destination in the hotel's business center that the next morning, he skipped the complimentary continental breakfast except for a cinnamon roll snagged on the way out.

The early morning was still, beams of sun treading the chilly, blue water. Others paid him no attention, runners checking their pulse, a middle-age couple letting their dog run off the leash, a youngish woman oblivious in headphones, a something-something clumsily wanding a handheld metal detector over the sand in search of booty.

J.J. took off his shoes and socks, rolled up his jeans, and walked up the beach. He walked a short distance, turned, and admired. Soon the rippling lake washed away his footprints, one by one, but it didn't matter. He had put them there, finally, and that was enough.

Chapter 19

The divine words resonated as they always did and chastened as they deservedly should. Looking out the window of his motel room, Bible open to Matthew 7:5, Father Thomas read the verse again. "You hypocrite, remove the wooden beam from your eye first; then you will see clearly to remove the splinter from your brother's eye."

By all rights, he should be heading to the train depot in a couple of hours to return to everything that was right in his life back in Los Angeles. But he was not in charge of rights and right, and because of that, his insides churned like never before in the years since he left Vietnam in one piece. Instead of the comforting arms of Sunday morning Mass at ten a.m., Father Thomas was waiting for Peter to arrive and take him to reunite with his mother.

He slept little over the night, stunned and challenged by the introduction to the man at the back of the reunion hall and the conversation that followed.

"You're who?" Father Thomas demanded. His eyes squinted.

"I'm your brother, Peter. I know you find this hard to believe…"

"That is certainly an understatement."

He had to admit that having a brother wasn't all that surprising. In fact, the only surprise was that more of them, and probably sisters too, hadn't come out of the woodwork. Growing up, the only ones in the house were he, his mother's boyfriend *du jour*, and Doris, a still-insatiable woman of thirty-eight, when he slammed the door behind him and went off to war. As a teenager, he wondered why no other kids hung around. With her endless trysts, his half-siblings could be on youth baseball teams scattered all over Cicero, maybe Berwyn too.

But why now, after all the absent years, was this happening? There were times, body bent in prayer, that he had thought of his mother and asked for the Lord's forgiveness, and his own too, for the way he left and never went back. Priests go to confession, too, and he had brought this sin to his confessor. But he never seriously considered reaching out to Doris. What would it prove? Would she want him back? What might he find?

Now it was out of his hands, reacher the reachee.

Without an offer to go someplace quiet and talk, Father Thomas ordered, "Prove to me you're my brother."

Peter obeyed orders, describing their mother in physical detail, the house Father Thomas fled, even producing his and Thomas' birth certificates.

The priest rubbed his eyes. "I still find it very hard to fathom that you not only found me but that we meet now and in this place."

Peter offered a smile. "Well, it's not that we haven't tried."

"What do you mean?"

"Who do you think is behind the invitations to the reunions?"

"So it's you?"

"Absolutely. You can check with the reunion committee if you don't believe me. When I found out your class was having one this year, I figured why not add the handwritten note alongside. And I'm happy it worked, or at least helped."

Father Thomas' classmates filed out, many stopping for final words of well wishes.

"Looks like it's time to leave," Peter suggested. "Maybe we can continue our discussion? I know of a nice twenty-four-hour coffee shop nearby."

The priest straightened his ponytail, figuring he'd come this far, so why not keep going.

"Lead the way, Peter."

"Wonderful, Father Thomas."

"Please, call me Thomas."

Peter, as best he could, recaptured the absent years for his long-lost brother.

Despite his rude and abrupt departure, Doris never stopped thinking about her son and lamented all that had gone wrong. She vowed to change though it didn't come easily. One Monday two years later, her car broke down as she drove back from Champaign after yet another in her string of weekend losers, this conquest a squirrely college kid who scribbled "Jon Dow" on the motel register. Sitting inside her crippled vehicle and sobbing in despair and shame, she pounded the steering wheel and choked out, "Serves me right, a loser in a loser car."

A persistent tapping startled Doris to attention.

The man talking through her window smiled thinly in greeting.

"Is there anything I can do for you, ma'am?"

"No, you can't. No one can," she snarled. "Get away or I'll call the cops."

Traffic hustled by. A truck driver aired out a double blast.

"I thought you might need some help, is all."

"And why would you think that?"

He pointed at the front of her car. "Your hissing radiator is kind of a clue."

She sighed and wound down the window. "Yeah, I guess it is."

"I'll take a look if you like."

Doris wiped her eyes, stared absently straight out the windshield, and shifted her glance sideways. The guy seemed nice enough, neither young nor old, of modest manner and with the calloused hands and chiseled chin of a laboring man, just her luck that her knight in shining armor would be a mechanic in a rusting pickup truck.

She shook her head ruefully. *What choice do I have stuck out here? AAA's for rich people.* "Sure, go ahead," she answered the man.

A minute later, he returned to her window and wiped his hands on a rag. "Not a huge problem, just a burst radiator hose."

"Out here that might be a huge problem for me." Doris started to wind up her window.

"Uh, ma'am, I have a spare in my truck."

"I'll bet."

"No, really. I own an auto-repair shop back home in Cicero and always keep parts on hand for myself and good folks like yourself who might be stranded."

"Good folks like myself," she muttered under her breath. "Right."

"I can fix it pretty quickly and get you on your way. I do suggest, however, that you have that radiator replaced soon. It's on its last legs."

"Thank you, kind sir," she said. "I mean that sincerely. Not many decent folks around."

He shrugged. "There are if you give them a chance." He returned with the radiator hose and made the repair in prompt order.

She took out her wallet, knowing how little was in it. "What do I owe you?"

"Nothing. Just do a courtesy when you can for someone who needs it. Safe travels now." He handed her his business card and prepared to leave. "By the way, my name's Samuel, Samuel Williamson. Pleasure to make your acquaintance."

"I do thank you again, Mr. Williamson." She didn't offer her name in return, and Samuel didn't ask for it. He drove past, tapped his horn lightly, and waved.

A week later the car began to limp again, and Doris decided why not give him—and her—a chance. Samuel wheeled himself out from under a Suburban when she pulled up and, recognizing the face, offered a generous smile.

"It's good to see you again. Are you here about that radiator?"

"No, I already had that replaced," she said. "Now there's a funny noise when I start it. Do you have time to take a look?"

"Glad to. It's always something, right?"

Surprisingly gladdened that he remembered her, she added, "By the way, I'm Doris."

"Nice to meet you, Doris. Come back later today. I'll do my best to have that beauty up and purring."

She laughed. "A beauty, that it is."

Doris returned with her checkbook, and, having stuck her toe in the water this far, brought along a plate of chocolate chip cookies.

"How's the car doing?" she asked.

"Good as new, an easy fix."

"I brought you a tip. I baked them myself."

"That's very kind of you. They're my favorite."

"Really?"

"Yes, really."

Relieved that her meager checkbook had enough to pay for the repair, she shook his greasy hand and turned to leave.

"I was wondering…" he began.

Here it comes, she figured. "Yes?"

"Would you like to join me at my church service this Sunday?"

Over the years, Doris received any number of invitations from males wide-eyed in pursuit of Miss Right-Now, but to church? That was a new one. She amused herself, toying with the answer, *Why the hell not?* but instead replied calmly, "That would be very nice."

The acquaintanceship born that Sunday led to friendship then to courtship. A year to the day after they sat together for the first time listening to his minister, Samuel and Doris stood before him, hands entwined, vowing "to have and to hold, till death us do part."

She was forty-one, he fifty.

"That's a love story if I ever heard one," Father Thomas said. The clock ticked toward one a.m. in the coffee shop, yet the two men made no move toward leaving, mesmerized as if reading a book neither could put down. "Dad and Mom went to work pretty quickly on building a family. They weren't exactly spring chickens," Peter continued. "First came yours truly, then Mary."

"Mary?" the priest gulped.

"Yes, Thomas. You also have a sister."

"Oh, my goodness."

Peter let his brother collect himself. "In fact, the reunion invitations were her idea. She figured it was a pretty low-key way of reaching out to see if you were interested in getting back in touch. No harm no foul and all that."

"I'm glad it finally worked," Father Thomas said sincerely.

"As are we, Thomas, as are we."

There followed stories of births and anniversaries, celebrations and reunions, life and death.

Peter's eyes watered. "Dad passed away four years ago, a righteous man, father, and husband. He and Mom loved each other every day of their marriage, in so many ways, big and little. Her waving goodbye at the window in the morning when he went off to work. Them holding hands going into the grocery. It was almost like they were trying to make up for all the missed years."

"Missed years," Father Thomas mused, his own eyes moistening and mind racing around what was and what might have been.

"Missed years don't mean a lost future," Peter answered. "Mom and Dad are proof of that. Dad never tired of talking to Mary and me about how God answered his prayers later in life to bless him with a good woman to love and to love him in return. And Mom was always happy to tell us how Dad's inner beauty melted the ice around her heart and showed her all the good there was in the world." He rubbed his eyes with the palms of his hands. "I'm sorry you never got to meet him."

"Did he," Father Thomas said and took a sip of water, "I mean, did your dad know about me?"

Peter offered a small smile and said softly, "Yes, Mom told him all about you. He always promised her that one day you would come back. He just knew you would. We, my sister and I, thought of calling you, even before you made it to LA We talked about it quite a bit actually, even picked up the phone once or twice, but stopped. No, it had to be up to you to want to come back. It was Mary who suggested trying the reunion. That you didn't answer the first times didn't stop her."

The conversation lagged, and the men watched the soothing rainfall dampening the sidewalks, drops decorating the window of the cafe. Father Thomas didn't know that two miles away in an assisted living apartment lay Doris, anxiety building at the thought of seeing him. When Peter had told her of Thomas' signed willingness to attend the reunion and that Peter intended to meet him there, Doris pleaded that Peter tell Thomas she was dead.

"I'm afraid to face him after all I used to be."

"I won't hear of it," Peter pronounced.

"What if he hates me and refuses to come?"

"He will want to see his mother. Our mother."

The rain gave way to a brilliant morning when Peter arrived at Father Thomas' motel a sleepless five hours after they had parted outside the diner. Other than Peter updating Thomas that their mother, now in her late eighties, was in frail health and loved having the Sunday newspaper comics read aloud, the two drove wordlessly. Once inside the building, Peter took a seat in the lounge.

"I'll let you two get acquainted. Mary is coming in a bit, and we'll wait for you here."

"Okay." Father Thomas had no idea what to expect, of himself or of her, when he walked down the hallway. He hoped for the best, but if the worst happened, well, he could deal with it. He straightened himself at Apartment 115, took a deep breath, and knocked.

There was no answer.

A television set blared through the heavy door.

He knocked harder.

The volume tapped lower about a dozen decibels. "Please come in," came a trembling voice.

Father Thomas took another deep breath, turned the doorknob, and entered. Resting in a recliner, she seemed smaller than he remembered. An afghan warmed her lap and legs, light blue slippers with worn white fringe covered her bony feet. He surprised himself by feeling a sudden warmth after all the empty years between them.

"Please sit, Thomas." The voice of a mother to a son hadn't changed.

He went to a chair at a corner of the room.

"No, here, near me."

He moved closer.

"It's nice to see you."

He'd rehearsed this moment a hundred times with a hundred opening lines and a hundred responses, and yet now, actually here, he couldn't recall a single one. Finally, to rescue himself, and maybe her too, he looked over at the TV. "What're you watching?"

"Something on Turner Classics. The new movies think only

about violence and sex."

"I agree."

They paused, long enough for it to be awkward, not too long to be a showstopper.

Finally, he asked, "How long have you lived here?"

"Coupla years."

"Seems real nice."

"It is. Everyone's friendly, and the workers are good to us."

They talked lightly getting more comfortable with each other until, after an hour, Peter cracked the door. "Everything okay?"

"We're doing fine," Father Thomas said. He smiled at Doris. "Aren't we?"

"Yes, we are," she said and smiled back.

Mary came in and introduced herself. "I can't believe I'm meeting my bigger brother."

Father Thomas, stifling a chuckle that his sister in ponytail appearance struck him as a mini-me version of himself, shot a playful smile and surveyed his own bulk. "I'm bigger alright."

"*Touchè.*"

The levity broke everyone up, and they settled in getting acquainted and feeling at ease with one another. Brothers and sister agreed to meet up later at Sunday afternoon Mass where Father Thomas beamed in the company of his newfound nephews and nieces and delighted in singing along with "From the Inside Out," a Hillsong tune new to him and one he took note of for sharing back home.

On the way out of church, Peter offered, "We've reserved the party room at Mom's place tomorrow. That okay with you?"

"Sounds great. Tonight, I'd just like some time to absorb all of this."

"Sure thing."

The priest turned down the offer of a drive to his motel. "I believe I'll stay here a while and catch a cab back. See you tomorrow."

"Till then."

He returned inside the dim, quiet church, lit a votive candle, and knelt in prayer.

Heavenly Father, thank you for leading me back home.

His Bible open to 1 Peter, he read the verse aloud, "Announce the praises of him who called you out of darkness into his wonderful light." A sparrow flew through the open door, perched on a nearby pew, tilted its head, and observed for a short while, then returned to freedom.

A time later, Father Thomas walked out into the approaching night, having never intended to return to the motel. He leisurely covered the mile walk to his mom's place, making a random stop and singing along the way his new favorite son, "From the Inside Out."

Two residents sat outside on rocking chairs when he arrived. "Here to see your mother?" greeted a woman, whose years had not and would never diminish her smile.

The question stopped him in his tracks. "Do you mean Doris?"

"Who else would I be talking about?"

"How did you know I was her son?"

The woman poked her friend good-naturedly, and they grinned at each other. "She talks about her son the priest all the time."

"She does?"

"Why should you be surprised?"

"I don't know. I just am."

"Well don't be. Have a nice visit."

He served himself a cup of apple juice in the lobby and sat awhile, thinking about the surprises piling up. A brother, a sister, now a mom who talked about him all the time after he walked out on her decades ago. What next? Only one way to find out. He swallowed the rest of his juice, walked down the hallway, and knocked softly at apartment 115.

"Come in, Thomas. I hoped you'd come back tonight."

"Hi." He stopped, unsure how to address her.

She motioned him to the dinette. "What've you got here?" she asked. "It smells delicious."

"Still like thin crust veggie pizza?"

"My goodness yes! You remembered!"

He held up a six-pack.

"And Dr. Pepper too?"

They clinked glasses in "Salut!" and ate and spoke and sipped, neither reliving the good old days, of which there were none between them, both relishing the prospect of good new days between them, of which now there could never be enough.

During a break in the conversation, Father Thomas got up to stretch his legs and look around the tidy, one-bedroom apartment. Plastic red and yellow flowers in a glass vase sat atop a doily on her coffee table. A Stiffel lamp lit one side of the living room, a table lamp the other. Above the sagging sofa, he admired a wall chock-full of framed photographs of children and parents, of weddings and baptisms, of Christmases and parties, of happy times past and present. In the center of the top row stood a picture of Samuel, a handsome, beefy face, engaging smile, and gentle eyes, silver hair groomed into a swirl in front.

The two photos on either side took the priest's breath away. Looking back at him was a young man, proud and defiant, in Marine dress uniform, and an older man, wizened and serene, in clerical collar.

He turned. "Where and how in the world did you get these?"

"A mother has her ways. You've made me very proud with what you made of yourself, Thomas. Not a day goes by that I don't...well I don't..." She started to cry.

Father Thomas moved to kneel beside her, wrapped a bearlike arm around her tiny frame, and kissed her cheek. "It's okay, Doris." They looked into each other's eyes. "It's okay, Mom."

They held each other and then remained sitting close together watching another Turner Classic until she eventually nodded off. Father Thomas pulled the afghan up to cover her shoulders, found a spare pillow, and lay down on the couch, for the first time in his life feeling that this was something like home.

Next morning, he beat the sun up, spent breakfast with his mother and other residents in the dining room, then set off on a mission.

First, he headed back to the motel to empty his suitcase and donate it and the contents to the Goodwill, followed by a stop at a big-box store, and finally to the train station to trade in his ticket. A call to Father Damien, the retired priest standing in at Saints Peter and Paul while he was away, left him reassured that all was in order at his parish and that there was no need to rush home.

Father Thomas told no one else of his plans.

The rest of Monday was an affair of chitchat and potluck with his family, sadness of departure softened by promises to stay in touch and meet again. All held hands in thanksgiving as night arrived and the family prepared to go their separate ways, bound together in their hearts.

"The world owes us nothing," Father Thomas began his farewell prayer and looked into his mother's eyes, "but thanks to the blessings of our Lord, we here tonight have been given everything. He has been kinder to us, to me, than any could ever imagine, and for that, we are eternally grateful and in his service."

"Amens" resounded.

Doris watched from the window when everyone left, raised a hand as her oldest child got into Peter's car, and called, "I love you, son."

Thomas smiled and without hesitation answered back, "I love you, too, Mom."

Over the years Father Thomas learned to appreciate daybreak, first in Vietnam, for having survived another twenty-four hours, and since then, for what the previous day had brought and for what the new day promised to bring. So it was at sunrise the next day when he climbed into the taxi waiting outside his motel, the cabby surprised but compliant when Father Thomas told him the destination.

Thirty minutes later, in clerical shirt and collar, jeans, new Cubs cap, and hiking boots, he stood alone outside the Chicago city limits on what promised to be a spectacular day.

"Arise, let us go hence," he proclaimed, and with that, his back to the west and face to the east, Father Thomas shrugged the new knapsack into place and hoisted a thumb.

Chapter 20

J.J. loved but two women over the course of his six decades. One was his mother. The other he met in New York, lo, these many years ago on a crisp March afternoon so generous with sunshine it seemed as if God himself was renewing his pledge to let there be light. Maybe magic like this can't be recaptured, but it can be revisited, and such was his intent when, with resolution, he stuck green pushpin to map in his garage and now cruised ever closer to the place of his heart's desire.

The leaden skies that greeted J.J. on arrival in Chicago returned to bid him farewell on this, day fifty and mile 2,704 of his quest. Any last-minute qualms he may have had when he had set out on his trip were long gone, and he fully embraced the adventure, feeling nowhere near the point of wanting to head back home. Car window wide open, toes still a bit damp from the walk along the shore of Lake Michigan, he drove south, then turned left, mind occupied in search of the precise word to describe his mood.

Content? Relieved? Serene? He pursed his lips. Serene. That sounded right. A long day and many miles lay ahead, and that was good. They would allow him to daydream of the immediate destination that awaited and of the city to come after that.

To top it off, the journey would include a nine-hour bus trip.

Since boyhood when he first hopped aboard public transit in Billings, J.J. loved bus rides and took them every chance he got, sitting back, looking out the window, and thinking his thoughts. As an adult, he rode buses around cities and to distant points. The only negative, he thought wistfully, was when the bus drove past a rest area and he missed the opportunity to visit.

When planning his trip, the decision of whether to first visit New York or Cleveland, the two cities on his horizon, occupied no small amount of time. He went back and forth and forth and back until finally yielding to a higher power to make the choice. New York heads, Cleveland tails.

The flip of the quarter dictated the former, whereupon another idea struck. Instead of driving directly to New York, why not take a bus there and leave Ruby in Cleveland where he would end this leg of his journey anyway? Internet to the rescue as always, the plans fell easily into place, providing a 10:40 p.m. departure due to arrive the following morning at 7:50, and long-term parking just a short walk from the bus depot. Things got even better. A quick call to friends from his days in New York revealed that their delightful bed-and-breakfast in the Brooklyn Heights brownstone was still open for business and would welcome him with open arms.

The seven-hour drive from Chicago to Cleveland—including pit, rest, and summer-sausage-on-rye stops—passed uneventfully. This was followed by parking, securing his seat on the overnighter, discovering and purchasing an ultra-lean pastrami on rye for the ride ahead, and people-watching at the bus depot.

At long last settling into the window seat in the empty sixth row from the back, he was so wound up over the forthcoming walk down memory lane and the bus ride to it that even the thought of sleep eluded him.

Everything was perfect.

Too perfect.

J.J.'s red flag fluttered the instant she climbed up the steps and thereupon greeted every single fellow passenger as she leisurely made her way down the aisle until the driver told her to sit so the bus could start its journey.

He muttered to himself, "Please sit anywhere but next to me."

J.J. enjoyed conversation as much as anyone, even more than some, but there's a difference between conversation with the friendly and inundation by those in love with the sound of their own voice, who don't cross the line so much as obliterate it. From experience, he had developed keen radar to detect an incoming verbal barrage and thereupon employ effective evasive maneuvers. Picking up his cell phone for an imaginary call worked as did ducking and weaving to the other side of the street or into a restroom. But there was no escape hatch here trapped in the window seat of a Greyhound, cell phone stored with his belongings in the overhead bin.

The woman moving his way was aging not aged, dyed black hair pulled back in a bun, happily plump, eyes searching, smile beguiling. In one hand she clutched a small purse, in the other a cloth Boston Red Sox giveaway bag stuffed with food for the trip, a romance novel, darning needle, and balls of yarn in red, white, and blue, the collection brought along perhaps not so much to pass time as to serve as backup in the event she landed no prey on the ride. She passed four perfectly fine seats until she spied the one next to J.J.

"Is this one taken, young man?"

His line against talkers, as he labeled those in their own little world, did not include in-your-face rudeness, however, and even though he wanted quiet time to himself more than anything, he put on his best face. "All yours, ma'am."

"That would be wonderful."

She squirmed herself and her paraphernalia in. "I'm Lydia Mathews. And you are?"

Before he could answer, she opened up. The bus pulled away, and Lydia went to work. No deep breaths to slow her down, no punctuation of any kind, no periods, commas, colons, question marks, semicolons, or exclamation points, just an endless stream of nouns and adjectives and pronouns and verbs and adverbs, as if coming up for air would pose risk of death or, worse, allow the listener to interject a word or two.

…and I told my friend you know the lady who used to live next door to me I like to think you and I are friends too even though we just met my name is Lydia by the way but I didn't catch yours or maybe I did I'm not so good with names you look like a Jerry or maybe a Mark well I'll get it before leaving you know my friend next door she got her hair done and it was the most awful sight to see and I wanted to tell her about my hairdresser when the phone rang and it was my sister that's who I'm going to see now…"

Coming soon, J.J. knew again from experience, had to be the conjunction junction that enabled a talker's complete switching of subject without breaking stride. It arrived, right on schedule.

"…so anyway I read in the newspaper or did I see it on TV you know some of those newscasters are so handsome there was a bad rainstorm down in Florida I feel badly for those people and it reminded me of my sister her name is Belinda who heard about the storm too she has the same last name as mine Mathews neither of us ever married though we had our chances believe me so it reminded me of the bad storms we had growing up in Pennsylvania and she called me to talk about it and I said to her we've got to get together and remember the days back when we were girls and I'm going to buy the two of us a large cheese pizza as soon as I arrive both of us so love pizza we never got it growing up..."

His feeble "really?" from time to time, in hopes of, by some miracle, slowing the onslaught, bounced like BBs off a T-Rex. For all he knew, maybe it only encouraged her to talk more. J.J. finally surrendered and pressed his head against the window, peering into the blackness and wondering when it would end. And mercifully, it did after four hours, five minutes, and many thousands of words, when the driver announced their arrival at the terminal in Milesburg.

"Have a nice visit with your sister," he dry-mouthed when Lydia went to collect her untouched, uneaten, and undrunk belongings. J.J. realized she never once went to the restroom. Nor, for that matter, had he, fearing she might follow him inside to talk away obliviously.

"...Oh I will thank you I never did get to tell you about the time Belinda and I she's my sister you know talked about going over Niagara Falls in a barrel that's the truth Tony as God is my witness..."

"Last call, ma'am, time to leave," the driver ordered. "The bus is about to depart with or without you."

"Okay, okay people are in such a rush these days..." She pushed forward, legs and mouth moving in tandem, and with a final "...so anyway..." to all within earshot waved at the door. J.J. returned the bye-bye, achieved solace in the pastrami sandwich, put his head back, and drifted off, mind occupied with twin thoughts of the days ahead and how his trip thus far could have been so much worse. Just imagine if he had been stuck somewhere between Lydia and Belinda. The crossfire was too awful to contemplate.

He awoke in daylight, a face peering above.

"Hey, buddy, we're here, the Port Authority Terminal," came a male voice from the row in front of him. "I looked over to make sure you hadn't died during the night after all that talking."

"You heard it too, huh?"

"How couldn't I? I'm just glad I brought earbuds to drown it out."

J.J. noted to himself: *Earbuds. GET SOME!*

He and the anonymous benefactor shared a laugh. "I'm just thankful she got off at Milesburg."

"Me too."

Emerging from the bus, J.J. ventured over to catch the subway, Times Square alive with activity on Saturday morning. Billings and New York City stretched a ways apart in distance, a world apart in dimension, yet for J.J., both would always mean a great deal to him. He took in a deep breath of the place, and in so doing caught the unmistakable and irresistible whiff of hot pretzels drifting from a street vendor. Quickly purchasing one, he bit in. If heaven has a taste, this was it.

His friends stood at the top of the steps when he departed the subway in Brooklyn, and after a short walk to A B&B Grows in Brooklyn, the three sat down to eat and catch up on the years behind.

Rich and Gayle Henderson managed the business, having taken over from Rich's mom and dad when they retired to sunnier and more relaxed climes. With the parents at the helm, the bed-and-breakfast forged a well-deserved reputation as an oasis of comfort and tranquility in the big city, along with a sumptuous breakfast, and J.J. was delighted to find that Rich and Gayle kept the tradition intact on both sides of the ledger.

His room offered all the appointments of home, and the breakfast table was even better. Awaiting as he entered the dining room were eggs poached, toast buttered, oatmeal creamy, potatoes golden, bacon crisp, ham browned, kielbasa sizzling, orange juice chilled, and coffee hot. J.J. cannonballed into food and conversation.

"Rich, how are your mom and dad?" he asked, reaching over for another slab of ham and hunk of sausage.

"J.J., I see you haven't lost your appetite," his host answered. "And my parents are well, living the good life just outside Phoenix. They're regulars at spring training every year."

"And yours, Gayle?" J.J. asked.

"Mom and Dad sold their house in Braintree last year and have been caravanning with friends around the country ever since. Quite a life, and they deserve all the good they can get."

The Hendersons and J.J. talked and ate for the better part of two hours until finally, stuffed with food, memories, and good feeling, they adjourned, each to their assignments for the day.

Much awaited J.J. in the week ahead. A ballgame against the Blue Jays at Yankee Stadium, visits to the Museum of Modern Art and the New York Public Library, a walk down Wall Street, a spin on the Staten Island Ferry to catch a bird's-eye view of the Statue of Liberty and other harbor sites, spectacular food everywhere, a return to Times Square to bob in the sea of humanity on a workday. But all of them were mere details compared to the first place on his agenda, and, despite the long overnight bus trip, J.J. headed there without delay.

Central Park glittered in the morning sun. Audubon trove of singing birdlife, joggers serious and wannabe, locals starting their weekend, out-of-towners of all ages, sizes, and colors, the iconic setting mirroring that of when, as a recent arrival in the city, he went for the first time to get some sunshine and bask in the park's tranquility.

J.J. followed the pathway still so familiar after the flight of thirty-four years that it felt like he had been here yesterday and, deep within himself, desired it were so. But he held no grudge against time and knew that his wish could never be, so instead, he traded it for another.

Please be there.

It had to be there.

It was.

The bench stood in place, steady, unmoved by months and years, day and night, sun and gloom, wind and calm, tears of joy and cries of sorrow. Caressed by the summer's warmth as if he were the only one in the universe, J.J. set himself tenderly and stretched out an arm as if to embrace what once was and might have been, the memory of her not a shadow in his mind but a ray of light that, at times, shone brighter than others.

Today it gleamed when he pictured the moment they met.

On that March afternoon, J.J.'s first sight of Darleen Dancer was her luxuriating where he now sat. Dressed in all black from head to toe in stirrup pants, sweatshirt, wool socks, moccasins, and beret, she wore her chestnut hair cut short, a rebellious wisp partially covering one ear. No makeup and no need for it, she permitted a touch of perfume that kissed the breeze.

Darleen's charm lay not in her dress but in her demeanor, reflective of a free spirit and infectious contentment. Hoping to make her acquaintance, J.J. gathered up his courage and walked over. "Hello there. Beautiful day, isn't it?"

The man didn't necessarily believe in love at first sight, but he did find, at that moment, that there can be such a thing as smitten at first syllables when she answered in a lilting Australian accent, "G'day, love."

J.J. couldn't help but smile, and Darleen did too.

So it began, not with bells ringing or doves descending, but with words followed by more words, his and hers, until they parted, agreeing to a first date of lunch and people-watching at JFK International in the innocent, fear-free airport days of pre-9/11.

The more J.J. got to know Darleen, the more he liked her. And the more he got to like Darleen, the more he loved her. The two spent days and afternoons and evenings in Manhattan and Brooklyn, sometimes after work, usually on Saturdays and Sundays, she busy during the week with her post at the Australian Mission to the United Nations, he immersed in the investment business. They talked little of plans together, taking things day by day—a new experience for J.J., a lifelong practice for Darleen—and never tired of each other's company and cute mannerisms, like saying "the same" instead of "I love you," snatching a quick phone chat at work, or her mouthing "kiss kiss" jammed face-to-face on the subway. Theirs were enchanted evenings of Broadway shows and simple pleasures of reading in the public library, a merry-go-round J.J. never thought would end. He entertained asking Darleen to marry him.

One Sunday morning she called him unexpectedly, they having already made plans to hang out in the Village.

Darleen sobbed into the phone.

"What's wrong?" he asked.

"I just got a call from back home. My mum's got cancer."

J.J. offered words of consolation that he hoped would comfort and encourage, but she interrupted after a few sentences. "I have to go to be with her and help her."

J.J. knew how close Darleen felt to Georgina. The two women had only each other, her father having died in an auto accident nearly twenty years before, a wayward brother nowhere to be found. But that she might go back to Australia for any length of time never entered his mind.

"When are you going?"

"As soon as possible."

"How long will you be there?"

"I don't know, J.J. I am so sorry."

They parted tearfully at the airport two days later. "See you when we can," he said.

"Yes."

Back when mail was air not "e," global calls operator-assisted not cellular, and texts were books not an *–ing*, frequent letters and occasional telephone conversations kept them in touch. During the ensuing weeks and months, whenever he inquired about her return, the answer was an unwavering, "I don't know, J.J." But they couldn't continue this way forever. He feared it, and she knew it.

Georgina's battle with torment was long and difficult, and while she ultimately survived, she required near-constant care and companionship that took a life-changing toll on mother and daughter alike. Communication between longing American and dedicated Australian became less and less frequent and finally stopped. Their romance, birthed in spring, passed away after three autumns, not of indifference or hardening of heart but of circumstance. If, indeed, it is a truth that absence makes the heart grow fonder, an asterisk warns that it carries an expiration date.

Over the years, J.J. didn't find anyone new, not out of fear that his heart might be broken again but from the simple fact that the right person never came along, the blessing of a band of gold being a matter of choice not commandment. And while the memory of their fateful conversation and Darleen's departure faded, his image of her never did, always bringing a bright smile to his face and an occasional tug at his heart. Both feelings kicked in as he sat, these years later, in the place where they first met.

A voice interrupted. "May I join you?"

Immersed in his memories, J.J. hadn't noticed someone stop in front of him.

"Certainly."

"You looked deep in thought," the woman stated.

"I was reminiscing about someone very special."

She sat without being asked. The woman beside him bore her age of perhaps eighty with dignity, her stoop with determination, her loneliness of heart with grace. She took out a book of crossword puzzles and put down her work from time to time to point the pen at a bird or a flower or a tree and talk softly.

"I've not seen you before," she said after some time had passed.

"I moved away a long time ago and am back here for a visit."

"I come here every day," she offered, "weather permitting, to sit on this bench."

"Interesting."

"On this very bench is where my husband proposed to me. We returned here many, many times, sitting hand in hand, often not speaking and simply enjoying the presence of the other."

"I know exactly what you mean."

"My Ivan passed away four years ago after fifty-three wonderful years together. Ever since he went to heaven, I have come here to pray and talk to him, to be near him and point out God's beauty around."

"It's not painful for you?"

"It was at first, but now I feel his presence when I am here, me in body, he in spirit, faith that one day our souls will unite for eternity."

She put her face to the sun then turned to him. "And what brings you to this place?"

J.J. told his story about him and Darleen. She listened patiently and patted his knee when he finished.

"Love is love. What matters is not length of years but depth of feeling."

The two sat and talked a while longer until she slowly stood and offered her hand in farewell. "I am Inez. God be with you."

"I am J.J. God be with you as well."

Watching her walk away made him think. *Why couldn't Darleen and I have been together all these years and more? It's my fault, isn't it?* Some of his dad's words resonated. "Time marches on, son, and nobody has the luxury of standing still." *When time marched on for Darleen, I stood still. Why didn't I move to Australia to be near her, to help her, to love her?*

J.J. sat without moving.

A bird flew up and perched on the back of their bench, its sweet chatter as if to scold that he had traveled too far and this was too nice a day, time, and place to spiral into regret and recrimination. Shortly, he agreed, strolling through the park in the lingering afternoon with a double cone of chocolate ice cream and whistling "Downtown," Darleen's favorite song.

Chapter 21

The five days in New York following his tripping down memory lane in Central Park delighted J.J. from morning to night. He visited the sites on his agenda and more, window shopped on the grand thoroughfares, experienced the nonstop pummeling of his senses, all fueled by hearty eating at restaurants, vendors, and the Hendersons' breakfast table. But he was certain these pleasures would place no more than runner-up to what lay ahead.

Of all the points awaiting by whim of red pin or determined by placement of a green one, Cleveland ranked far and away at the top of the list. In fact, had the artillery landed pretty much anywhere east of the Mississippi, he would have declared The Forest City, whatever its charms and bright lights, to be his destination by acclamation for the singular place tucked away in a quiet neighborhood that had fascinated and attracted him for more than a decade.

Pinching himself that he was really here when the bus pulled in just shy of seven in the morning, J.J. offered a wave and heartfelt if sleepy-eyed "thank you" to the driver, hopped off, and headed directly for Ruby. He had things to do and a place to go and no time to lose.

Brown bagging as an alternative to overpriced and overrated restaurant food for lunch ranked among his greatest simple pleasures, and he renewed the habit with gusto within a block of exiting the overnight garage. The treats from Moth and Rudolph a taste bud memory, he stopped at a grocery for three cans of Spam, a pound of pepper jack cheese, a jar of dill spears, a loaf of dark rye, another of light bread with caraway seeds, and a variety pack of potato chips. He checked in to his motel, where he dropped off the load, dipped into it to make the day's lunch, and set out.

A short drive took him through city streets in the Sunday quiet, along the way reciting "The Lord's Prayer" twice in lieu of attending Mass, certain that God would bestow a pass. And then, suddenly, he turned a corner, and there his destination lay, glittering dead ahead in the morning, the Holy Grail of moviedom.

Even before stepping a foot inside, A Christmas Story House and the Museum across the street was even more magnificent than he had imagined. A fan of the movie *A Christmas Story* since watching it at the theater the first time on a date, he vowed a pilgrimage to this place featured in the film ever since reading of its opening to tourists in November 2006.

Now here he was. And there was free parking to boot.

Other than eating, sleeping, and transporting himself, J.J. planned to spend every moment here for the next five days. If some might accuse him of obsessing, so be it. After all, he was a man who, in a younger version of himself, ordered a Big Mac, medium fries, and small Coke five days a week for six consecutive months because the McDonald's up the street from where he worked provided good food and service and, from his invariable corner table, overlooked a picturesque church of gray stone.

Let the critics laugh, snort, or whatever. There was no place on earth he would rather be, and he intended to make the most of it.

A decent-size group of visitors was on site when he arrived, some talking in hushed tones as if walking on sacred ground. J.J. shared in the sentiment but not in the inhibition and bounded in to inquire about what was to be his first of many tours of the campus.

"Hi," he chirped to the cashier.

Identified as Rebecca on the employee badge pinned to her blouse, the woman facing him featured a bony nose, a touch of blush, and a smile that broke only because it was a job requirement. J.J. pegged her to be in her mid to late fifties.

"How can I help you today?" she offered.

"I'd like to buy a pass for the next tour and am wondering if there are discounts for going multiple times."

"You mean you want to go on the tour more than once today?"

"Actually, I will be here several days and want to go on the tour at least once every day, and probably more."

Rebecca sized him up. "I've seen my share of fans in the eighteen months I've worked here, sir," she said, "but you are the first wanting to go on the tour more than once. And to answer your question, no there are no discounts."

Chipped, faded pink nail polish tipped the slender fingers that rang up his admission fee on the cash register. She handed him his change.

Her hands were cold.

"Thank you all the same," J.J. said and headed off for the first of his many tours as full of anticipation as Ralphie was on his first sighting of the Red Ryder BB Gun with a compass in the stock.

He spent the rest of Sunday exploring the gift shop, garage, and museum and taking the ultimate tour of the house that was the set for the filming of the movie. His instincts about coming here proved to be spot on. The more he saw, the more he wanted to see. Props, memorabilia, fan mail, scenes and scenery, costumes, the grounds, every square inch of the vintage house available to the public, nothing escaped his attention or intention to see them again, lest he miss the smallest detail. Even the address, no grand name like Broadway or Fifth Avenue or Michigan Avenue, but a pedestrian West Eleventh Street, intrigued him.

He returned Monday faster than a jackrabbit on a date when the doors opened at ten and remained until they closed at five. For a break from his wanderings, he set himself in front of the gift shop TV showing the movie on a nonstop loop.

"You weren't kidding, were you?" Rebecca said on Tuesday when he booked an afternoon tour, his second of the day.

"Nope," he said and set off to yet again look over the main characters' costumes.

At one o'clock, he went to the car to grab his lunch and noticed Rebecca on a bench eating a salad.

"Mind if I join you?" he asked.

She looked up from her book and narrowed her eyes. "I'm sorry?"

"I'm about to eat my lunch and was wondering if I might join you."

"You're not a weirdo, are you? I mean, a weirdo who goes on a tour over and over?"

"You've got me there," he laughed, "but I don't think of myself as a weirdo."

"Weirdo or not, I know nothing about you and don't make a habit of sitting with strange men." Her lips curved upward into a tight smile. "Maybe that didn't come out quite right."

"It's only lunch," he said, holding up a hand in surrender as he turned to walk away. "But I'll leave you alone. Sorry to have bothered you."

She pursed her lips. "I guess it'll be alright. Just don't try anything funny."

J.J. held up a three-finger salute. "Scout's honor." She scooted to one end of the bench, and he sat at the other. "I'm J.J., by the way, visiting from Los Angeles."

"And I'm Rebecca, from Cleveland. But you knew that."

He held up a soft drink he had purchased inside and offered to buy her one, which she rejected with a terse "No."

The two chatted of this and that of little consequence, of his fascination with all things *A Christmas Story*, and what it was like to work there.

"It's a job," she said.

"Any ambition beyond cashier? Maybe be a tour guide?"

"Actually," she said with a roll of her eyes, "I'm going to night school and studying to be a brain surgeon."

He stifled a groan. "That'd be an interesting change."

"I'm sorry. I don't mean to be a smart aleck."

"No offense taken."

"To be honest, my life is very quiet and boring. I'm content with what I do, live in a one-bedroom apartment, have a cat named Bumpus. I'm in a bowling league."

"Bumpus. Cute! And you like to bowl?"

"No, I'm in a bowling league because I hate it." She shook her head. "There I go again. Sorry! I do like it although I and our team sucks."

"I like bowling too. And I'm terrible. Maybe we can go sometime."

"I'm surprised you'd be able to tear yourself away from Ralphie and company." She laughed despite herself.

"How about tomorrow night after work?" J.J. asked.

"First lunch, now bowling?" She hesitated. I'll think about it."

Wrapping up her lunch bowl and utensils, she asked, "So what does J.J. stand for?"

He was about to answer and caught himself. "Guess."

"Guess?"

"Sure."

"How about Jeffrey Julian?"

"No."

"Justus Jehoshaphat?"

"*Nein.*"

"Jerry Jerome?"

"*Nem.*"

"*Nem?*"

"It's Hungarian."

"You're a bit strange," she said.

"I guess so."

"Actually, don't tell me your name," she said. "I like Jerry Jerome. I think I'll call you that."

"Go for it."

The next morning, J.J. arrived once more at A Christmas Story House promptly at opening. When he paid for the first of his two tours planned for the day, Rebecca gave a half smile and announced, "If you still want to go bowling, we can meet outside at 5:30."

"Hey, thanks. See you then." J.J. killed the half-hour wait after the museum closed by heading up the street to replay in his mind the scene from the movie when Ralphie, brother Randy, and buddies walked this very sidewalk toward school. He arrived back outside the gift shop just as Rebecca showed up at 5:30 on the dot. She either lived nearby or brought a change of clothes because she had exchanged her work outfit for blue jeans and a pink top, her right hand clutching a red knock-off purse. J.J. felt a twinge of embarrassment that he hadn't changed his own clothes, but Rebecca, either oblivious, courteous, or not minding, did not mention it.

"It's not too far to the bowling alley," she announced. We can hoof it."

"Sure. It's a beautiful evening."

Neither had lied about their ineptitude on the lanes. In two games, Rebecca scored a combined 221 and J.J., 219.They retired to the attached coffee shop, where he ordered the two-hander hot dog smothered in fried onions, she the more modest regular dog painted with ketchup. They split a plate of fries and ate quietly for a time. Both drank coffee, J.J.'s black, Rebecca's white and sweet, and were on a second refill when she picked absently at a crumb on her plate and ventured, "Ever been married, Jerry Jerome?"

"Why do you ask?"

"You seem kind of nice."

"I thought I was weird."

She smiled over her coffee cup. "I still do, but you seem…a gentleman."

"I was close once, but it didn't happen." He hesitated before asking but figured why not. "You?"

"You what?"

"Ever been married?"

Rebecca rubbed her eyes. A young couple walked in, hand in hand, giggling together.

"Once."

Not one for greeting card platitudes, J.J. said, "What happened?"

"He ghosted me."

J.J. ran a hand along his face. "I'm sorry to hear that. No sign of it coming, just like that?"

"Nope, flat-out disappeared without warning. One day I came home from work, and he'd cleaned out his closets and taken all his stuff. No goodbye note, no nothing."

The young couple nuzzled.

"Why don't they get a room?" Rebecca sneered.

J.J. looked at her with what he hoped came across as compassion.

"I tried calling his cell," she continued, "but he never picked up, and two weeks later, there's a voice prompt that the number was no longer in service. Finally I get served with divorce papers. Irreconcilable differences. We'd been married eighteen years. Shoot, I didn't know we had *any* differences. I was happy. I thought he was happy."

J.J. reached to take her hand. She flinched and pulled back.

"Don't. I should never have talked. This has got to be so boring for you." She rubbed the back of her neck. "It's getting late."

He shook his head. "You're not boring me. Not even close."

The waitress came by offering a third refill.

"Sure," J.J. agreed.

Not so Rebecca, who stood abruptly. "No, let's go."

"Really? I'm happy to..."

"No, I mean it. Time to go."

J.J. wanted to stay, the night still young and more to be said, but knew he had no choice. On the way out, it felt worse, as if she had opened a curtain to expose vulnerability and instantly regretted it. At the street corner, she asked in a near whisper, "Do you think you know the way back by yourself?"

"I'm sure I can find it. Why do you ask?"

"I suddenly remember there's something I have to do." She refused to return his look.

"Okay then," he said. "See you tomorrow morning?"

"I'll be there. And thanks for the bowling and the company, Jerry Jerome."

She turned away and strode up the street.

J.J. returned to the campus easily and quickly but was in no mood to head to his motel, so he sat on the bench where he and Rebecca had spent lunch together. Two boys played catch up the street. Moms and dads and grandmas and grandpas sat on porches or on lawn chairs. Dogs on their constitutional pranced and smiled. If there were a more perfect summer setting in America, J.J. couldn't conceive where and what it would be.

The night grew older, and he sat a while longer, hoping Rebecca would stop by despite his certainty that she would not. Finally he got up and left, praying for words of affirmation to soothe if not mend her sadness.

An unfamiliar face greeted him the next morning when he

arrived for his daily tour. "Hi, how may I help you?" she asked.

J.J. looked around. "Is Rebecca here?"

"No, Thursdays and Fridays are her weekend. I am Amanda and would be happy to assist you."

He tried not to let his feelings be hurt or his last day at the place be diminished and succeeded to a degree, even finding a bit of gallows humor when he ate his brown bag lunch and announced to no one, "Now who's doing the ghosting?"

Near closing time, J.J. went back to Amanda. "If you are in contact with Rebecca, could you let her know that I'm leaving tomorrow morning and would like to say goodbye?"

Amanda wrinkled her nose. "How does she know you?"

"I've been in every day this week, and we became acquainted."

"I'll try calling her tonight," she said. "What's your name?"

"It's J.J."

"Ah, it's you," she said and playfully pulled back. "She mentioned your name to me earlier this week when we chatted on the phone. Says you're a real *Christmas Story* freak."

He frowned. "That's me."

Amanda blushed. "I mean, she did say it in a nice way."

When he arrived Friday, there was no sign of Rebecca. Amanda looked up when he approached the counter. "I called last night and gave her your message. This was taped to the window when I arrived for work."

She handed him an envelope addressed to *J.J.*, inside of which he found a note in cramped penmanship on lavender paper. It smelled faintly of citrus.

Dear Jerry Jerome,

Thank you for bowling. I still say you're a weirdo, but a nice one.

Stay happy.

Rebecca

J.J. read the note, read it again, and returned to Amanda. The two exchanged smiles.

"Please tell Rebecca that J.J. ...that Jerry Jerome says farewell and God bless."

"I surely will."

Visitors of all stripes and ages filtered in chattering and excited, as J.J. had on Sunday, Monday, Tuesday, Wednesday, and Thursday. He picked out a souvenir refrigerator magnet and departed, then leaned up against Ruby to soak in the August sun before heading back down the street and leaving town.

Chapter 22

The brutish Kearns may have morphed into the humble Father Thomas, but that didn't mean he had lost the instinct and assuredness of his former self. Nor had the rebellious streak that he possessed and redirected while serving within the domain of his priesthood been extinguished. By whichever measure, he set out all by his lonesome and within the limits of avoiding states where hitching was against the law. He was not going on a whim but with a desire for time to think, reflect on, and, indeed, celebrate the events of the previous days. Guided and confident that his journey home, whether in a line straight or jagged, would not be lacking in rides, characters, conversation, and drama, he was bolstered by the truth that a bruiser of a man in clerical collar with thumb upright was not an everyday sight on the interstate.

Some of his expectations came to pass less than ten minutes after Peter dropped him off. Two hippie wannabes, on leave from helicopter parents somewhere to the north, discharged from a VW bus, requested and received a selfie with him, indulged in little more than sixty seconds of self-indulgent conversation, and drove off without offering a ride. Then, about a hundred yards later, Father Thomas came face-to-face with a fellow traveler gripping a tattered duffel bag, a crucifix and bobblehead of an unidentifiable athlete tied to it by a foot of twine. Headphones, wires dangling to nothing, covered his ears. He was decked out in a wide brim straw hat, black long sleeve T-shirt, black sweatpants that stopped mid-ankle, black walking shoes, and socks that, once upon a time, were white. Deep, shifting eyes suggested a life spent alone, whether elected or imposed, recent or longstanding.

"My name is Saul," he offered, and without another word, hustled across the interstate. He did, to his credit, look both ways.

All of which made the priest 0 for 2 so far in securing a ride or meaningful communication. Not one to fret, the day still young and his yoke light, Father Thomas walked on, thumb out, losing himself in prayer, gratitude, and thoughts of his newfound family back in Cicero. He didn't notice the car pull off just ahead of him until the driver honked a second time to get his attention.

Father Thomas walked up to the open window and greeted the man inside with an amiable, "Good morning, my brother. I hope you are well on this fine day."

"I told my wife," the driver motioned to the passenger, "you don't often see a priest hitchhiking. As a matter of fact, we've never seen it. Where're you off to?"

"Los Angeles, but I'll take whatever comes my way to get there."

"Well, we're headed to Denver, doing it leisurely, taking a coupla days. You're welcome to join us until we bed down for the night."

"That's mighty nice. I'd be delighted to join you."

Over the next four hours, they shared stories. Father Thomas told of the high school reunion, reuniting with his mom, and meeting his brother and sister for the first time. Will and Ellie Dawkins spoke of their three grown children and their ambition in retirement to visit all forty-eight contiguous states.

Ellie turned from her seat to talk to their guest. "If your collar hadn't stopped us, the Cubs cap would have. We're lifelong fans."

At a little after noon, they pulled into a rest area. "Time for lunch, Father," Ellie said as Will dug a cooler from the trunk.

"You folks are very kind."

Sitting at a picnic table, they enjoyed croissant sandwiches of chicken salad along with sweet gherkins, kettle cooked salt-and-vinegar potato chips, and ginger ale in plastic cups, then hit the road again, driver and passenger switching seats until four, when exit signs popped up.

"We like to stop early for supper and a good night's sleep, so we're going to stay in Lincoln tonight," Will explained. "You're welcome to come into town with us and find a place to stay."

"It's still early," Father Thomas said, "so I'll travel a bit more. And thank you again. You've been splendid company."

"Our pleasure, Father," Ellie said. "I wish this was our West Coast trip so we could take you all the way home."

The three shared a laugh and waved goodbye, and within five minutes, Father Thomas secured another lift to twenty miles west of Lincoln with a farm couple returning home in their orange, weather-beaten pickup, loaded in back with eight bags of groceries braced by thirty pounds of potatoes. Father Thomas tucked himself in among the supplies and enjoyed the wind in his face.

"You'll be alright going on from here?" the driver asked at the window when they stopped at the long driveway to their farm.

"Sure thing." He waved as they drove off.

He walked along and alone. Mother Earth in wait for alfalfa seedlings stretched to the sky. A choir of finches performed from fence posts. Along with the beauty came ugliness, his legs taking him past the detritus of America, roadside reminders of loss and anguish, discard and despair, tears shed and silent.

In the dirt, a wheelchair on its side, seat ripped, handle busted.

Kicked up in traffic a rumpled poster:

MISSING:

Jennifer, now 14.

Last seen November 5, 2015

in Des Moines.

Please call.

In the road, a wedding portrait frame cracked, glass shattered.

Across the way, a child's blue boot; alongside it, a pink yarn doll, face down, one leg missing.

The blend of cars, trucks, and things in between barreling east and west provided drive-by white noise, supplanted by a flotilla of motorcycles that passed a Greyhound cruiser bound for Salt Lake City. With impending darkness, the notion arose that maybe it would have been better to call it a day back there somewhere. No matter and no fear. Father Thomas kept moving, one foot in front of the other, forward, always forward.

An 18-wheeler pulled up, and an arm motioned.

"You've got some *cajones* out here all by your lonesome," the man behind the wheel remarked when Father Thomas arrived at the window.

"I've been in worse."

"Hop in. Name's Art," the driver said after Father Thomas pulled himself into the cab.

"Father Thomas."

"Where're you bound for, *padre*?"

"Los Angeles."

"Got a load headed for Casper, so I can get you partway there."

"Much obliged."

"Welcome aboard. Relax and enjoy the ride."

They shared the starlight. Neither man uttered a word for the two hours until Art announced, "I sleep in the day and drive at night so you're welcome to bed down in my sleeper."

"That's very generous, Art. I believe I'll take you up on it."

"Do you mind a little music?"

"Not at all."

Father Thomas closed his eyes to Chopin's "Raindrop Prelude," and the next thing he felt was a nudge.

"It's 5:30, Father. Time to part ways."

The priest sat up and beheld the early light. "Best time of the day. May I ask where we are?"

"At a truck stop near the state line. I made good time, caught a shower before waking you, and am ready for some shuteye myself before heading on over."

Over breakfast of three-egg linguiça omelet, hash browns burned as ordered, and pot of black coffee, Father Thomas reflected with gratitude and praise on the Lord's guidance and help on this, just his first day and night on the road.

Father, I thank you for the goodness and fellowship of my brothers and sisters, especially for sending Art to befriend this stranger in the night, and for giving me a place to lay down my head. If thy will be done, may I be your instrument of peace and comfort in my walk ahead.

Whistling with contentment and a satisfied palate on his march back to the highway, he halted at the sight of a station wagon on the lip of the oasis. If grime were a color, the car's would be a dead ringer. A cardboard sign taped to the rear door announced in red marker

out of gas

will work

god bless you

he hasn't blessed me

Father Thomas walked to the driver's side and tapped. The weathered-faced woman inside inserted two fingers in the window's inch opening and pushed it lower.

"Yes?" she challenged and looked out in a retro Beatles cap. Her years clocked in at thirty-four, but a decade of trouble and stress gave her a much older face. Makeup tried but failed to mask bruising around her right eye and on her lower jaw.

"Where are you headed, my sister?" he asked.

"Anywhere but here."

"Let's go fill 'er up and be on our way."

"For real?"

"Certainly. You need gas, and I need a ride. Looks like a good match to me."

"Pleased to meet you then, and thank you." She extended a hand. "I'm Christine Decker."

"Father Thomas."

Forty-five minutes later, they took off, gas tank filled along with two bags containing enough food for four.

"A hitchhiking priest is a new one on me," she started, relief in her voice growing. "You run into some real creeps on the open road." She grunted bitterly. "You run into some real creeps everywhere, for that matter."

Father Thomas countered with the lite version of his trip to Cicero and his return to the West Coast, and then the two fell silent in the serenity of the High Plains. Thunderstorm clouds threatened but laid off.

The station wagon rumbled on until it was time to stop for a break and open the goodies. "No offense, Father Thomas," Christine began after unwrapping her second roast beef sandwich, "but I really do believe God has abandoned me."

He looked at her thoughtfully. "I gathered that from your wording on the sign, Christine. I am sorry you feel that way, but our Lord never abandons anyone. He is always there, waiting, and intervening at the time of his choosing."

"Well, if that's so, I wish he'd hurry up and choose."

A squirrel stopped by for lunch, crunching on a nut fallen from the branch of a cottonwood tree.

"May I ask who you are running from?" Father Thomas dared.

She teared. "Let's just say, I'm not the greatest at picking men...or in any choices for that matter. Everything I touch turns to dust."

"Escaping an ill-chosen past is all-too common, I'm sad to say."

Her eyes widened. "Even in priests?"

He smiled ruefully. "Yes, even in priests. It has been said that members of the clergy in witnessing at church are often preaching to themselves, and I can tell you that is very true. But it is never too late to start over, and I mean that sincerely."

Father Thomas took a pad of paper and pen from his knapsack and said as he wrote, "Christine, this is the name and address of the church where I am pastor in Los Angeles. If you ever find yourself in the neighborhood, please do stop by. Our parish is a wonderful one with some fine people always ready to reach out and help.

She folded the paper and put it in the glove box. After they started up again, however, Christine turned quiet, and soon she signaled and pulled over.

"Father, do you mind if we part company here? I really don't want to talk anymore or be with anyone. I'm sorry."

He put up a hand. "No apology necessary. I've been there myself and totally understand."

He leaned in after retrieving his belongings. "It was a pleasure sharing this time with you, Christine. Remember what I said about visiting my church, and definitely think about what I said about our Lord. He truly is always there for you."

"I will," she answered unconvincingly and opened her door. "Let me see how I can help pack the food that is left so you can take it with you."

The priest shook his head. "Please keep it, compliments of a grateful friend."

Father Thomas waved as she drove off, looked north, south, east, and west to get his bearings, and managed to hitch a ride shortly with a national park-bound outdoorsman in a Jeep, who paid for both of their motel rooms for the night on the outskirts of Santa Fe.

The morning started warm and promised to get hot quickly, but weather never bothered the priest, or at least he never paid attention when it demanded. He walked along, content to be left alone to meditate on the Word and thank the Almighty for leading him to perhaps bring some good to Christine. The reverie lasted all of twenty minutes before the horn blasted on an cattle truck approaching from behind. The driver, lean and browned and of even temper, stopped ahead, leaned out the window, and called, "I've got room if you want, preacher!"

Father Thomas appreciated the offer even more when Tex—as the man identified himself despite the admission of never having set food in the state—announced he was headed "down Tucson way," which would leave Father Thomas less than five hundred miles from Los Angeles. Their ride passed leisurely with jovial, pleasant conversation, and by mid-afternoon the two said goodbye at a rest area. Tex assured Father Thomas he would easily find a hitch straight home.

Racist cursing interrupted his walk to the restroom.

Ahead blustered two skinheads, one blubbery and pocked, the other smooth and bathed in tattoos. Both, like all bullies, puffed false bravado by picking on gentle people who couldn't or wouldn't fight back. At this moment, the skinheads were in the faces of a man, a woman wearing a burqa, and two young boys huddled at a picnic table.

"Sirs," the man said, holding his hands up, "we mean you no harm. My wife and I and our children just want to be on our way."

"Sirs?" One bully poked the other. "Get that." Their fists clenched. "You people need to be taught a lesson."

A voice boomed. "What lesson did you have in mind?"

The bullies turned, but their startle turned to sneer when they saw the priest approach.

"Well, if it isn't Father Time," one drawled, making the other snort with laughter.

"Actually, the name's Father Thomas."

Two eyes of defiance glared at four of contempt, which flickered with uncertainty as they tried to decide how to confront this huge man in clerical collar and Marine tattoo. Anyone possessing an ounce of brains or a pound of self-preservation would dig deep and decide on their next move very carefully. The skinheads possessed one or the other and decided to end the face-off.

"Let's get outta here," Pock yelped.

"And you..." Smooth pointed to the family. "Next time your bodyguard won't butt in to help."

When Father Thomas took a step in their direction they ran to their car and sped off.

The family crowded around, voices clamoring, tears of relief forming. "Thank you so much."

"*As-salamu alaykum,*" the priest offered.

The two adults took the priest's hands in theirs. "*Wa 'alaykumu s-salam.*"

"Please, let me introduce us. I am Ashraf, with my wife, Aleah, and our sons, Fadi and Ibrahim. And you are Father Thomas, am I correct?"

"At your service."

"You are a mighty man of peace. We will always be indebted to you."

"He speaks Arabic!" a wide-eyed Fadi said to his dad.

Father Thomas couldn't claim fluency beyond modest expressions of greeting, friendship, and respect. He had acquired these when a parish family invited him to dinner with some Muslim friends of theirs who, in turn, had taken him in to their house to enjoy good food, fellowship, and conviviality. And once they got to know one another, the new friends shared discourse about his Bible and their Quran and sent gifts to one another on Christmas and then at Ramadan.

"Please sit and let us talk a while," Ashraf said, leading Father Thomas to their shaded picnic table, offering some respite from the heat.

"I am sorry we have nothing to offer you to eat," Aleah added. "We had just finished our meal when those men came up. But we would be honored to have you join us for some refreshing tea."

The boys, one maybe eight and the other a year or two younger, couldn't stop looking at the priest. "What is that writing on your arm?" the younger one asked.

"Ibrahim!" scolded Ashraf. "Mind your manners." He turned to the priest. "I apologize for my son's rudeness."

Father Thomas smiled. "Ah, you mean my tattoo. The words are *Semper Fi*, short for S*emper Fidelis*, which means 'always faithful' in Latin."

"The United States Marines say that, do they not?" Ashraf said.

"Yes they do. It's their motto. I was in the Marine Corps before I became a priest."

"We want to be Marines!" the boys shouted, immediately silenced by a look from their dad.

"Once a warrior for country, now a warrior for God. Very special indeed," said Aleah.

"We must all, within our own power and circumstance, watch out for the other and not allow evil to triumph over good," he answered.

As the adults talked, the boys kicked a yellow soccer ball. Other travelers wandered past, having newly arrived or having kept their distance from the skinheads.

"It is proper," Ashraf said, "that people of different beliefs, you with Jesus Christ, we with Allah, can come together in harmony in a world of such hatred and arrogance."

Father Thomas told them of the tableside conversations with his Muslim friends back home and added, "People of goodwill are meant to share one another's company and enjoy the blessings of God."

Husband and wife nodded. Both started to speak, Aleah deferring to Ashraf.

"Our Quran teaches there is no such thing as blind chance and that things happen by design and for a reason, and blessings can benefit as well as teach. Truly, Allah sent you to us today, a man of character and principle, not only to help but to show that justice and goodness can prevail when we most need it and least expect it."

Sipping their drinks, the three adults turned to easygoing conversation, the boys played on as boys do, and time passed gently.

Ashraf and Aleah exchanged looks.

"We must be going. Can we offer you a ride?"

"Where are you headed?"

"We live in San Diego and are driving to a family reunion in Wichita."

"Looks like we're headed in opposite directions," Father Thomas chuckled, "but we are almost neighbors. I live in Los Angeles and am on my way home."

"I'm sorry we cannot be of assistance to you," said Aleah.

"I'll be fine."

Not that they expected the skinheads to have doubled back, Father Thomas and Ashraf nevertheless kept an eye out as they walked to the parking area.

"We must pray for those men; pray that they find salvation," Father Thomas said.

"Yes, we must and we will," Ashraf agreed, "that they may be guided to the Right Path."

The parting was joyful as Christian and Muslims shared a hug and vowed to meet again back in California.

"May God be with you, my dear sister and brothers."

"*Fi Amanillah.*, Father Thomas," said Ashraf.

Humming in prayer and praise, Father Thomas bowed until the car disappeared into the afternoon's sunlight.

Chapter 23

For the first time in sixty-five days, the compass did not point him to continue eastward. J.J.'s spirit was heavy with satisfaction from his trip's discoveries, spiced with a dash of regret. He wished he could have had the opportunity to show Rebecca that life, with its frailties and disappointments, can be filled with good that would not eliminate the bad but make it bearable, that joy can replace despair if you give it a chance.

His next predetermined visit was at least ten hours of driving from Cleveland, minus sixty minutes for switching to Central time from Eastern. J.J. settled himself comfortably in Ruby and drove along, content to send good thoughts Rebecca's way along with meditating in the peace of the open road and absorbing sights and sounds as he headed into a part of the country where he had never worked or traveled. Indeed, the closest he had come to anything related to the South was Bryan Jensen, the memory of him tweaking J.J.'s heart as he passed random markers. One sign caught his eye.

Biloxi—975 miles

The two met in Chicago at J.J.'s first job in financial services. Bryan was thirty years his senior, a man out of Mississippi and a true Southern gentleman, a lover of classical music and fine dining, and one of the very few decent memories from his two score years ago spent in the Land of Lincoln. As colleagues, J.J. and Bryan quickly became mentor and mentee and occasional partners for a club sandwich and iced tea at lunch. J.J. liked to half joke about how he and good folks like Bryan had once been bitter enemies on American battlefields.

"Bryan," he offered once between bites, "if I saw you coming at me over that ridge in Gettysburg, do you know what I would have done?"

"I suppose shot or bayoneted me."

"Nope. I would've pointed my rifle and blown you a kiss."

"You know, J.J., I believe you."

"What would you have done?"

Bryan winked, and they clinked glasses.

As J.J. moved on to posts in the East, he and Bryan exchanged phone calls, the occasional letter, and Christmas cards but, after some years, fell out of touch. Then one day while working in Boston, J.J.'s e-mail included an announcement from the head of his one-time Chicago office.

Colleagues,

It is with regret that I inform you that our friend and retired colleague Bryan Jensen passed away yesterday at the age of 72.

There will be no services, so please keep Bryan in your thoughts and prayers.

J.J. immediately called back to a former coworker, not believing his ears when the man told him, "The poor guy checked into a hotel and jumped from a seventh-story window."

J.J. knew little of Bryan's personal life other than he never married and was an only child. As he put the phone down, he could only wonder what profound despair could have driven this good and decent man to take his own life. Loneliness? Health? Aging? None of the above? All of the above? Whatever, it did not matter.

Later at home, going to his knees, J.J. prayed in anguish, "I wish I could have been there to help, Bryan. I apologize to you for not being a better friend."

That night he prayed for the repose of Bryan's soul in eternal life, made a point of doing so every Sunday in the years that followed, and threw in a bonus Our Father on this August Friday as he headed into the one-time stomping grounds of his Southern gentleman friend.

Such memories and contemplation made the driving hours pass not in remorse but in fond recollection of their better times, enhanced by unfolding settings, big city yielding to expansive fields of soybeans, and corn yielding to bucolic hills of bluegrass. As if further evidence of God's creation and splendor, a mother duck showed the ropes to her five ducklings in a meandering stream near a rest area where J.J. finished off a burger, fries, and Fanta grape soda along with a fresh peach purchased at a roadside stand.

As the ribbon of road stretched on and on, there finally came a time when J.J. needed some sound not from his own mind. He fiddled with the car radio, stopping the dial on a station at the tail end of its weather report and promising twenty minutes of uninterrupted Elvis. At the third entry of the medley, J.J. turned up the volume.

"Kentucky Rain" was his favorite from The King, its story the anxious search for a missing love. This time the song struck J.J. as amusing in a peculiar way since, at the moment, he was not looking for love, was no longer in Kentucky, and what rain was falling had stopped. The Tennessee countryside around him emerged from its shower clean and earthy and tingling. J.J. opened both the driver-side and passenger windows to give his senses a clear shot.

A signpost announced that his next city of choice, established by a red pin stuck on the wall back in his garage, was just ahead. Strange that the sailing dart would have landed on Lebanon and not on Nashville, a mere tick to the west on the map, but his was not to reason why. Internet research had at least pleased him when he found that the approaching destination was named after the biblical cedars of Lebanon in the environs of Jesus Christ and was nicknamed "Cedar City" by locals. Both facts seemed rather pedestrian to a state that boasted locales with such names as Bell Buckle, Glimp, Only, and Bugscuffle.

J.J. pulled onto the main strip of town shortly after seven, his first assignment to find a place to bed down. Hoping to skip the chain motels in search of a locally owned and operated establishment, he hit the jackpot when he found a small motel on a side street across from a park. In the lot were a rusting Chevy Bel Air, a gleaming SUV, and a tired panel truck. All bore Tennessee plates.

"Good enough for the locals, good enough for me," he declared and stepped into the night air, the car thermometer reading eighty-five degrees.

Neither the Ritz nor the pits, the place ranked skimpy in amenities but five-star in charm and down-home hospitality. In the small lobby, two pots of freshly brewed coffee sat on a small table along with creamers in a nearby refrigerator that invited patrons to store restaurant leftovers "for two days, or there ours." He fought the urge to correct the grammar when a matronly woman rose from her chair behind the check-in counter.

"Can I help you, young man?"

"Yes, ma'am, I'd like a place for tonight and the following three."

"Very good. So that will keep you here through Monday, am I correct?"

"You are, ma'am."

"Ma'am makes me sound so old. Please call me Bertha."

"A pleasure to meet you, Bertha."

She looked at his name on the register.

"Good thing your last name isn't Johnson."

"Why?"

"With those first initials, it'd sound like a stutter, J.J.J."

"Never thought of that." He repeated the triple J's back to her good-naturedly.

"Don't mind me, just messing with you."

"It's kind of funny, actually."

The coffee's aroma drew him, caffeine having long since lost its influence on his ability to sleep. "May I?"

"Take all you want. We have plenty."

"Thanks. Do you also run the restaurant across the parking lot?"

"Affirmative. My husband, Harold, and I inherited both of these places from his parents and will be here until we go to our Maker. You'll meet Harold tomorrow, I expect, if you eat with us."

"Count on it," and with that J.J. paid for the four nights, got his key, and went to his room. Before retiring, he called his neighbor Sahil to quiet his mind that all was well back home.

"No worries, my friend, we have everything in hand. Sai and Suneetha have taken quite a liking to tending your lawn and flowers, and Nandu and I go over your mail to make certain there is nothing urgent. It is the usual collection."

"Sahil, I can't thank you and your family enough."

"Think nothing of it...Oh, Nandu just reminded me, there is a postcard for you."

"A postcard?"

"Yes, from a place called Wisconsin Dells."

"The Dells? Yes, I stopped there a while back."

"Then it looks like you made a new friend. Now don't worry a bit and take as long as you like to return. We will take good care of your happy home."

Guessing and hoping Marie was the sender of the postcard, he recited her collection of names, even trying them in reverse order, as he stretched out on his bed and slept soundly in the tranquility of the pitch black.

J.J. awoke to another sensory delight. The pull of frying bacon got him dressed and out the door to hustle to the diner, where Bertha greeted and cashiered and Harold served, along with three chipper teenage girls and an even chippier graybeard cleaning tables.

"Would you like the social or order from the menu, J.J.?" Bertha inquired.

"Not J.J.J?" he teased. "And what is a social?"

"Are you from the old country?" Bertha laughed. "Or probably from the North? I believe you Yankees call it a buffet."

The name alone dictated the choice. "Ah, a buffet. . .a social. You've got it."

He chose wisely, the selection impressive, portions plentiful. Platters, plates, bowls, and pitchers of scrambled eggs, grits, biscuits and gravy, sausages, bacon, toast, jellies and jams, doughnuts, crullers, orange juice, and coffee presented the challenge of where to start and the regret of overeating.

J.J. dug in, chewing slowly to put off the inevitable saturation as long as possible.

During the course, or courses, of his meal, he could not help but notice that all three of the servers displayed "Terry" on their name badges. He motioned to Harold.

"How can I help you, sir?"

Bertha bellowed, "His name's J.J."

"Yes, dear," Harold answered over his shoulder. "Now, J.J., what would you like?"

In lowered voice, he asked, "I was wondering, are all three of your servers really named Terry?"

Harold looked confused. "Why wouldn't they be?"

"Well, I thought maybe they were fake so customers wouldn't know their real names, and, you know, try to bother them later or something."

"This is a friendly town. I can't believe that would happen."

"But you'll have to agree it's a coincidence for all of them to have the same name."

"Maybe so, but that's the way it worked out. Bertha and I did all the work here on the floor for a long while but last year decided to advertise for serving help. Just turned out all three of these girls applied. We liked them, and we hired them."

Terry, Terry, and Terry scurried about, serving customers and putting on their best smiles. J.J. pointed to the graybeard. "I don't suppose his name is Terry too."

Harold cocked an eyebrow. "Of course not. His name is Robert, but everyone in town calls him Old Bob." Harold straightened and called, "Hey, Old Bob, come over for a sec."

The name badge confirmed it.

"This is J.J., staying with us at the motel a few nights, and judging by the way he's piling on the food, I expect will be a regular customer here."

J.J. swallowed a clump of eggs. "A pleasure, Old Bob."

"Likewise," he answered pleasantly and returned to his dirty dishes.

The boss gave an affectionate look. "Old Bob came to us four years ago. You probably won't believe it, but he played football at Tennessee, joining as a walk-on and making starting linebacker for three seasons."

"Wow!" J.J. replied.

"Wow is right. And there's more. He completed his education there and stayed on in administration and student affairs all his working days. Over the years, he passed through here from time to time with his wife, Mattie, and came to us shortly after she passed."

A customer called, and Harold excused himself to refill the beverages of other diners, all the while greeting and thanking them by first name.

"Now, where was I?" he said back at J.J.'s table. "Oh, yes. Old Bob came here and asked if we needed help clearing tables. We didn't really need anyone, but he said it was a job he had always wanted. And then he said something kind of funny."

"Funny?"

"Here he was asking for work but told us that before we decided, he wanted us to accept three conditions."

J.J. put down his fork and listened.

"One, he wanted no paycheck, only to eat his meals here for free. Two, we were to never call him a busser. 'I'm a bus*boy*, not a buss*er*' is how he put it.' And three, we were to always refer to him as Old Bob."

"And the rest is history," J.J. observed.

"So it is. We love having him here every day, both as worker and diner. He's like a brother to us, and our customers adore him. And he never fails to thank us after each and every meal. After Mattie passed, he really had no one, and by his telling, she was a wonderful cook, and he could do little more than prepare Ramen and peas."

All good things must come to an end, and so it was with the Saturday morning social. Comforting himself that there would be another the next morning, J.J. decided it was time to get out and about and discover all things Lebanon. When he'd mapped this outing way back when, J.J. had allowed three full days to explore. With that in mind and plans in hand, he headed across the street to an inviting bench in a leafy park.

He was far from alone. A Rottweiler on its morning constitutional towed its petite benefactor, one hand holding onto the leash for dear life, the other throwing crumbs to swarming pigeons. Dog and owner barely avoided a senior in tattered brown suit, white shirt, green paisley tie, and black tennis shoes. A scrawny cat drank water from the gutter, oblivious to a butterfly fluttering frantically to free itself from a spider's web. Walkers and talkers and gawkers milled about, the Saturday morning farmers market luring many.

And there was someone else J.J. could not help but notice. In a world consumed by action, thrills, noise, a rhythm of life that allowed no let-up, the young man on the bench next to J.J.'s sat doing nothing at all.

In the eyes of humanity, he was not attractive in body, appearance, or deportment. He bore no bling or tats screaming out, no earbuds screaming in. No nose rings, lip rings, earrings, or cellular rings. His sandy-colored hair reflected a mere stab at combing, and his faded orange Volunteers T-shirt sagged at the neckline. Sitting there with legs crossed leisurely and fingers intertwined, his face glowed.

J.J. did not mean to stare but did. The man caught it, offered a lopsided smile, and nodded, to which J.J. nodded back. After sitting a minute longer, J.J. departed for exploration, which carried him first to the main and surrounding streets offering the variety of shopping emporiums one would find in a city of thirty-two thousand. After that it was off to tour a historic village and then rest his legs and read copies of the local newspaper at the public library. He stopped on his way out, overhearing two old-timers re-create with chess pieces the battle of Shiloh in "the War for Southern Independence." J.J. had never heard the four years of turmoil and bloodshed referred to by any name other than "the

Civil War." He retired for lunch to the Cracker Barrel in a tip o'
the cap to the restaurant chain that opened its first store in Lebanon
some half a century before, and in bonus to his platter of chicken
and dumplings discovered a flier for the county fair. Sure enough,
it had kicked off the day before.

No longer a country boy but still holding country in his heart,
J.J. loved the rustic, down-home, easy paced atmosphere at fairs,
along with all their accoutrements. In the years after Billings, he
attended as many fairs as he could and never tired of wandering
among the livestock, vegetables, flowers, fruits, jellies, jams,
cakes, cookies, woodworking, quilts, and crafts lovingly grown,
tended, prepared, created, and entered by locals wherever he may
be. Wilson County's fair was all he had hoped it would be, capped
before leaving by a large, chilled, pink lemonade and piping hot
footlong corn dog scrolled with spicy mustard.

Baked and beat from his hours in the sun, he returned to his
motel filled with good cheer, picked up a large Styrofoam cup of
coffee and a week-old copy of *The Wall Street Journal* abandoned
in the lobby, and headed over to the park to take in the splendor of
the lazy Saturday evening.

On the bench was the presence again, still the icon of
contentment.

J.J. took a seat on the same bench where he had sat that
morning, hesitated, and looked over in greeting.

"Hello."

"Hello," the man replied.

"I'm J.J."

"David."

J.J. left initiation of further conversation up to the other man. After a moment, David walked over to the popcorn vendor, returned with two bags, and held one out to J.J.

"Hey, many thanks. Please join me." J.J. patted the bench.

"Haven't seen you before," the man said and sat alongside him.

"Staying a few days as part of a long trip," J.J. explained simply.

"Ah."

The popcorn was freshly popped and salted just right.

"You?"

David Gentry spared J.J. the extended story of his life, which went like this. Hard driving in high school and bent on leaving Lebanon after graduating, he made good by attending the University of Georgia for undergraduate and graduate degrees in biotechnology, and, diplomas in hand, swiftly found corporate employment. In not so many years, he advanced up the management ladder and thereby paid for a condo in downtown Atlanta, was in the market for a second one for a getaway and rental, took annual cruises in the Caribbean and Mediterranean, was a regular on the club scene, and filled his life with toys and trappings that left him unsatisfied and constantly yearning for more.

A phone call from his dad one weekday afternoon opened his eyes to the joyful humility of yearning for nothing.

"Son," went the conversation, "your mother and I, well, we could use your help back here."

"What's wrong, Dad?"

"Nothing's wrong, Davey. I'm sorry, I feel a little guilty calling you like this."

"Pop, tell me. What is it?"

"Well, if you could come back for a month or so, maybe take a long vacation or some kind of leave, we, the both of us, are just plain tired and need some time to rest."

"Let me think about it, Pop. I'll call back."

It took all of five minutes for him to know what he wanted to do.

"I'll be there by the end of the week."

"You're sure?"

"Absolutely."

He returned to Lebanon four days later and never regretted it.

In his Cliff Notes abbreviation to J.J., all David said was, "I went away for a while, but everything I wanted in life was waiting for me back here. Finally, I admitted it, turned my back on who I had become, and returned to be who I really am."

"I can tell that you're happy."

"More than I would've thought possible."

The two men finished their popcorn and sat within their own silence until darkness fell.

J.J. attended Mass the next morning in a quaint church of old wooden pews and worn kneelers, followed by another hearty helping of the breakfast social and company of Bertha, Harold, Terry, Terry, Terry, and Old Bob. After a leisurely reading of the Sunday newspaper in the motel lobby and a nap in his room, he took off on a stroll. At the far corner of the park, he happened on a small gathering that he soon realized was a Bible study group attended by a young couple, the man in the tattered brown suit, a woman head bowed and hands clasped, and David.

"Join us, J.J.," he invited. "No pressure. Just listen if you like."

The young couple motioned him to move closer. Over the next hour, all gave testimony on the day's message in Psalm 27:11. "Teach me thy way, O LORD, and lead me in a plain path." J.J. sat thinking, not talking, then he rose and joined the circle in the concluding intercessory prayer led by David. "Lord, our dear friend Sylvia cannot be here today, and we just pray for her return to health, to her family, to us, and we pray for her doctors, for their guidance and wisdom. And most of all we pray that your will be done whether keeping Sylvia here or bringing her home to you, our Lord and Savior. In Jesus' precious name, Amen."

David motioned to a picnic table decked out with red-and-white checkered cloth, three cheese pizzas, and two pitchers of Arnold Palmers.

"J.J., please stay and eat with us."

"Thank you," he replied and prepared to offer some money but David stopped him. "Anthony," he explained, nodding in the direction of the brown suit, "he always picks up the tab."

That night, welcomed once more by the sturdy armchair in his motel room and the lullaby of frogs in a distant field, J.J. held a paperback but did not read, instead settling into the comfort of these new friendships that wrapped around him like a fleece blanket. He genuinely liked these people and their city and, while not willing to tarry, he resolved to spend every waking minute in their company.

Which is what he did.

During a final conquest at the restaurant, he turned to the menu to devour the half-pound burger buried in condiments and its equal in fries at lunch and to master the turkey platter that sagged under the weight of white meat, dressing, and mashed potatoes at supper. Through both feasts, he reveled in the stories and antics of Bertha, Harold, the three Terrys, Old Bob, and the assortment of regulars. Between the feeds, he sipped coffee in the motel lobby talking to other travelers and walked in the neighborhoods and among the local proprietors, stopping to check out the music store, a news stand, and even a vacuum cleaner merchant. Finally, he went to the park for his evening constitutional to spend one last time with David, the bags of popcorn J.J.'s treat this time. The two idly discussed matters of no consequence until it was time for them to part.

"Thanks for the popcorn and the company," J.J. said.

"I enjoyed both immensely," said David.

They shook hands, and J.J. watched David leave.

David crossed the street to climb a flight of wooden stairs into a modest apartment above Gentry Jewelers.

"Hello, Davey," chimed his parents.

"Hi, Mom and Pop."

Everett in wheelchair and Betty adjusting her macular degeneration glasses sat across from each other at a card table in the living room assembling a 500-piece jigsaw puzzle of a waterfall scene. David joined them.

"Some tuna casserole left over in the fridge, Davey," Betty offered.

"Thanks, Mom. Yours is the best."

He leaned in for her to kiss his cheek. His nose twitched at her pungent perfume.

"Day go well in the store, Davey?" Everett asked.

"Yes. Eric and Beth from Bible study came in and put a down payment on an engagement ring."

"That's nice," his father said. "I'm happy for them. I sold engagement and wedding rings to their parents."

The three worked a few more pieces into the puzzle, said their "sleep wells," and turned in for the night. Lying in his tidy bedroom, David prayed and gave praise. "Lord, thank You for leading me to this paradise."

A short ways away, J.J. switched off the bedside lamp. He, like David, drifted off under the spell of the frogs' reprise.

Chapter 24

State capitals and capitols intrigued J.J.—the cities for their atmosphere of drama, the buildings for their atmosphere of dramatics. He had visited more than a few during vacations, none the equal of their granddaddy in Washington, DC, where he had once pleasurably spent a carefree week. Lately he was keen on Arkansas', to traipse around the stomping grounds of the Clintons, having voted twice for Bill and once for Hillary.

Tennessee faded in the distance four hours later when he crossed a mighty bridge over the Mighty Mississippi. When pulling away from the curb in front of his house back in June, J.J. had reset Ruby's tripmeter to zero. It now registered a mileage tick over thirty-six hundred, and after all the time and distance, he was starting to feel antsy around the edges to return to his familiar turf. But this was quickly dispatched by the majestic waterway below, the memories of Lebanon, all the wheres, whats, and whos before that, and his eager anticipation of those that surely lay ahead.

The dart directing him on this humid Tuesday southwesterly

along the interstate to his penultimate destination of chance had stuck so precariously when he approached the map on the garage wall that he thought it might fall to the floor and require a do-over. But there it stayed, for an as-yet unknown reason. Perhaps, he admitted, after all the pleasantries thus far, one of Father Thomas' Sunday admonitions might come to pass: *Looking for the good doesn't mean you will find it. And if you are the good yourself, that doesn't guarantee others will embrace you. Even the make-believe of movies doesn't always have a happy ending. That's life. Deal with it.*

The Arkansas state bird did a flyby, perhaps in welcome, perhaps in warning, and J.J. declared, "There's only one way to find out which it is, Father, wherever you are." He forged head on.

Whatever the mockingbird's intent, from the moment he arrived, J.J. liked Little Rock. His first full day passed quickly at the Clinton Presidential Library, where, among the exhibits, he hoped, perhaps, to even meet the former president who, rumor had it, made random walkthroughs to press the flesh with visitors. J.J. struck out on that score, but no matter, the exhibits and sense of the place and the man were well worth the trip, as was a later visit to the capitol. There, he stumbled upon the delightful basement cafe, a throwback place whose luxury lay in its unpretentiousness. Even more, the day's trifecta of chicken breast, rice, and greens provided the opportunity for his summer concession to healthy eating. But organic orange juice rather than a chocolate shake? Let's not go overboard.

After making his rounds of things political, there was no lack of other sights and sites to keep him engaged in enjoyment and discovery. Before he knew it, his four assigned days dwindled to the final evening. Only one late entry remained on the to-do list, a random place that caught his eye while strolling nowhere in particular on the previous afternoon. He decided to make good on his pledge to visit before heading out.

Undeterred by a driving rainstorm, he parked a block away. Lightning lit the sky, thunder rumbled, and the downpour would have doused him were it not for the passerby who shared her umbrella.

"Thank you, ma'am," he offered when arriving at the door of Joe and Angie's Restaurant.

"No problem," she remarked and resumed her way up the street.

As with the city, he liked Joe and Angie's immediately, even more so. It was perfect. He had his choice of seating at a counter of six tired stools or at two rows of four booths dulled with age and separated by an oft-traveled narrow aisle. Family and customer photographs covered the walls. A determined fan churned overhead. The back doorway opened to a Dixieland pinball machine and two-lane miniature bowling alley.

Accepting the invitation on the entranceway sign to "seat yourself," J.J. settled into a middle booth. A vintage jukebox in the far corner played "It's Gonna Take a Miracle," not obtrusively loud but unobtrusively gentle, as if a breeze, not a gale. He daydreamed. *If Darleen were here, I'd ask her to slow jam, right now in the restaurant, and she'd oblige.* But she was not here, just he and five other patrons, and all, like him, sitting alone.

A bubbly waitress appeared. He declined to ask if her name were Terry.

She said, "Fresh lemonade to whet your whistle?"

"Maybe later. How about coffee for now?"

"Coming right up."

Everything on the menu, Early Bird or not, appealed. Under "Beverages" came the notice, "Drinks Free on Tuesday's." Too bad this was Friday. He chuckled at the erroneous apostrophe, his mom's insistence on proper grammar staying with him still. But he did call over the server to inquire about some small block lettering carved just above the lip of his tabletop, its shiny red scrubbed down by customers over the years to a mellow pinkish.

BD LOVES LD

"What's this all about?" he asked and tapped the inscription.

She smiled lightly and slid into the seat across from him. "You noticed."

"It does catch a person's eye."

"Most people guess it's from a love-struck teenage boy to his girlfriend. What do you think?"

"I've no idea," J.J. said, intrigued by the woman's mischievous manner, "but tell me, please."

She leaned over and spoke in a tone of reverence. "Actually, it was carved by an eighty-nine-year-old man to his wife on their sixtieth wedding anniversary. Both of them ate here every day, all three meals, and all of us just loved them both. After she passed away, he would come and sit and trace the letters with his finger." A patron waved the waitress over for a coffee refill.

"I shall return," she promised, and in a short time did so, refilling J.J.'s cup from the pot in her hand.

"What was I talking about? The old couple, right. Then he passed not many months later. We couldn't bear to replace the table, and so we kept it as a memorial to their wonderful love together and as a reminder of how much they meant to us as friends."

The waitress dabbed a tear with the corner of her apron and got herself back together. She announced, "I'm Melanie, by the way." She stood and said, "I'll be back to take your order," and returned to duty.

Rain drooled down the window.

Determined fan churned overhead.

Vintage jukebox in the far corner played on, not obtrusively loud but unobtrusively gentle, as if a breeze not a gale.

He sat there, holding a menu in hand but not reading it, instead thinking of the old couple.

A voice crackled, interrupting his thoughts from the booth behind him where a hulking frame slouched. Her mottled ankles protruded from a red skirt, feet pinched into white sneakers, and weight bulged in ill-fitting blue blouse and maroon sleeveless sweater. Turquoise plastic eyeglasses missing one arm hung loosely on her face, and four pink barrettes tidied a mop of hair once blonde. She sang out a second time. "Got to go to Kansas City, yep Kansas City, that's in California, to see my niece, Kansas City here I come."

"Woman's crazier than an outhouse rat," barked a man sitting in a booth across the aisle. "Hey, maybe you should give yodeling a try, you nutty old bat."

Either not hearing, minding, or caring, she carried on with her warbling, finally slurped the remainder of a bowl of tomato soup and tumbler of milk, struggled to her feet, and pushed out into the storm.

"Shirley, you forgot to pay!" the waitress called after her.

J.J. took in the proceedings. "That's okay," he said to Melanie. "Put it on my bill."

"You're kidding me."

"Why not? How much can soup and milk cost?"

Watching Shirley lurch sideways past the window in a futile attempt to avoid the rain, Melanie grabbed a yellow slicker from the coat rack and hurried out to wrap it around the woman's shoulders.

"Would you look at that?" sneered Across-the-Aisle.

The waitress returned and went over to J.J. "You're sure about paying?"

"Certainly."

"Well, well, looks like we've got a do-gooder in our midst," squawked Across-the-Aisle, his tone as shrill as before but maybe down a notch in volume.

J.J. looked sideways at the antagonist. His black hair receded into a widow's peak, lips thin, eyes slate and boring—not as in dull but as in piercing. The man clocked in somewhere between fifty and who cares. A dime-size mole punctuated his right temple.

He glared at J.J. and then the wall.

The wall glared back. J.J. didn't.

"Sir, there's nothing wrong with paying forward to help people in need."

The antagonist answered, his glare returning to J.J.

"In the first place, the name's Meyers. In the second place, I'm sure that biddy's got plenty of money to pay for her keep."

"Still, Mr. Meyers..."

"And in the third place, Mr. Meyers is my old man. He's dead. So's my old lady for that matter. Any questions?"

J.J. retreated to the safety of his menu.

Meyers lit a cigarette off the end of the dying one, his body language shrieking "buzz off," to which anyone within the ZIP code happily obliged, including J.J. after his failed attempt at civility. But he made the mistake of momentarily glancing away from his menu and down at the checkerboard linoleum floor, where, midway between himself and Meyers, sat a half-open wallet.

Valor won out over discretion. "Is that yours?" J.J. asked.

"Is what mine?" Meyers grunted across the aisle.

"That." He pointed.

"How in the world?" Meyers started, and after snatching the wallet from the floor, he sniffed, "I suppose now you want a do-gooder reward."

J.J. said nothing, intently studying the menu.

"Maybe you expect me to buy you supper."

Still, J.J. said nothing.

"So, I'm not good enough to buy you a meal?"

Now J.J. looked over at the man. Free food was free food, after all. "Okay," he said. "You can buy me supper." J.J. returned to his menu, which, by now, he had had time to practically memorize.

"Well, are you going to join me or not?" Meyers demanded.

"You mean have supper together?"

"No, nitwit," Meyers snarled. "I'll eat mine here, and you have yours at Pizza Hut. Of course I mean together. Besides, I don't want you ordering anything expensive," a statement ridiculed by Meyers' slick threads, spit polish Allen Edmonds loafers, Blancpain watch, and emerald pinky ring. The snappy Panama hat beside him defied anyone to take a seat uninvited.

J.J. slid in diagonally across from Meyers and introduced himself. He added, "Thanks for supper, though kindness requires no compensation."

Meyers rolled his eyes. "Shut up and order."

J.J. decided to obey his dining mantra of, when in doubt, order the meat loaf. His instinct was justified when the platter arrived bearing a generous portion of meat alongside a heaping scoop of mashed potatoes, both drenched in gravy, and a ladling of corn.

His entrée was preceded by a tossed salad topped with ranch dressing and two packets of croutons. A large glass of water with lemon but no ice did the job nicely as beverage of choice, lest anything more substantial prematurely sate his appetite.

Meyers ordered another beer along with his prime rib and baked potato. He rejected the dinner roll and demanded in its stead an English muffin toasted borderline black. Neither man spoke until their food arrived, whereupon J.J., hands folded, silently said grace.

"Are you done?" Meyers growled.

"Done with my prayer? Yes. You don't pray before a meal?"

"Take a wild guess."

"I have always believed it is right to thank God."

"So do you want a medal?"

"No, I'm good."

"Yeah, yeah. Pass the pepper and stop talking for a minute if that's humanly possible," Meyers commanded.

J.J. looked out the window, wishing himself to be anywhere but here. But was there really a choice, this rowboat of irresistible food inches in front of him?

The men ate. Other diners came and went. Melanie greeted and bid farewell to each with a smile and a thank you.

The rain continued.

Meyers took a swig of beer. "So you're a Bible thumper to boot." He took another swig and muttered, "Great."

J.J. chewed and swallowed and said, "I can't recite the Bible

240

chapter and verse, and Lord knows I'm not perfect."

"That's a relief."

By now J.J. had become adept at parrying Meyers's punch lines. "I read the Psalms a lot. Can't say I understand or accept all the Bible's teachings or its admonitions. I focus on prayers to him..."

"Enough already," Meyers said. "You're giving me a headache and spoiling my steak."

J.J. changed the subject. "Are you from around here?"

"Yes." Another swig of beer. "You?"

"Passing through."

"So was I. Twenty-two years ago." Again, Meyers glared at the wall. Still, the wall glared back. "You work all your life, you retire, you die."

"I like to think there's more than that," said J.J.

"You don't say."

"I do say. There's family, faith, love, fulfillment..."

"Stop." Meyers clapped his hands on the table. "I didn't ask for your self-indulgent commentary and judgment, nor do I need them."

"I wasn't..."

Melanie tiptoed to clear the table and mouthed to J.J., "You okay?"

He grinned and mouthed back, "Never better."

She stifled a laugh, cleared her throat, and asked, "Can I offer you two some apple pie? You do know that *stressed* spelled backwards is *desserts.*"

"I'll pass on the pie," J.J. answered, "but remember the line."

Meyers said, "I'll take the pie but pretend I never heard the line. Do you really think it's funny?" He pointed across the table. "Go ahead, have some."

"Really?"

"No, I just made that up. Of course really."

"Alright then, I'd love some apple pie," J.J. told her. "Homemade?"

"Is there any other kind?" Melanie said.

Meyers rubbed his forehead. "Make them à la mode."

"Coffee for you?" she asked Meyers.

"Go for it."

"Another refill, J.J?" she asked.

"Sure thing."

They sat and waited. Pie à la mode and coffee arrived, dessert and drink both proving more than satisfactory. The only other remaining customer arose, put three quarters on the table, and, bent with scoliosis, she shuffled over to the two men.

Meyers demanded, "What do you want?"

Palms open, the woman said, "Psalm 125:1, gentlemen. 'They that trust in the Lord shall be as mount Zion, which cannot be removed, but abideth forever.'" Without further word she walked away and out.

Meyers watched, mouth agape, and scraped off the last of his pie. "What was that? Can't a man be left alone?"

J.J. said, "He can be, except…"

"Except what?"

"It can be okay for a man to be left alone, so long as the privacy is a gate that can be opened and closed and not a fortress never to be left or approached."

"That's almost poetic."

"Thank you."

"I said almost."

Melanie swiveled on the near stool, winked at J.J., and shook her head as if to say, "You can't win."

J.J. finished off his pie and said nothing more. Meyers' self-indulgent hostility was bringing him face to face with his own weakness and lack of faith at the time of his layoff, when he wallowed in self-pity. Maybe the Spirit in God's wisdom pointed him on this trip, indeed to this very encounter, to force him to a time of testing.

"What?" Meyers asked.

He answered, "Just thinking."

"Bad for a person. Are you done eating?"

"As a matter of fact, I am."

"Then maybe it's time for you to leave."

J.J. maneuvered himself out of the booth.

"This is the longest conversation I've had with one person in the last ten years," Meyers said without looking up. His audience of one did not find that difficult to believe. The hand J.J. extended in thanks for the meal was not reciprocated, nor was the remark,

"It's been a pleasure."

He offered his calling card to Meyers. "What's this?"

"Something from me to you."

"Put it on the table."

Neither man looked at the other when J.J. exited after paying for Shirley's meal. Melanie sat at the counter and watched him through the window, then returned to flip through an old issue of *People* magazine.

Meyers scanned the card, tore it into four pieces, and stubbed out his cigarette on them in the ashtray.

Determined fan churned overhead.

Vintage jukebox in the far corner played on, not obtrusively loud but unobtrusively gentle, as if a breeze not a gale.

The rain continued.

Chapter 25

Father Thomas strived to never puff up to be of a proud heart, but that did not rule out taking pride in some things. One of them was refusing to be a slave to the regimen of three square meals a day. Another, along with hitting the open road on a spontaneous hitchhiking adventure, was taking the occasional gamble. Which meant, after the fellowship and budding friendship with Ashraf and Aleah and their kids, he elected to skip supper and a motel room and stay right where he was and take a chance that the edict against overnight stays at the rest area would not be enforced and confident that he would not awake shaky with stomach rumbling.

Both sacrifices panned out. After a restful night beside the restroom building, a patch of soft grass for a mattress, knapsack a pillow, scattered high clouds a blanket, Father Thomas woke with the sunrise, stretched to gain his senses, chose a package of vending machine peanuts for breakfast, and got back to work hooking fingers into knapsack and fixing eyes homeward.

The priest walked contentedly alongside the highway and

softly sang, "Be Thou My Vision," the hymn's words and message resonating in his heart and mind.

"Be Thou my best thought in the day and the night, Both waking and sleeping, Thy presence my light..."

In pondering all the good that had come his way in and since Cicero and thanking God for his many blessings, Father Thomas had to admit that, after hitting the road one way or another for going on two weeks, he was ready to return to his church family. They needed him and he them. Plus, there was another commitment drawing him back to Los Angeles beyond the walls of his church.

Men and women clothed in missionary zeal carry goodwill and the Word of the Almighty to all corners of Gods' kingdom. In that spirit and of the one in which Jesus sent out his twelve apostles to spread the Gospel and minister, Father Thomas for a decade had tended to the lost sheep in Los Angeles. He took up the yoke on the city's public transit system, crisscrossing the bus and subway routes once a week in the dead of night to break spiritual bread and bring the manifestation of Christ's compassion to the broken and the brokenhearted, the addicted, the homeless, the depressed, the alone, the angry, the rejected, the runaway, the criminal, the dropout, the lost, miseries often overlapping, sometimes myriad.

On one such occasion, among the burdened going to and from jobs that paid the minimum and provided the same, the marginalized lugging groceries or laundry in overstuffed backpacks, the lost heading nowhere with nothing, he encountered a very angry young man named Roberto Alvarez, boarding at the 7th and Figueroa stop shortly after 12:30 a.m. on what passed for a wintry night in Southern California. The priest sidestepped Roberto manspreading over two seats reserved for the handicapped and daring anyone to challenge him. Recently turned nineteen and middle finger raised in defiance to the odds of making it to twenty, Roberto did not know or care where he fit on the spectrum of despair. And he was in no mood for the priest glancing his way from across aisle.

"What are you looking at, *guero*?"

"At you, my brother."

"Well quit it," he snorted, "and I'm not your brother."

Other passengers took no notice, or they did and kept their distance.

"We are all brothers and sisters in the eyes of the Lord."

"I said quit it. Now leave me alone or I'm going to mess you up."

Father Thomas shot him an amused look. "I rather doubt that," he said and reached out a hand. "May I know your name?"

Roberto clenched his fists. "No, you may not."

Making it a practice to carry a backpack of Bibles, peanut butter sandwiches, and bottles of water to dispense on his Metro missions, he opened one of the books and beseeched the Lord to help this lost soul who was so much like himself a lifetime ago.

Four stops later the priest got up to leave.

"Here," he said and offered the book to Roberto.

He slapped it away. "Let it go, man."

Father Thomas put the Bible on the seat next to Roberto, disembarked, and ritually pronounced, "All glory to God," as the bus pulled away. That night marked somewhere around his five hundredth outreach, and to date, only a few ultimately had managed to find their way to Saints Peter and Paul, where they, like the Prodigal Son, were joyously welcomed into the parish population. But numbers did not matter to him; rather, he was blessed to present the door to the Word and the Way and the Lord's invitation for them to knock.

Father Thomas often recollected the encounter and prayed for him in the years that followed, but if pressed to think about it, he would figure Roberto to be perhaps the last person in the world he'd run into on his walk outside Tucson. And then a silver minivan roared past, suddenly pulled up on the shoulder, reversed to about ten yards in front, and stopped. Never one to back away, Father Thomas maintained his stride, arriving at the driver's open window.

"What are you looking at, *guero*?" the question delivered this time not with a snarl but with an ear-to-ear smile.

Father Thomas surveyed the man behind the wheel and the woman in the passenger seat and was momentarily at a loss for who this could be. Then he rubbed his eyebrows in surprise of recognition. "Praise God," he beamed at the man. "Can it really be you?"

"It's me alright."

"What's it been, five years?" Father Thomas asked.

"Actually nine."

A voice tinkled from inside the van. "Who's that man, Daddy?"

Father Thomas craned to look into the back seat. Wide eyes looked back. "*Señor*, you are very big," a little girl said from her car seat.

The two men howled. "She does have a way with words," Roberto said, his voice thick with pride.

"What's your name?" the big man asked.

"Emily."

"That's a pretty name."

"Thank you."

"May I ask how old you are?"

She looked to her mom who nodded it was okay to answer.

"I am four and a half," she announced.

Traffic barreled past.

"Perhaps you'd better get in before you end up as very big roadkill," Roberto said.

"Sounds like a fine idea," answered Father Thomas.

With the priest safely inside the vehicle, the woman in the passenger seat up front nudged Roberto. "Perhaps you could introduce us, sweetheart?"

"Where are my manners?" laughed Roberto. "This is my wife, Veronica."

"I'm pleased to meet you," Father Thomas said.

"I've heard a lot about you," she answered.

Roberto drove and glanced in the rearview mirror.

"I found your name and the name of your church a month after we met on the bus when I was led to open that Bible and read the handwritten inscription inside. I was tempted to contact you so many times but, for some reason, I never did."

"No matter. We're here now," Father Thomas said and gave out a hearty laugh. "It seems we all know each other's names except for one."

Roberto looked at him confused. "Whose is that?"

"Why it's yours! Of course we could continue as 'my brother' and '*guero*' if you want."

Roberto slapped himself on the forehead and did the honors. Father Thomas grinned in turn at each of them. "I'm pleased to be with all of you." He clapped Roberto on the shoulder. "I'd long prayed our paths would cross again."

Before anyone could talk more, a small ball of white fur barked from the back of the minivan, bounded into the seat, and snuggled up against the priest, muscling her teeny freckled nose into his mighty palm.

"I see our guard dog found you," Veronica said. "During our honeymoon in Las Vegas, we spotted her walking on a street just off the Strip, ribs sticking out, so dirty we didn't know what color she was."

The dog wagged her stump of a tail.

"A warm bath revealed this cute white thing," Roberto

explained. "When we thought of a name, Cute or White didn't sound quite right, neither did Thing."

Veronica chimed in. "After the dog dried, I said she looked so fluffy, why we don't name her that? She answered with a happy bark, and Fluffy it was."

The car fell silent except for Fluffy's rhythmic breathing curled up on the priest's lap.

"Father, I'm deeply sorry for not contacting you and expressing my thanks," Roberto finally said. "I was nervous and embarrassed about who I had been and never found the right words to say to you."

"No need, Roberto. Let's rejoice that the time has arrived."

They decided to head to a fast-food restaurant advertised up a ways, and soon thereafter, with trays full of breakfast treats, all four settled into a booth. Fluffy came along with them in a carrier that Roberto slipped under the table in hopes that the teenage manager would not notice their violation of the posted "Service Animals Only" rule. She did, however, but smiled and said in a quiet voice, "I love my dog, too, so no problem." She looked down at Fluffy and put a finger to her lips.

Emily hummed to herself, filling in a coloring book, and Roberto persevered to fill in the blanks between his first and second meetings with Father Thomas.

He started by explaining a young man's dissatisfaction that built to resentment that boiled over to outrage, the worst part being that there had been no reason for it. On the contrary, in fact. His mom and dad were deeply devoted parents who had worked their way up from kitchen help to owning a prosperous breakfast and lunch restaurant. Their example and financial assistance motivated and put his sister through UCLA and then on to medical school, but Roberto wanted none of it. Whatever they tried to do for him was never right in his eyes. He spurned their pleas to let them love him, dropped out of high school in a fit of pique, and hit the streets to hide in plain sight. On that winter night after his encounter with Father Thomas, Roberto shoved two women out of the way to get off the bus a few stops later. Despite himself, stewing on the steps at the bus exit, he went back to his seat, picked up the book, and slipped it inside his jacket.

"To this day, Father, I can't believe I did it. I hated you, my parents, my sister, myself. I know the Lord works in mysterious ways, but that was something out of '*The Twilight Zone.*'"

"How did you survive on the streets?" the priest said.

"I lived and slept wherever. The streets, shelters, benches, the bus. I had no friends, no family, no nothing. When I finally opened that Bible, the prayer card you enclosed spoke to me and has been with me ever since." He took the holy card, folded and dog-eared, from his wallet.

Anyone who listens to my teaching

and follows it

is wise,

like a person who builds a house on solid rock.

Matthew 7:24

"I returned to my parents' house soon after, got my GED, and from there went to school to learn aircraft mechanics. Now I work out of LAX. But the best thing to happen to me was meeting my beautiful Veronica at a Bible study."

Husband and wife squinched closer and held hands. "Thank you for marrying me," Roberto whispered.

Veronica kissed his cheek. "Forever."

Emily sipped her milk. "May I move over and sit next to Mister Father Thomas?"

"Of course, honey," mom said.

Emily wrapped her doll-like fingers around the priest's thumb and said, "Wow."

Their laughter turned heads.

"Enough about me, Father. Are you still on your Metro mission? And what brings you out here in the desert?"

"The answer to your first question is definitely yes. I have been doing this for going on a decade and consider it my life's work outside my parish. Believe it or not, Roberto, I once was lost like you before a Marine chaplain showed me the Way. It is now my sacred calling to carry that mission forward."

He spoke more. Emily would not let go of his thumb. "Now as for your second question, I'm headed back to Los Angeles after a visit to the Midwest to see my family."

Roberto and Veronica looked at each other. "Surely you're not walking back."

"Hitchhiking. When you passed me, I was taking a breather

and enjoying quiet time. I started in Cicero."

"Cicero?"

"Yes, it's a suburb of Chicago."

"I know where it is. You're kidding, right, about hitching from there?"

"I've made it this far."

"You mean all the way from Cicero?" The couple looked at each other in amazement.

"It's been a great ride, or rides, I should say."

"We're returning to Los Angeles ourselves from visiting her family in Las Cruces," said Roberto.

"Yes," added Veronica, "and would love to have you ride with us back to Los Angeles."

"Even take you to your front door," said Roberto, "if you don't mind one stop we have to make."

It did not take long for his decision. "Sounds wonderful. Thank you."

Piling back into the van, Roberto told the priest of his volunteer work with runaway kids on nights and weekends. "Heaven knows I can identify with them. The stop we're making is to visit one of them now, a girl reunited with her parents not long ago after two years on the streets."

The miles passed merrily with idle chatter and quiet time looking out the window until Roberto announced, "Here we are," and proceeded along a winding, half-mile gravel driveway. At its end stood Patrick and Lucille Murphy and teen-age daughter Karen arm in arm in arm. As soon as Roberto stepped out of the van, the girl ran and wrapped her arms around him. "Thank you so much for coming, Mr. Alvarez."

Her parents walked up and, after hearty greetings, Patrick offered with a sweep of his arm, "Welcome to our home." On the rim of their two-acre homestead rested a double-wide, manufactured house, pretty in pink with white trim. Window boxes filled with happy petunias in salmon, blue, and purple stretched around on all sides.

Veronica said, "Your house is beautiful," the compliment echoed by Roberto and Father Thomas.

"Roberto, we thank you from the bottom of our hearts for all you did for our Karen. We were beside ourselves after she ran away and hoped and prayed for her return, and you answered those prayers."

"I am happy I could help in my own small way," Roberto answered. He affectionately put a hand on the shoulder of Father Thomas. "It was this good man who showed me the way."

"All glory to God, Roberto," Father Thomas offered. "I was blessed to do his bidding."

Lucille guided them to a brightly decorated red table under a canopy. "We were hoping you could join us for lunch."

The party chatted, sipping ice cold orange Kool-Aid tapped from a picnic thermos and dining on baked beans, homemade potato salad, and charcoal-grilled hamburgers and hot dogs, whose exquisite aroma and taste rivaled any steak from any five-star restaurant. The laughter and voices performed a cheery melody in the stillness of the desert, paper plates and cups and plastic utensils sparing them the clank and clatter of regular tableware. Soon the girls slipped away with Fluffy, leaving the adults to talk.

"We," Patrick started, "had Karen rather late in life. Kids are always a challenge, and when you have one in your forties even more so."

"I can only imagine," Veronica said. "Emily is already a handful."

"Amen to that," agreed Roberto.

"Karen was our only child," explained Patrick. "Both of us tried too hard and were overindulgent, and then when she became the typical teenager with rebellion in her, we went the other way and became overly strict."

Lucille spoke. "It was too much for her, and finally, she ran away the day after she turned fourteen. We tried filing a missing person report with the police, those fliers you see all around in stores and freeway stops, but nothing worked. And then out of the blue, Roberto contacted us and told us he had been working with our beloved daughter at a shelter in Los Angeles."

Patrick picked up the baton. "When the time was right for us to reunite, we went there and slowly put the pieces back together. Karen is back in high school, making friends, and doing well."

Patrick put his arm around Lucille, and she leaned into him.

The girls returned from their play, and Karen walked up to the priest.

"Father Thomas," she said simply. "That's a good name."

"Yes, Thomas; it's a good, strong, biblical name and it suits you," Patrick said.

Father Thomas was about to respond when Veronica broke in.

"Actually, there's a lot more to it."

The girls sat and listened too. Fluffy snoozed at their feet.

"Let me tell you what the apostle Thomas was really like," Veronica began. "He is often demeaned as Doubting Thomas, the apostle who demanded physical proof of the risen Lord. He should really be praised as Steadfast Thomas, a man of great conviction, courage, and adventure who was relentless in pursuit of truth, even requiring it of our Savior before proclaiming 'My Lord and My God.'"

Patrick said, "I never thought of that, Veronica."

They watched a prairie dog skitter past the house, stop to survey a stand of yucca, and hightail it away.

"There's more," Veronica continued. "During the years after the Resurrection, Thomas ventured far, preached, and started a church in what is now Iran. After that he traveled to India where many Christians to this day consider him to be the country's patron saint. Indeed, Thomas is a popular name among the Saint Thomas Christians of India."

Father Thomas knew all of what Veronica offered about his namesake, and more, but kept his silence other than to say softly, "You are very gracious."

Veronica addressed him. "After Roberto told me about his

meeting with you and how it changed him, I was determined to know about you, so I researched your church and your own patron and realized how you were traveling in his footsteps with your mission. I even went to Mass at Saints Peter and Paul myself once."

Roberto looked over to her in surprise. "I never knew," he said. "If you go again, I'd like to come along."

"Perhaps the three of you will make a habit of it. Our parish would love to have you," Father Thomas said warmly.

"We just may," Roberto said.

Lucille smiled broadly. "Just as God's will is done in bringing back our precious Karen, so has it brought all of you together."

"Hear, hear!" Patrick agreed.

The two hours Roberto had allotted for the visit stretched to three, no one wanting the feeling of unity to end. But as the day grew later it inevitably became time to go.

Headed away down the driveway, four arms in the van waved out the windows in farewell and affection, reciprocated by six waving arms in front of the house. Not wanting to inject his own public display into the two families' day of rejoicing and celebration, Father Thomas resisted the urge to shout his favorite exclamation in praise. But then he decided to go for it, his cry embraced by a glowing Roberto and Veronica, applauded by a clapping Emily, and endorsed by a barking Fluffy.

"Hallelujah!"

"Again!" Emily shouted, and he complied.

Chapter 26

Another capital lay ahead, this one not on any list and, for the moment, not on his mind. J.J. thought back to Meyers. Offering prayers that the man would find answers and comfort, J.J. recalled his own funks.

"There but for the grace of God go I," Little Evie pronounced in motherly attempts to straighten him out from teenage bouts of melancholy.

"Always keep your perspective, son," seconded Big Al from another room.

So wound up in himself in the angst of puberty, he did not realize, or could not admit, how right they were. But in the years and growing up that followed, he acknowledged within himself their correctness, a point brought home once again in the not-too-distant past when he spiraled downward after his job loss. With not a clue about what could have put Meyers in such a seemingly permanent state of mind, J.J. debated whether to return to the restaurant in the hope Meyers would be there, undoubtedly seething during a meal or coffee break, and try to open his heart a crack. But to find what? Tranquility, forgiveness, contentment? As far as Meyers was most probably concerned, J.J. was nothing more than an interloper who spied a dropped wallet.

Head dizzying in a circle of who was right and who was wrong, or if there was a right and a wrong, J.J. gave up and elected to enjoy the morning.

After he departed Little Rock, the next and final destination of the dartboard journey lay a tick over a thousand miles away on the far fringe of New Mexico. But this trip had never originated as an endurance test, and he was not about to consider it one now and mindlessly submit to blasting across Oklahoma and its Panhandle, letting the sound of his own wheels drive him crazy. Which meant that shortly out of the Arkansas capital, he detoured southwest toward Austin, a city in Texas he had wanted to visit for as long as he could remember, and what better time than now. To make matters better, there came a detour from the detour when he saw mileage signs to Dallas.

The Big D had not registered on J.J.'s radar when plotting this trip or in all the years preceding, but he was glad it did pop up out of the blue on this sweltering Saturday. He ended up spending three days feasting on Tex-Mex and exploring, the highlight of which was a visit to the Texas School Book Depository from where the infamous Lee Harvey Oswald fired his fatal shots at President Kennedy, an incident of fifty-four years ago that felt more like a thousand, if you bridged the America of then and now.

A drive-by of the Texas Rangers baseball stadium in nearby Arlington followed, along with taking in the game on Ruby's radio. This jogged memories of a pristine boyhood, when baseball was not so much watched as heard, its joys savored by the Werth family on many a backyard Sunday afternoon, complementing their together time with golden ears of corn and red meat cooked over an open charcoal fire.

From there J.J. headed back onto the original detour to Austin, where he spent a leisurely day crossing another capital city off his to-do list and concluding with a grocery stop to restock provisions. The newly purchased Spam and rye bread sent his empty stomach into a frenzy that demanded he pull up at the first rest area outside the city. Seated at a sun-fried picnic bench, J.J. and his taste buds braced for the first exquisite bite when an Alaskan malamute bounded up, a young woman trying and failing to keep up.

"Stop!" she shouted, her tone somewhere between command and plea.

The dog blew off the instruction, settled on its haunches up against J.J.'s legs, and gazed with pleading eyes on the sandwich.

Surrender was a *fait accompli*.

"Okay with you if I share a chunk with the pooch?" J.J. asked.

"Yeah, go ahead," she answered with a shrug.

He broke off a piece of the sandwich, which the dog scarfed in one bite, and nosed in for seconds.

J.J. obliged.

"Sorry," the woman offered.

J.J. thought of the plenty of remaining tins of Spam piled in the trunk and said, "He's fine. It's all good."

"He's a she."

J.J. blushed slightly. "Sorry. What's her name?"

"I call her Karl."

"Unusual name for a girl. Cool."

"I like to think so."

"I'm J.J., by the way."

"A pleasure, I'm Magda." She sat next to him, and he offered her a Gatorade from his stash.

"No, thank you."

Neither spoke further for a short while. With Karl snoozing in a content clump at his feet, J.J. polished off the last corner of bread and observed this new acquaintance. He guessed her to be in her early twenties. Her twinkling navy blues missed nothing, and her jet black hair was cut short atop three dangling pig tails. A thin, two-inch scar formed a horizontal sliver across her slender throat, which, rather than being off-putting, defined the woman's features as naturally as did her dimples. Drenched, she might have weighed in at a tick over a hundred.

Her attire and embellishments consisted of high-top black hiking boots, jeans in one piece *sans* the trendy gaps and rips, an aqua polo shirt, large, silver loop earrings, and a bracelet of small seashells. Attractive and aware of it but not pressing the point, she wore no body art, makeup, or head covering of any kind. Were Magda inclined to trace her roots, she would have found they led to a Sioux maiden and a buffalo soldier, who hooked up back in the day somewhere in the Dakotas. Lacking any such compulsion for discovery, Magda took strength from an instinctive sense of blood and pride.

She broke the silence. "Where're you headed?"

Dallas and Austin had put J.J. in a wandering state of mind, and he was determined to keep it going.

"San Antonio," he blurted.

"Any particular reason?"

"I've always wanted to go there to visit the Alamo."

She rolled her eyes.

"What?"

"The Alamo. A chapel back then in the middle of nowhere that could have been abandoned by the Texicans and bypassed by the Mexicans. But no, their leaders had to have bragging rights at the cost of hundreds of lives."

"Whoa," J.J. managed to squeak out.

"Just think about it—J.J., is it?—what did all the testosterone and bloodshed prove? Nothing. It's a battle that never should have been fought, but it was, uselessly, and then instead of apologizing, what do we do?"

"Pray, tell me."

At least that got a laugh from her before announcing, "The authorities memorialize it, Hollywood makes movies glorifying it, and people flock to see it."

"People like me."

"Don't take it personal. But places like the Alamo really bug me," she said and got up to leave.

"I'm sorry," J.J. said in genuine contrition. On an impulse he called out, a bit more loudly than intended, "Hey!"

"Hey what?" she said and stood over him.

"Want to join me?"

"Say again?"

"Want to ride along?"

"To the Alamo?" she screeched. "You've got to be kidding me."

"Not to the Alamo. To San Antonio."

Magda turned her face to the sun, closed her eyes, and got up to stand on tiptoes, the pause sufficiently long that J.J. took this for a no and gathered himself to depart.

Then to his surprise, she answered. "Sure. Why not? It's a nice day for a drive."

He suddenly remembered Karl, who remained lying down oblivious to the Alamo ruckus. "I forgot about the dog. Might be a problem."

"Oh, she's not mine. We met on the road, and, like me, she's her own person, content to be with someone for a while but not wanting to be tied down."

As if on cue, Karl got up, walked over, touched noses with Magda, and ambled away. "See you, girl," she called out. The dog woofed and trotted in search of new conquests.

"Got any luggage?" J.J. asked, to which Magda displayed a

slim bedroll knapsack, deposited it in Ruby's backseat foot well, and took her place in front.

J.J. stuck to the slow lane, whatever that meant out here in the open range, leaving him and his happenstance companion to converse and observe the flora and winged and four-legged creatures along the way.

"Magda suits you."

"I beg your pardon?"

"Your name, Magda. It suits you."

"Thanks. My birth name actually is Helen. I mean, do I look like a Helen?"

"What's a Helen supposed to look like?"

"I don't know, but certainly not like me."

"Helen is a fine name."

"I chose Magda from Mary Magdalene, a strong, courageous woman and follower of Jesus, at the cross when he died, and the first person at the tomb to witness his Resurrection."

"I'm aware."

"And she knew how to pick her friends. Do you realize that aside from John, all the others staying with Jesus at his crucifixion were women? Those supposed brave and devoted men who professed allegiance either fled or hid. Even Pete, the rock of the church, denied Jesus."

"And this means?"

"Just sayin'."

He redirected the conversation.

"You took a chance traveling alone with me."

"How's that?" she asked without taking her eyes off a grazing remuda, J.J. preferring the random patches of swaying wildflowers.

"Driving alone with me out here. I could be a serial killer."

Magda glanced over and wiped away a smile. "Really?"

"Well, maybe not."

"Maybe I'm one," she dared.

"Are you?"

A bug took on the windshield and lost.

"I suppose we'll find out."

Traffic streaked past, some of them annoyed and annoying tailgaters who, after zooming around, slowed briefly in front to make a point. J.J. ignored them. He was in no hurry and refused to be swayed from puttering along in good company and even feeling a little disappointed that San Antonio was but a two-hour drive away.

Mentally searching for the perfect word to describe Magda, he rejected captivating as too strong, interesting as too weak, and settled on invigorating.

"Do your parents live in Texas?" he asked.

"I've no idea. I went through the foster system until the day I turned eighteen, when I gave myself the best birthday present ever."

"Which was?"

"I emancipated myself from the ties that bound me, changed my name, and got out of Dodge. That was six years ago. I've gotten by just fine ever since. I live pretty low to the ground, am not afraid of hard work to get some spending money, and always find a place to eat and sleep."

J.J. started to ask where her Dodge was if not in Kansas, but thought better of it. "You're pretty brave and creative to do that. Not many people could."

Magda shook her head. "You'd be surprised to see how easy it is to live off the grid, or better yet, to create your own with little more than the clothes on your back. Everyone now has to have their RVs, ATVs, Humvees, TVs, you name it. I don't begrudge them. To each their own. I just prefer living in the moment, finding satisfaction and light and good from within."

"It's too bad you never got to know your mom and dad. Parents can be very special. I was blessed with mine, and they treated and taught me well. Both passed away many years ago, first him, then her. I feel their presence all around but miss and think about them all the time, even these decades later."

Magda didn't interrupt.

"Even though I was grown and gone from home, after Mom died, it felt strange with both parents gone, sort of like a ship without an anchor. I suppose a person never really gets over the loss of loved ones, do they?"

He took on a distant look. Puffs of cloud all shapes and sizes freckled the azure sky. Two vultures landed on the rubber-beaten yellow stripe up ahead to engage in a game of chicken with onrushing traffic, only to quickly reconsider upon realizing that they were in the company of motorists disinclined to swerve or slow for man, woman, or beast.

She answered. "Those we have loved in this world await us in the next when our time comes to join them for all eternity in heaven, paradise, garden, rebirth, whatever word you choose to define the other side. Until then, we are to carry on and feel their presence and communicate with them soul to soul."

J.J. nodded lightly, confident Big Al and Little Evie were in heaven along with Charlie, and he recalled the several occasions, when meditating in backyards here and there, that a pair of finches flew up, chattered, and flitted from daisy to daisy, then flew off together. Perhaps they were nothing more than two birds dropping in, or perhaps it was something more, as if a parental greeting from beyond of love and affirmation to stay strong.

Magda said, "During my time before the everlasting reward with the Wakan Tanka, I mean to live a life of simplicity and worshiping of life in all its forms. It is that which enriches us, and you would be wise to follow the same path."

"I do try to do that as a good Christian."

She hummed an undefined tune and folded her hands in contemplation.

"I'm a Spiritualist, a Buddhist, a Taoist, a Christian, a Jainist, and more, believing that God is God in whatever form you want, or in no form at all, and that no one's deity or beliefs are greater than the other. A shaman once told me when I was searching for my own way, 'Heaven is many rivers flowing into one ocean.'"

J.J. turned the idea over in his head. "I have a friend back home, a parish priest, whom I believe you would enjoy talking with if you ever take a vacation back on the grid."

"We'll see."

"Wait. We'll see about talking to him, or we'll see about going back on the grid?"

"Both."

San Antonio exit signs popped up, and soon they found themselves at the Alamo. The entrance line snaked out front.

"Last chance, Magda," he teased as they climbed out of Ruby.

"Right," she scowled, upraised eyebrow adding an exclamation point to her reply.

"Just thought I'd offer. What'll you do in the meantime?"

"Maybe I'll split."

"Whatever."

"Or maybe I'll stand out here and whistle the '*Himno Nacional Mexicano.*'"

"Eh?"

"Mexico's national anthem, silly. You don't get out much, do you?"

"Looks like it, I guess." He closed the car door and locked it with a beep of its remote. "If you do decide to stick around, what say we meet back here in two hours?"

"We'll see. Take all the time you need."

The anointed 120 minutes later, J.J. walked up to Ruby. Magda leaned against the car reading a two-day-old newspaper she found on a park bench.

"I'm glad you stuck around," J.J. said.

"How was the tour?"

"Interesting and enlightening."

"I'll bet." She returned the paper to its place.

"I'm getting hungry," said J.J. "Want to go for some barbecue? No, wait, let me guess. Carnivores are scum, and the idea of eating meat infuriates you."

"Actually, it does, but I do lapse," Magda admitted. "In fact, I fight the impulse of gorging on barbecue every minute of every day."

"You surprise me."

"That's the general idea."

They found a place for a late supper, ordered at the counter, and took a seat at a long wooden table. A short while later, they were strapping on bibs and digging in, he to brisket and sausage, she to beef ribs and pulled pork, sharing sides of pinto beans, sweet potatoes, coleslaw, and corn. After a while, music started up in an adjoining dance hall. Wiping their chins and tossing their trash into a receptacle, the two went for a look and found the dance floor packed with bodies moving, round tables unoccupied except for purses and jackets. A woman in a wheelchair, gray hair tied back in a bun and nose tethered to an oxygen tank, watched the proceedings. Her fingers tapped and head swayed to the beat.

J.J. and Magda both loved line dancing, partly for the music but mostly because no partner was required when the mood struck to bust a move, and it turned out that they shared a fancy to "Boot Scootin' Boogie," which the local band began to play.

Departing a few hours later, the place still rocking in full swing, J.J. and Magda walked past the car to a bus stop bench. The dark embraced them.

"I love the night," Magda said and breathed in deeply. She talked more, of her appreciation for connection with The People, the rivers, the mountains, and the Creator. Hers was a feeling of belonging J.J. had not imagined and perhaps could not.

A bus turned the corner and rumbled toward.

"But that doesn't mean I can't enjoy BBQ and getting out on the dance floor," she said with a smile. "I enjoyed our time there."

"I did too."

They waved the bus driver on and walked back to Ruby. At the car, Magda spoke again. "I know this area pretty well, and there's a nice cluster of motels just west of the city where I'm sure you'll be able to find one to suit you."

"And you?"

"There's a campground close by where I can bed down for the night."

He shot her a look. "You don't worry about your safety?"

"There's nothing to worry about. I can take care of myself, always have, always will. I've slept in campgrounds, parks, and rest areas across the western U.S. My bedroll and knapsack have everything I need."

"May I drive you?"

"Thanks, but no, I'll be fine. Just pull up at a motel you like and I'll take it from there."

"Would you like to meet for breakfast?"

"Maybe."

"How's seven?"

"I'll come by and wait at your car. Maybe."

J.J. woke early the next morning and prepared a cup of the complimentary coffee to cool while he showered. As always fashionably early, he walked out at 6:50 and posted himself half sitting on Ruby's trunk to wait and breathe in the morning air. He greeted other crack of dawn devotees with a nod and a smile and happy thoughts of the day ahead.

The minutes ticked to seven and later. Thirty minutes passed and he quintuple-checked his watch, straightened up, and walked a lopsided circle around the car. It was then that he noticed the piece of paper folded tightly under the driver's side windshield wiper.

"Wopila tanka, J.J. Toksha ake wachinyanitin ktelo.

Magda"

The translation could come later, but he was pretty confident it wasn't, *Hey guy, I'm running late and will meet you in the restaurant.*

His eyes searched the parking lot. He got in his car and drove a mile east and another west looking for her, but to no avail.

Magda was gone.

Chapter 27

One thing J.J. had to admit. Being blown off in handwritten notes of farewell was getting old real fast.

Breaking from his habit of coffee black to stir hazelnut cream into the mugful, he wallowed in sour grapes to assuage his disappointment at Magda's abrupt departure. A free spirit like Magda's would undoubtedly recoil in revulsion were he to revel in his happiness over his pedestrian lifestyle in the three-bedroom bungalow on the LA grid. For all he knew, she might have bolted from the car in the middle of nowhere—not that she would be out of her element—or to his horror, she might have flung his souvenir Alamo refrigerator magnet out the window.

That got him laughing, as did the admission *at least she didn't ghost me.* He contemplated more in the restaurant across the parking lot from his motel over coffee refills accompanied by a three-egg omelet and a slab of ham trimmed of any semblance of fat. Bottom line, he immensely enjoyed his day with Magda and had looked forward to their meal together this morning. And, he dared to hope that despite the lurking landmines, he had anticipated sharing more of her company and conversation in the next day or two. Penultimate line, she and Meyers were cut from the same cloth of yearning for aloneness, the latter just drawn from a darker bolt. He thought back to his conversation with Magda of the day before.

"Generally you like to be left alone, I take it," he said when circling for a parking space at the Alamo.

"I value my private time but wouldn't say I'm a hermit."

He told her about Meyers.

"Certainly aloneness can be taken to an extreme, but extreme to one may not be extreme to another. Live and let live is how I see it," she said. "In fact, I think people who impose themselves on someone who wants to be left alone are practicing a form of theft."

"That's an interesting twist."

"Time, like money, is finite. Each of us has a certain amount. If someone has five hundred dollars and is robbed of a hundred, that means they have that much less money for things they need or want. By the same token, if a person has sixty minutes and someone interrupts or imposes for an aimless ten, they have stolen time of value. Who is the selfish one for not wanting to share—the person who doesn't want to give up their time frivolously or the one who wants to take it away?"

After a last swig of java, J.J. smiled warmly at the good memory of her and her unorthodox ways and ordered himself to get in gear, which he did, the first stop being the motel's business center for an internet translation of Magda's note:

Many thanks, J.J. I will see you again later.

Magda

He refolded the paper and put it alongside Marie's Santa and the other keepsakes in his duffel and whistled along with Brooks & Dunn's "That Ain't No Way to Go" playing on the overhead speaker as if to prove that the gods have a sense of humor.

It was the last day of August, and he determined to spend the rest of it in a perfect peace. Not that he had anything against Avenged Sevenfold, Santana, or Tanya Tucker, even favoring them when the mood struck, but J.J. chose to spend his next open-window radio interludes listening to and occasionally singing along with Fleetwood Mac, War, and Jefferson Airplane, bands to forever wrap himself around. Four hours out of San Antonio, he traded in the west-bound interstate for northbound roadways less traveled into the underbelly of New Mexico. Over the following days, he supped on a very special corned beef blue plate special topped off by an even more special hot fudge sundae at a third-generation hole-in-the-wall in Hobbs, looked for aliens and UFOs in Roswell, and sat up eating delivery service pizza on lumpy beds in forgettable motels while watching *The Three Stooges*, *Perry Mason*, and *The Twilight Zone* into the night.

At other times, he did nothing of consequence.

A week went by in the blink of an eye, and before J.J. knew it, he had covered the final hundred miles and change on Route 66 from Albuquerque to arrive at his final objective in the summer of '17.

Gallup laid out the welcome mat with a spectacular sunset that swallowed him whole and an unseasonal early September chill that drove him to retrieve his windbreaker.

It did not take too very long to locate a modestly priced and well-appointed establishment to lay his head for the next five nights. Before tucking himself in, he reviewed the places highlighted in his AAA travel book. But first things first, and following the obligatory free breakfast of Danish and coffee the next morning, he wandered the neighborhoods to find what the city offered in the way of his favorite hangout.

He went out looking for a laundromat.

To some, make that many, make that all, of his friends and coworkers, J.J.'s fascination with laundromats was more than a little strange since he had a perfectly usable washer and dryer at home. More to the point, laundromats to them were joints to dutifully take soiled clothes and linens and spend ninety minutes dully staring out the window or absently leafing through a six-month-old copy of some ratty magazine. To J.J., the naysayers had it all wrong. In the first place, many laundromats now featured spiffy snack and beverage counters, DVDs, and video games to while away the many minutes. But more than that, even without those embellishments—and he frankly preferred it that way—he felt in these establishments a serenity, a contentment, a place to read or people-watch amid the tumbling machinery and swirling humankind.

As with so many things, it all depends on how one looks at it. J.J. rejected the protests of his coworkers and often found himself speaking up for characters and clothing that provided far better company than talking heads at a cocktail party. He relished building his defense. "I don't go there all the time, just when the fancy strikes me," he told incredulous challengers.

"Then why go there at all?" shot back the retort, to which he sighed and explained, "They're no longer the dingy places you remember. The modern ones are clean, some serve food and beer and show movies. Besides all that, you meet all kinds of people in laundromats. Travelers, young newlyweds, moms with kids, dads with kids, boys looking for girls, girls looking for boys, college kids, lonely seniors. They all have a story whether they're telling it or not. Often I just like to observe."

And that was that.

Everywhere in J.J.'s adult life had been a multitude of laundromats from which to choose, certainly so in the Los Angeles area. And one side benefit of his road trip was that it fed his fetish because there was nowhere else to clean his clothes along the long way other than at the laundromats at his overnighters, which, more often than not, were fully occupied. He had found several great venues thus far, and Gallup did not disappoint when his expedition hit pay dirt seven blocks from the motel.

After separating his laundry by color and fabric into two washers, he settled into a seat just inside the door and looked over the top of his book to survey the clientele. Many of the usual were there. An elderly couple wordlessly watched CNN. Two teenagers played hooky to hide out and smooch. A young mother bribed her two kids with suckers so she could indulge in a semblance of quiet. And then a man walked in singing to himself. He emptied two bulging plastic bags into a single machine and took a seat two places down from J.J.'s. After scrounging for the sports section of the day's newspaper, he said over the top of it, "Nice laundromat, eh?"

J.J. answered, "Yes, it is." He prepared for more conversation, but it didn't come, the newspaper instead stretched upward. A curl of corncob Captain Black floated above it; indistinguishable words sang behind.

He went for it anyway. "If you don't mind my asking, what's that song you're singing?"

The stranger lowered his broadsheet. "I don't mind at all. It's 'In Heaven There Is No Beer'"

"Catchy."

"I like to think so."

J.J. watched as the man went to deposit his laundry into a dryer. His manner of dress undistinguished, the only standout a red Make America Great Again cap, he moved nimbly and delicately like a tap dancer on eggshells and with a boundless energy, as if perpetually running five minutes late. His hazel eyes seemed kind, shaded by brown brows thick enough to paint a wall. More outstanding was the nose, once or twice broken and once or twice not returned to its original place. Whether this was from defending himself as a boy against bullies who teased him about his name or from his hours in the ring as a young man in Golden Gloves competition—and in fact both were true—what mattered was that despite his slender size, Lucky was a guy you wanted on your side in a brawl.

After depositing coins and looking in the window to make sure the dryer was running, the stranger stopped by J.J.'s chair. "Do you like going to the movies?"

"Movies? Do I like going to the movies?"

"That's what I asked, partner," the man grinned.

"Sure do. Why?"

"I run a drive-in theater in these parts and like to drum up business. I keep a bunch of fliers on that shelf over there."

J.J. put down his book and went for one.

LUCKY'S NIGHT AT THE MOVIES

Two shows and a cartoon

$5 adults

$1 children under 12

Bring yourself, bring 7, bring 7 million

"This is you and your theater?"

"Yup. That's me." He extended a rough hand that J.J. accepted.

"My name is Fred Frederick Hupchek, but I go by Lucky. And who might you be?"

"I'm J.J. Werth. Nice to meet you, Lucky."

"J.J., huh? Sounds like I'm stuttering. How's about I call you

J?"

J.J. thought of Bertha's joke about his last name being Johnson and agreed. "Why not? And maybe I will take you up on the movies. I'm passing through but should have an evening free. Is there a phone number or website I can check out for shows and times?"

Lucky pointed to the phone number and address on the flier. "No website. People who know me say I should have one so's customers can look me up on their or iPads or iPods or iHops or whatever they call those confounded things. Me, I'm old school, probably even ancient school. I don't advertise, just post these announcements around town in fun places like this."

Anyone who called a laundromat a fun place was okay in J.J.'s book, and without saying so, he immediately decided to check out Lucky's drive-in.

The minutes and the tumbling and the swirling passed until J.J. rose to leave. He carefully folded his laundry, placed it into his duffle bag, and announced, "My work here is finished," and turned on the way out.

"Hope to see you there, J. By the way, you dropped a sock."

J.J. searched the floor.

"Made you look," his new friend chirped.

After absorbing Gallup's Native American culture and exploring its historic gems over the next twenty-four hours, J.J. decided it was time to go Hollywood.

The drive-in's personality reflected that of its owner: nothing fancy, everything appealing in a good-natured way. The gravel lot cradled eighty-five speaker stations, and all but four of them were taken by the time the opening credits rolled. From the forefront of the movie screen, a play area beckoned. Old Glory fluttered from a forty-foot pole to the left of it. The snack hut offered the usual movie fare. On the wall at the back a ten-by-ten oak sign, words woodburned in, read:

I spend most of my money

on women and beer.

The rest I just waste.

The owner was nowhere in sight.

While paying for his heap of popcorn and large beverage, J.J. inquired of the cashier, "What's that racket out back?"

She giggled. "Oh, that's Lucky. He always bangs his cymbals before the movies start."

J.J. settled in for the double feature, *Shawshank Redemption* preceded by *Cinderfella,* the two separated by a Popeye cartoon.

At intermission he went for refills of bucket and tanker. Lucky waited on customers, declaring, "That'll be seventy dollars, *amigo*," to a bald, portly patron at the head of the line.

"What!"

"Inflation."

"Since when?"

Lucky offered a wink-wink. "Tell you what, I'll settle for eight."

"That sounds better." The customer offered a ten. "Keep the change, wise guy."

"I'll put it toward my yacht."

The two shook hands heartily.

J.J. stepped up.

"J, my man! *¿Qué pasa?*"

"I love your place, Lucky. Very homey."

"Glad you like it."

He turned to leave with his popcorn and drink.

"J?"

He turned back.

"Your fly's open."

Not about to fall for another gag, he answered tersely, "Uh-huh."

A young woman in the next line tapped his shoulder and whispered, "Sir, it really is."

He looked down. They were right.

J.J. so enjoyed himself that he returned to the drive-in the next night for seconds even though the double feature was the same. Popeye, however, yielded to Road Runner.

During and after the cartoon, an assortment of children danced a merry jig to "It's a Small World" belted out on Lucky's harmonica just outside the snack hut. J.J. stood near taking it all in and was about to return to Ruby for the start of *Cinderfella*, when The Association's "Cherish" started up over the speakers.

J.J. had not heard the song for a good many years, but it was nice having the clock turned back. He was not alone. Watched by the twinkling heavens, men and women long past teenagedom stood outside their cars, some with eyes closed in memory, others slow dancing on the gravel. A few made their way to the play area to maneuver around slides and swings in two- or three-step. No one wanted the music to end, but it always does, no matter who or where you are. And when it did in this corner of J.J.'s world, appreciative applause decorated the night.

A teen-age cashier out on cigarette break during intermission spotted J.J. at the water fountain and nodded toward the boss. "He likes doing this a coupla times a week unannounced," she said to JJ. "The guy sure loves music. And not just the oldies but goodies. You should see him break dance and hip-hop."

"You're kidding."

"No, I'm not."

He declined her offer of a smoke.

"Been here long?" he asked.

"A year or so. That fella out there," she motioned a wave of her Marlboro toward Lucky, "he saved my life."

J.J. moved closer, intrigued.

"You'd never know it," she confided, "and he'd never tell it, but he's a savior to people like me who fall between the cracks." She went on to describe Lucky's many years as a foster father and otherwise savior to lost kids. "I was just another junkie on a street corner when he approached me. I thought he was a john and went to slap his face, but he caught my arm and asked me to join him for a soda where he offered his phone number and said to call anytime. Doing it was the best decision I ever made. He got me clean and brought me here. There must be a dozen of us who love him like a dad and consider him to be exactly that. Most everyone who works here owes their life to him in some way."

Lucky walked over, harmonica in his pocket. "What are you two jawing about?"

"Nothing, Papa," she said and kissed his forehead. "Nice talking to you, sir. I didn't catch your name."

"It's J."

"I'm Cindy."

She returned to her snack station, Lucky to his lawn chair anchored outside the hut, and J.J. to his movie. As he prepared to fire up the car after the second feature, a tap came on the window.

Lucky looked in. "Got time to stick around for a cuppa?"

"Certainly."

Lucky brought out two large coffees and unfolded another chair. "It's great here this time of night."

Crickets sang in agreement.

For the first time, J.J. noticed the tattoos on Lucky's left arm, four names all in a row. *Maggie Donna Josie Michelle*

He pointed. "Girlfriends?"

He made a fist and held up the arm. "Those? They're the names of my four wives. Make that ex-wives. Hope springs eternal, y'know? Every time I tied the knot, I figured it would take, so I tattooed the name of my beloved on yours truly."

"The new wives didn't mind?"

"Nah. They loved me for it. Still do. We go out sometimes, though one at a time. I've always enjoyed the company of a good woman. And a bad one now and again."

Another wink-wink, and an angelic smile.

J.J. waited for Lucky to continue.

"Don't bother me. I'm thinking."

After a minute or two, J.J. broke the silence. "Will you ever try again?"

"What, marriage? Why not? More than likely, there's another ex or two in my future." He traced the tattoo superfecta.

"You know, J, I haven't had and probably never will have a happily ever after. But all in all, I've led a charmed life that's given me plenty of happy durings and surely will give me more. And that will be good enough until the Good Lord comes calling."

At times when two people meet, it is best not to reconnect lest the magic they had dissolve into anticlimax. Such was J.J.'s decision the following day, his last in Gallup, when he slept in, enjoyed a leisurely brunch, and took in the El Rancho Hotel, where he imagined John Wayne, Ronald Reagan, and Katherine Hepburn roaming the hallways. That night sitting in his room, bedside lamp the only light, wind the only sound, he treasured what he knew would be a lifelong memory of Lucky. He, like so many of the places and personalities encountered along these many miles, cannot be found on any Chamber of Commerce website or boastings on social media. And that was what made them all the more special, the most endearing surprises and joys and goodness to be found not by design but by accident and serendipity.

After not too long a time, J.J. turned in for the night, gladdened by the memory of Lucky and his drive-in. Not far away, under the darkened marquee, a harmonica played, its melody lighthearted, its performer equally so and silently wishing his new friend well, wherever he went from here.

Chapter 28

A cell phone chirped forty-six miles west of Las Vegas, which is to say 224 miles east of Los Angeles, depending on whether you are intent on running from or rushing to.

Roberto tilted his head backward. "Must be yours, Father."

Father Thomas picked up, or more accurately flipped open, his phone. "Hello?"

"Sergeant Thomas Kearns?"

Father Thomas had not been addressed as such for so long that his anxiety radar immediately lit up. It proved to be on the mark.

"Yes, this is Thomas Kearns."

"Dexter Jones asks that you come as soon as possible."

"Where is he?" He listened for a moment, jotted an address on his hand, and said, "I'll be right there."

"Trouble?" Roberto asked.

"Yes, I'm afraid so. I have to get to Las Vegas. Please drop me off when you can, and I'll hitch."

Veronica said, "There's nothing and nowhere we're driving to that can't wait. We'll take you where you need to go."

"I don't mean to put you to any trouble."

"No trouble at all," agreed Roberto. "Now if you'll tell us the address, we can enter it into our GPS and be on our way and get you there."

Father Thomas forced a smile and raised his palm.

The van stayed quiet on the way, and he took advantage, gazing out the window at the landscape, thinking and reflecting.

The last time he and Dex met was two, no it had to be three years ago during the weeks before Christmas in a tradition traced back to their return from Vietnam. After re-entering civilian life, whatever that meant, Father Thomas and a tight collection of Marines gathered when they could, not to relive or, heaven forbid, to glorify warfare but to luxuriate in surviving it in reasonably one piece. Over the years and decades, time and circumstances diminished their number but not their enthusiasm.

Nine gathered at that most recent circling of the wagons. They spent the better part of four days hosted by a lieutenant who went from military service to a lucrative liquor distributorship just outside Detroit. In his man cave, they abided by their ritual of a champagne toast to *Semper Fi* followed by cheap pizza and greasy hamburgers—or maybe it was greasy pizza and cheap hamburgers—a bottomless keg, a box of fat cigars, and roaring laughter to the antics of *Bad Santa*.

Never knowing when, where, or if they would meet again, the aging men, who were warriors once, bid farewell with hearty handshakes and crisp salutes. And when it was over, Father Thomas and Dex went off for one last beer together at a bar that was just this side of a saloon and had never heard of, let alone put out, a doily.

"Do you remember how we met, Kearns?" Dex asked over their second cold one.

"Who could forget?"

As miracles go, Dexter Jones and Thomas Kearns becoming best friends does not merit the same ranking as Christ's distribution of loaves and fishes near Bethsaida, but it deserves consideration to rank among the top one hundred.

Back then, when both were grunts, the men had but three things in common. Both were young bucks full of venom and of themselves. Both were Marines. And neither had it in his DNA to back down from a fight—good, bad, or indifferent—when the opportunity presented itself.

Such an opportunity arose one evening outside a latrine when Kearns and Jones hustled up simultaneously. With a gratuitous bow and patronizingly exaggerated wave of the arm, Kearns gave out a haughty, "After you, blood."

Jones stiffened and marched up to Kearns. Jones was mean and big, and his opponent was mean and bigger, but that was of no consequence to either man. Jones' head tilted upward and Kearns' downward, and they squared off in confrontation, not of tempers flaring but of fury igniting.

"I'm not your blood!" Jones snarled.

"I beg your pardon. Blood," Kearns barked in retort.

That they did not come to blows that night remained a friendly bone of contention in the decades that followed. Father Thomas maintained that the intercession of a nearby chaplain stopped him from sending Dex to the infirmary. His counterpart recalled that chow time intervened and that "who did you say would have been the one laid out?" The angry exchange of so long ago in a place so distant in miles and circumstance gave way to what could only be described as a divinely directed truce sparked a month later when the two returned from a catastrophic search-and-destroy mission and ended up seeking and finding in each other a shred of sanity amid the insanity of killing. And that small measure of discovered humanity blossomed into an abiding friendship and love over the ensuing decades.

None of that mattered, or better, all of that mattered, now that their relationship was near its end, at least in this world, when Father Thomas arrived at the VA hospital and entered a new jungle in Room 210. Monitors and wires and contraptions of medical technology, for all their sophistication, declared an irreversible reality: Dexter Jones' health was failing, and rapidly.

His arm rose weakly. "Thanks for coming. Blood."

Father Thomas smiled. "Thanks for asking. Blood."

Dex smiled back.

After an embrace and a salute, they kept each other company holding hands in silence, one lapsing in and out of consciousness, the other on duty at bedside, praying and contemplating. The end and beginning arrived at 6:01 a.m., after the dark yielded to the light in the cool of a new day, an altogether fitting time of passage, Father Thomas would tell those others grieving.

Hours and a catnap later, the priest sat in a corner of the hospital cafeteria nursing a large cup of coffee and reading from Psalms. No one is disgraced who waits for you, but only those who are treacherous without cause. Make known to me your ways, Lord, teach me your paths. Guide me…

A tap on the shoulder interrupted his prayer. "Pardon me. Father Thomas?"

He looked up.

Simeon Walker had recently celebrated forty-eight, looked thirty-eight, and lived with the energy of twenty-eight. If a fashion magazine issued a call for workmen models, it need look no further than he who reported in rugged boots, pale jeans with a slight tear on the wallet pocket, and a black and white checkered shirt, sincerity of character a bonus.

None of that mattered here. Simeon stood motionless, eyes cast down and rimmed with tears.

"The nurse told me I could find you here. I knew Dexter." He introduced himself.

"Please sit with me," Father Thomas said. "Can I get you something?"

The man produced a supertanker soft drink. "I'm fine, thanks. I know you were also a friend of Dexter's."

"A very good friend, yes."

"Dexter and I worked together running a food kitchen here in Vegas."

Father Thomas brightened. "Yes, now I place your name. Dex talked highly of you in our times together. The two of you are very blessed in your calling."

"That we are, Father, or were, I suppose."

Simeon slumped in the chair and sobbed. Father Thomas placed a gentle hand on his shoulder and after a while said, "As we miss our dear friend and cry for his passing, in time we'll be able to rejoice in our years together with him and the glory he has achieved in heaven."

Simeon wiped his eyes. "You are right, of course, but at the moment…"

"Our mourning honors him." The two sat a bit longer. Simeon promised to call Father Thomas with details of the funeral, which he did that afternoon, and extended an invitation to spend Sunday, the day before the service, at the food kitchen.

A line at the food kitchen extended along the sidewalk when Father Thomas took him up on the offer and looked in at the unremarkable storefront, green neon in the spotless window declaring

THE LORD'S KITCHEN

Tables and chatter filled the modest dining room, where singles, couples, moms, dads, kids, and teens enjoyed heaped plates of turkey, gravy, mashed potatoes, and peas.

Simeon spotted him, and the two exchanged warm greetings.

"So good of you to come. Please, let's go inside, and I'll find you a place to sit down and eat."

Father Thomas held up a hand. "No, I will take my place in line like everyone else. Or maybe I can help in some way?"

Simeon chuckled. "You may be sorry you asked. One of our servers called in sick. You have any interest in manning the gravy ladle?"

"Love to."

By mid-afternoon, the gravy was gone, along with the turkey, mashed potatoes, peas, and staff, except for Simeon and his guest worker. "Let me show you around," he offered.

Forty chairs arranged along four long tables gleamed, as did the hardwood floor, commercial appliances, and stacked pots and pans. The men conversed over plastic cups of apple juice.

"What's next for The Lord's Kitchen?" Father Thomas asked.

"We'll continue in Dexter's name and inspiration, and I'm sure with some firm guidance from above." He looked at Father Thomas. "Dexter told me about how your friendship got off to, shall we say, a rocky start."

They laughed. "It was rocky, all right, but from there on, it was as much a blessing as anyone could hope for. If I may ask, how did the two of you meet?"

"I came to Vegas from Long Beach four years ago. Broken marriage, broken heart, broken spirit. Lived here on the streets by day and in bus shelters by night. Finally tired of being hassled all the time, I settled in the dumpster area of a motel nearby this place.

The owners had kind hearts, gave me a place to stash my meager belongings and sleep there. Mornings I would sweep up debris left by the motel guests with a short-handled broom I carried with me on my backpack, and later I'd catch a donut and cup of coffee from the lobby once the breakfast hours were over."

"And then?"

"And then one day, Dexter walked past and said he'd seen me do what I did day after day and that I seemed like a responsible person. He asked if I would like to go to work for him as caretaker at his food kitchen. I'd get my meals, a room in the back, and a few bucks a week. I went with Dexter that day and have been with him ever since. That man lifted me up, showed me to God..." Walker finished in a cracking voice, "and I could never and will never be able to thank him enough."

Quiet knocking at the back door brought a pause in their conversation. Simeon went over. "Grace, so good to see you."

A stooped, white-haired woman entered, her arms not quite able to hug all the way around Simeon's waist. "I was so sorry to hear about poor Mr. Jones."

"We all were, Grace. He's with God in paradise now. Please come in and meet Father Thomas, one of his good friends."

A feeble hand extended and drowned in the priest's. "A pleasure to meet you, Father."

"And you as well, Grace."

After quick pleasantries, she announced, "I must be going, gentlemen. I just stopped by to make sure of the time and place for the funeral."

Simeon wrote the details on the back of an envelope, and the two bid goodbye. "A bunch of us will be taking the bus. See you there," she said at the door and departed as meekly as she had arrived.

Father Thomas stretched. "Been a long couple of days. Time for me to go so you can get some rest and be ready for tomorrow." As they returned to the dining room, Father Thomas smiled at the words neatly scrolled in red on the white swinging door.

Inasmuch as ye have done it unto one of the least of these My brethren,

ye have done it unto Me.

The men walked shoulder to shoulder to the front. Simeon said, "After all is said and done about Dexter's goodness and decency and contribution, he told me more than once that he responded to our Heavenly Father's calling because, beyond all his love and devotion to the Lord, the Guy Upstairs dug food. 'Look at the loaves and fishes,' he'd say. 'Twice the Lord did it. He wanted those around him to eat,' he'd say. Not only that, Jesus liked food himself, and we're not talking spiritual bread here. After the Resurrection, the Lord joined two disciples in Emmaus for supper, and later in Jerusalem with the eleven he asked 'Have ye here any meat?' Even on the shore of the Sea of Galilee, he made breakfast of fish and bread to join the apostles for a meal when they came in on their boat."

Father Thomas rubbed his forehead in amusement. "I've never

thought of things quite that way. That's Dex for you. And I do remember how much he loved to eat, too, never shying from the food fests at our Marine get-togethers."

"All of it healthy and good for you, I'm sure. And probably washed down with apple cider."

"Absolutely."

Early the next morning after an Egg McMuffin, Father Thomas hailed a taxi in hopes of spending some final alone time with his comrade before the funeral. At the cemetery, the cabby turned and asked, "Friend of yours here?"

"The best."

She waved off the bills with a "God bless" and watched until he faded from sight among the headstones.

Father Thomas took a seat on a bench at the back. An attendant wordlessly handed him a prayer card.

Dexter Jones

December 25, 1945–August 4, 2017

All of Thee Are My Neighbor

Birds talked and squirrels skittered. Any hint of a cloud or breeze was merely a rumor, and the August heat laughed at the notion of moderating. The minutes passed.

Mourners and well-wishers appeared gradually, then more and more for the graveside ceremony on the nondescript hillside. Those who arrived, a rainbow of colors and a melting pot of every ingredient imaginable, stretched out in a parade of horsepower and leg power and willpower. They came in cars and vans and buses and motorcycles and wheelchairs and on walkers and canes and crutches and foot, striding in or shuffling forward, some barely able to move, others not at all without a benefactor's push. Whatever their background or foreground, in groups or one by one, they all occupied the common ground of paying respect to a man whose mission was doing his small part to make the world a better place. From nowhere materialized a guitar, a tambourine, a violin, voices loud and soft, on key and off to produce "Go Make a Difference" in spiritual and spirited harmony.

Several addressed the crowd. One, grizzled and leaning uneasily on a hickory walking stick, pronounced with no other ado, "If anyone gives you even a cup of water because you belong to the Messiah, I assure you, that person will be rewarded." Many talked among themselves, nodding or smiling, occasionally laughing. Afterward, comforted by the Lord's oil of joy for mourning, Simeon delivered a reading from the book of Isaiah, and they departed in cars and vans and buses and motorcycles and wheelchairs and on walkers and canes and crutches and foot, striding out or shuffling back, some barely able to move, others not at all without a benefactor's push.

Simeon, his usual Monday apron dispensed with in favor of a crisp, beige suit, found Father Thomas afterward. "Can I give you a ride somewhere? I gather you've found a place to lay your head these past days."

"Very kind of you, Simeon. I've been staying at the Catholic rectory up the street from your kitchen, and I'd appreciate a ride there."

Simeon did most of the talking on the way.

"In all the years I knew him, Dexter never accepted accolades or even a pat on the back, and insisted on no acknowledgement of any kind. Helping to him meant helping in humility, in invisibility. Funny thing, every time we turn around these days, someone is being a called a hero. Once, just once, when we were cleaning up after supper, I told Dexter he was a hero to me and to these people we served. He stopped what he was doing, eyes on fire. And anyone who has crossed Dexter with eyes on fire knows that is not a comfortable sight."

Laughter rippled in the car even as melancholy tugged at Father Thomas' heart with the memory of the latrine stare down.

"'I'm no hero,' he told me," Simeon continued. "'I'm just another ant on the hill carrying my weight and doing my part.' Well, he was a mighty big ant, if you ask me. Whenever we were running low on food, he found a way. We even jokingly called him Elijah after the flour and olive oil produced for that widow woman in the book of Kings. To me, Dexter Jones was a saint."

"Amen to that. All praise to God that we knew him."

No more needed to be said. The two men hugged outside the rectory and went their separate ways without lingering. The priest hitchhiked to the city's outskirts with young newlyweds, giddy in the freshness of their love, and shortly thereafter, he caught a ride with the owner of a print supply business, who graciously dropped him off at the curb in front of Saints Peter and Paul church.

Chapter 29

Six thousand four hundred miles and eighty-eight days in his rearview mirror, all that stood between J.J and his own bed was an easy, straight shot west. And yet with home's embrace so near, he was not quite ready to bring his wanderlust to a close. One more stop had to be out there. He just did not know where.

The mission of the garage map completed, he would select this last place on the fly and up to him alone, not making it any more special or less special than the others, or even special at all. And in that lay its attraction and its charm.

After tossing and turning like the tumbleweeds Ruby had dodged on the road, he finally surrendered and checked out of his motel when dawn was still nowhere near. Hours later, outside Kingman, he veered toward Las Vegas, arriving shortly after ten and stopping at a Sonic to reflect over a footlong smothered with diced onions and sweet relish along with a large cup of water, easy on the ice.

J.J. chewed, sipped, and meditated. To this point, the places he had visited he had chosen by chance of the dart, circumstance of the past, or happenstance of the present. This last one needed something else, something different. And that was when he made up his mind.

Why not go someplace simply because he liked the name?

Next step. Find a place with a great name.

He hurried to the car for his map, a well-worn guide turned companion after these months. Spread out on the restaurant table—several curious patrons looking on as they passed by—the map contained the solution to his search but demanded that J.J. do the work. Nothing to the west appealed. Ditto south, and he was not about to retrace his steps and head east. That left but one direction. He traced the map's gray sliver up, up, finally stopping and pointing, not certain of the dot's pronunciation but dead certain that it was his destination.

Tonopah.

In high gear, off he went, heading north, window open a notch, AC on just enough for effect.

The scenery alone made the trip a winner, the landscape a non-stop fascination of sagebrush, sand, dust devils, and Joshua trees, distant mountains shimmering in blue. Along the way, he passed historical markers of events and characters long since passed and forgotten, shuttered shacks and rusted trailers in stretches once home to civilization and now only to the elements and occasional vagrants. Mostly, the wildlife kept J.J. company, the family of burros kicking back at a watering hole, a solitary coyote dashing across the road. A cathouse appeared on the side of the road, its banner snapping in the wind:

TRUCKERS WELCOME

The sign's discretion amused J.J. because he imagined it could have advertised:

HUSBANDS AND RV GRANDPAS WELCOME

So majestic was the drive that J.J. felt almost sad upon arrival just over three hours later, and he even toyed with the idea of turning around and doing it all over again. But as with every stop along the way, he had come for a reason, uncommon as this one may be, and was determined to see it through. Without further thought or wavering, J.J. checked in at a motel on the outskirts of Tonopah and there asked a local the question that had gnawed at him ever since Las Vegas.

"How do you pronounce the name of this town?"

He scored the answer, with a little help from the local man, on his second try.

TOHN-uh-pah

Satisfied, he set off on foot.

Unarmed with any of his usual advance internet research to guide him, he aimed for the main drag. On a side street just shy of it, he passed a plastic bench on which sat a woman in turquoise sweat pants, an orange and yellow flowered blouse, a wide straw hat, and hiking boots with frayed, mismatched laces. Her bronze, leathery features were a byproduct of decades-long oneness with the desert climate.

"How are you today, ma'am?" he asked politely.

"Maintaining," she answered impolitely. "How does it look like I am?"

J.J. started to walk on.

"Hey stranger," called out the woman's throaty voice, "is there a bus that goes east? Colorado is east from here, isn't it?"

He returned. "Yes, ma'am, Colorado is east of Nevada, but you have to travel through Utah first." He took a shot at some levity. "That is, unless you go as the crow flies."

"Huh? I ain't no crow. And what's this Utah? Never heard of it. I just want to go to Colorado."

"Greyhound can take you there. I'm not from around here, so I don't know where the station is."

"I don't like Greyhound."

"It might be your only choice."

"Who cares? I'm thirsty. Do you know where I can get something to drink?" She accepted his unopened bottle of water, unscrewed the cap, and put it down without drinking. "I don't like this, it smells funny. Hey, where can I get a bus to take me east?"

J.J. got off the merry-go-round and set off anew. Around the corner, he happened on a half-filled parking lot, whose bold sign nailed to a heavy post barked in black:

NO LOITERING

NO ROLLERBLADING

NO SKATEBOARDING

NO BICYCLING

There being sufficient room at the bottom, a tagger post scrawled in red spray:

NO BREATHING

Not among the unfortunates afflicted with phasmophobia, he asked a kid on a bike if he knew where the Mizpah Hotel was. "Sure do, mister," replied the boy, "but you don't want to go there."

"Why not," J.J. asked.

"It's filled with ghosts!" the kid said and sped off in the opposite direction.

J.J. arrived soon thereafter, actually wanting to see the hotel partly because of the glittering accolades as a place to browse, spend a night or two, and enjoy a fine meal, but more to see for himself if the stories of ghosts in residence were true. A visit of thirty minutes convinced him of the acclaim but forced him to take the tales of the supernatural on faith.

Which brought him to his next stop.

Thirsty from his afternoon sightseeing, he spied a casino/hotel/RV park that he figured had to contain a place to quench it, and perhaps something more. During his college years, J.J. picked up the pleasantly peculiar habit of checking coin return slots in vending machines and pay phones whenever he passed by. Graduation did not end the quirk, and the quarters, nickels, and dimes added up with regularity, allowing him to use his findings to indulge in a modest dinner every New Year's Eve somewhere in the Greater Los Angeles area. On this trip alone, he had collected to date $11.85; his best single score was three dimes and a nickel from a candy dispensary at a rest stop. But that was before he walked past the disinterested Tonopah casino patrons who had nowhere to go or, if headed somewhere, were in no hurry to get there, absently playing slots.

The temptation of hitting three cherries did not lure J.J. in the least on his path to the beverage machine, which delivered two-fold: a forgotten, unopened 20-ounce Coca-Cola and four shiny quarters that jingled in his pocket when he stood back on the street. After retrieving the rest of his booty back at the motel, he looked around for a place to squander his now $12.85

Which brought him to Augie's Barber Shop.

Surveying himself in the storefront window, he realized these weeks away had left him shaggy, and he reasoned that getting a haircut now would not be like stepping out on the longstanding Lilah and her salon back home. What better place than the here and now to spend this found money?

Perhaps reading his thoughts or just wanting company, the barber opened the door and motioned. "Come on inside and sit a spell, friend."

In uniform of brown suspenders, white dress shirt, black trousers, and spit-polish wingtips, the barber had pinkish jowls, a slightly hunched back, and a dark mane swept back with not a hair out of place. Augie had a gentle and jolly way about him that made a stranger feel instantly at ease. The business, like its proprietor, carried not a hint of pretension. The shop was a model of simplicity, one chair for the work at hand accompanied by two for waiting customers and a thrift store cast-off reserved for Augie's leisure time. A 2017 San Francisco 49ers calendar was tacked to the wall opposite the mirror, and the other wall was empty except for a small crucifix.

J.J. told his name and settled in. "Wild guess," he said. "You are Augie?"

"At your service."

"Square it in the back, please, and short on the top and sides."

"You've got it."

"Augie, an uncommon name and a good one," J.J. said.

"My parents named me for the month I was born. I have a sister, June. We used to laugh and joke, 'Thank God we weren't born in something like February or November.'"

The men laughed, and Augie's soft, silver eyes twinkled with the spoken memory of his mom and dad.

Augie barbered.

"What have you seen of our fair city so far?" Augie asked after J.J. explained that he was a visitor to town.

J.J. told of his looking for ghosts but spared him the story of the woman in turquoise or the parking lot.

"For a burg of a couple thousand souls and change, we have some pretty neat things. There's a huge mining park, a pretty cool museum, at night there's some spectacular stargazing, and perched in front of the hardware store is an old-timer named Harold. He sits day after day just happy to be there and greets everyone with a hello and a smile. His cheer is reason enough to walk by."

"I'll try to check them out. Especially Harold."

J.J. looked left then right as best he could without moving his head, and repeated, squinting into the mirror to see the wall behind him to make certain of a peculiarity that had dawned on him. No price lists were posted.

"By the way, Augie, how much is this gonna cost me?"

"I wondered when you would ask. There's no charge."

"I beg your pardon?"

"Two years ago, a fella came in here, got his haircut, and prepared to pay me with a few rumpled bills and an assortment of change, mostly pennies and nickels. It was obvious this guy had very little and undoubtedly panhandled and sidewalk surfed to scare up some dough so he could make himself feel human again. Well, I didn't have the heart to charge him, and that night I figured, why not let everybody get their hair cut for free? I've been doing it ever since. And if anyone does want to pay something, there's an empty gallon pickle jar I put in back and give the money to the local food bank."

A passerby in olive green T-shirt inscribed *Violence Is Ignorance* stopped, cupped his hands, looked in the window, waved, and left. Augie waved back.

"If you don't charge, how do you support yourself?"

"God, Social Security, and the stock market provide."

"I suppose so. But what do your competitors in town think about this?"

"I like to believe we're one big, happy family. And if anyone minds, I've never heard about it."

Augie barbered.

"If you don't mind my asking, what brings you to town?"

J.J. answered in twenty-five words or less.

The barber chuckled. "I do something like your trip myself, but on a much smaller scale every year."

"Do tell."

"To make a short story long, the missus loved road trips to spend time with relatives, and during our time together, we hit places in our RV all over. Little Chute, Wilkes-Barre, Murfreesboro, even up to Wasilla once to visit a distant cousin. I always knew she was plotting something when I'd catch her poring over a map of the USA. 'Another F-bomb, dear?' I'd ask. I can still hear her answer back in that sweet voice, 'Yes, beloved, another F-bomb.'"

"F-bomb?"

"Family."

"That's a good one."

Augie stopped barbering.

"After my sweetheart, bless her heart, went home to God sixteen years ago, I thought of selling the RV, me being a more solitary sort than she. But I decided, in her memory, that wouldn't be right."

"You don't seem solitary at all."

He chuckled. "You'd be surprised. After being here and talking with customers six days a week, I do like quiet time."

A panel truck passed, horn honked in greeting. Augie raised a high five. He resumed barbering.

"Well, the year after my wife passed, I was watching the Super Bowl. It was in New Orleans, and, man, can you believe Tom Brady was the winning quarterback? The guy may never leave. Anyway, I said to myself that it would be fun to visit there and travel around Louisiana. I thought about it some more, and the next day went to the AAA, got a map of the state, and mounted it on a piece of construction paper."

J.J. jerked his head.

"Easy fella, you'll lose an ear."

"Sorry."

"So I took out a felt tip pen, closed my eyes, and made a dot on the map. The city marked by the dot or the nearest one to it is where I started my trip. I drove to Louisiana shortly thereafter, traveled all over the state for two weeks, and loved it so much I've done the same thing every year since, making it my routine to always set out on the Monday after the game. My Agnes would be very proud."

J.J. couldn't help smiling. "I'm sure she is."

Augie observed him in the mirror. "Without getting into anything too heavy or profound, what have you found on your travels?"

"I don't know how profound it is, but a friend back home says people should see beyond themselves and look for something good. That it really is all around if we'll take the time to seek it out. That was what I set out to do back in June."

"And?"

"I've done exactly that on this trip and have had the time of my life."

"My friend, I applaud you."

"How about yourself? Any blockbusters from your travels?"

He answered without missing a beat. "All I can say is that I've been at this shop for many years and looked out the window watching couples and families walk by and telling myself how fortunate I've been to grow up in Tonopah, meet a nice girl in high school, marry her, and settle down here."

The barber pulled up a chair.

"It may sound strange, but I believe I could have been equally content in many of the cities Agnes and I visited together or that I have been to alone since. My point is, we can find the good, as you put it, far from our roots or in our backyard. All we need to do is look, really. And what counts is what we make of ourselves wherever we choose to be."

Their conversation continued awhile until another customer came in, sat down, announced, "No rush," and opened his newspaper.

After a last trimming around the edges and a souvenir comb offered and accepted, J.J. added his $12.85 to the stuffed pickle jar on the way out.

He delayed out front to catch the day's declining rays before moving up the street, trading a hello with Harold, and stopping into a restaurant where the harried waitress struggled to keep up with the supper crowd. "Be right with you, sir," she said and handed him a menu.

She returned shortly. "Sorry for the wait. What can I get you?"

"I'd just like a glass of water, please."

"Surely. Anything else?"

"No, that's it."

Moments later she brought the water without word of complaint or attitude of irritation.

"What's the charge?" he asked.

The woman's laugh was genuine. "For water? It's nice to know a few things in life are still free."

After she went to another table, he quickly drank his water, put a twenty and a five under the empty glass and left.

J.J. walked with spring in his step the last few blocks to his motel. Tonopah had given him all he could have hoped for and more, and there was no need to linger. It was time to go home.

Out of confusion or concern, the receptionist did not understand when he asked to check out early.

"But you haven't spent the night. Is anything wrong with the room?"

"No, it's perfectly fine. I'm just ready to leave."

"Okay then, if you're sure. Allow me a minute to cancel your credit card billing."

"No, please don't. Keep it to pay forward for someone who

comes in short."

Her eyes widened. "That is very kind. Thank you so much and safe travels."

At the car, J.J. breathed in deeply, and along the drive back to where it all began, he allowed himself a single mini-mart break for a soft drink and beef taco grande.

A full moon's glow mingled with the stars when he closed his garage door and turned on the kitchen light a little before two.

Chapter 30

Hand off nine days away, fall was in the air, summer in denial. J.J. rose with the dawn, the night surrendering to a radiant sky of lavender and pink, and he shrugged off any fatigue that dared lurk after his short sleep.

It felt good to be home.

He rubbed his eyes and prepared to pick up the pieces from three months on the road. First things first, however. He walked through every room in his house, beloved like never before, then did so a second time. Somehow the place felt larger. As it turned out, aside from the large cardboard box filled with his accumulated mail, the old homestead looked as if he had just returned from a drive around the block. He seized the opportunity to relax and savor all that he had accomplished.

Lounging on the lawn chair in the garage, fresh cup of coffee in hand, he gave himself an *atta boy* and underlined it with a final entry in his daily calendar.

Mom and Dad and Charlie, I did it!

He tapped the page and, eyes wandering, noticed the map on the wall, pushpins in place save two that had fallen to the floor. Then the real fun began. On the floor, he lined up the keepsakes from his travels in chronological order and examined them one by one.

Ceramic church bell from Juanita's shop.

Laminated ID from Bobby's school.

Menu from Yellowstone cafeteria.

"Are you home, J.J.?" interrupted a voice from the front door. J.J. returned to the house where Sahil greeted him with smile wide and arms stretched wider.

"Welcome home, my dear friend." He surveyed J.J. "You don't look any the worse for all of your time on the road. Indeed, I have never seen you looking better."

They talked a few minutes before Sahil hustled off to work, and J.J. called out a promise to bring over gifts later.

He went back to the garage. The lineup resumed.

Gideon Bible from Billings motel.

Porcelain Santa from Marie Beatrice etcetera.

Program from Milwaukee baseball game.

Plastic bottle, half-filled with sand from Lake Michigan.

Ticket stub from Greyhound bus ride.

Goodbye note from Rebecca and refrigerator magnet from Christmas Story Museum.

Twig from Lebanon park.

Plastic ornament of Arkansas capitol.

Another goodbye note, this one from Magda, and refrigerator magnet from the Alamo.

"Lucky's Night at the Movies" flyer.

Embossed comb from Augie's Barber Shop.

J.J. placed each of the items in a curio cabinet he had once picked up at a rummage sale but which sat empty in the garage ever since, and he positioned the cabinet directly below the pinned map.

Many years from this day, a group of mourning parishioners from Saints Peter and Paul would gather at J.J.'s house to go through and distribute his things, among them in the garage, the fourteen cherished memories of his trip, treasures to the end and meticulously maintained in the curio cabinet, kept company by the long-faded map and colored pushpins affixed to the wall.

Stopping for nothing more than to refill his coffee and catch his breath, J.J. went next to assault the months-long mound of mail, and in doing so, uncovered two delightful surprises. Under a batch of solicitations and whatnot was the postcard from Wisconsin Dells that Sahil had told him about on the phone call back in August. He snatched it up.

Welcome Home, Fred Astaire.

Love,

Marie Beatrice Claire Elizabeth Ruth Julietta Paulina Josephine Esmeralda

(I added two more. Hope you like them!)

Lower in the pile leaped out an Amazon package encasing a book whose title induced a bittersweet smile, more sweet, to be sure, than bitter, of remembrance. *God Is Red: A Native View of Religion.* He kept the attached note for a bookmark.

You guys on the grid aren't all that hard to find.

Be well.

Magda

Precious pieces of mail put aside lest they be accidentally tossed with the recyclables, the sorting continued.

By the time J.J. returned to the garage and to his life, Father Thomas had been back for weeks, joyfully picking up with his parish where he had left them. Filled with a bounty of new inspiration for his Sunday messages, in his first he declared, "As Christians, ours is not to focus on high and mighty deeds and expect high and mighty effects and accolades but to serve and do good among the lowly and unesteemed, where blessings meet with no fanfare. Look to Bartimaeus, a blind beggar. After the Lord's miracle of restoring his sight, the Bible does not go on to say the crowd applauded, but simply that Bartimaeus followed him." The sermon's closing inspiration, "My dear brothers and sisters, let us never grow tired of serving and doing good," became a signature line at his Masses from that day forward.

Soon after Father Thomas resumed his pastoral duties, among the Sunday faithful who greeted him were Roberto, Veronica, and Emily. A fortnight later, when the church emptied after weekday Mass, a woman approached out of the shadows.

"Do you remember me?"

Father Thomas did not hesitate. "I do, indeed. Christine, is it not?"

Her face lit up like the sun in the morning sky. "My goodness, yes!" He and she walked together down the front path. "You know," she confided, "after we parted that day on the highway, I did some serious thinking and ended up driving straight through to LA. I found a shelter for battered women, got counseling and financial help, and now I have a part-time job. I'm even working on getting my GED. It's not much, but it's a start."

He put his hands on her shoulders. "It's a wonderful start, Christine. And I hope you'll consider joining us here. Our church has much to offer, and you have much to offer in return."

"Thank you."

If all good things come in threes, an afternoon in his church office made it so when a call came through from Ashraf.

"Father Thomas, I am happy to say Aleah and I and our two boys made it back safe and sound."

"Wonderful to hear from you," Father Thomas said. "I'm so glad you and your family are well."

Ashraf said, "I do believe you put the fear of the Almighty, both yours and ours, into those bullies back there that morning at the rest area. We never saw them again, and I hope they went away changed young men."

Father Thomas had his doubts but said nothing.

After a bit of lighter conversation, Ashraf extended an invitation to the restaurant he and his family owned in San Diego, along with a pledge of lifetime meals on the house, an offer the priest found impossible to pass up and accepted for the initial time three days later.

While maintaining his weekly calling to search and spread joy aboard the public transit system, his life of mission became enriched in new ways. One of them was volunteering Sunday afternoons at a food kitchen in memory of his friend Dex. There were moments of sadness to be sure, but Dex's passing did not overwhelm Father Thomas with sorrow. Rather it left a glow at having known him and a confidence that he was resting in the arms of the Lord. And whenever the spirit might waver, there were phone conversations with Simeon to rejuvenate and restore either or both of them.

The mealtimes at Feed My Lambs presented another opportunity. Accompanying the rattling of dishes and discourse, he tried his voice and violin. As the weeks went on, sometimes a few dozen or more joined in the singing.

During his time in the Word every night, Father Thomas practiced an equally fervent new calling that harkened back to one afternoon on his way home when he was scanning the horizon for a good Samaritan willing to befriend a hulking solitary hitchhiker. A small, white, wooden cross, chipped by weather and years, caught his eye, block letters in black paint inscribed

RICHARD SIMON

February 23, 2012

A touch of wind had ruffled the roadside vegetation and went away as suddenly as it arrived, leaving the priest alone with the simple handmade memorial to a man or boy about whom he would never know age or circumstance. For that matter, Richard Simon maybe was not even a first and a last name but a first and a middle, leaving the surname unspoken out here between the earth and the sky.

All things being equal, a life and death deserve better than a makeshift piece of lumber located on the way to somewhere else. But all things are not equal and never will be, and Father Thomas did what he could for Richard Simon, kneeling at the cross in prayer and recognition of one unknown to him. The remainder of the day passed in the bed of a pickup truck driven by an itinerant welder, but the incident stayed with him and then struck a chord back on his home turf.

Over coffee one morning looking through the newspaper obituaries, he was stopped by a death notice, two lines of black in a sea of type and ink that, like Richard Simon's marker, stood out not for what they said but for what they didn't. No word of age or circumstance, of a life well lived or of a death by despair. He immediately went to cut out the notice and paste it in his prayer book, and at day's end, he knelt in prayer as he had on that lonesome landscape, a stranger reaching out in spirituality and fellowship. "Dear Lord, if there is no one else to mourn or remember this soul passed to new life, let it be me."

His new ministry of anonymity, as he liked to call it, built up clipping by clipping, as did tending to the growing flock at Saints Peter and Paul and beyond. And evermore enriching and blessing him was the discovered and rediscovered family he had kept at arm's length for so long, sinfully acting out as a hearer of the Word and not a doer, declaring devotion to Christ with everyone else while failing to manifest it with those closest to him. Determined to make up for lost time, attention, and obedience, every day without fail, Father Thomas called his mom—or she him—brother and sister chiming in from time to time, with news or prayer requests or talking about the Cubs.

Once when Doris attempted to choke out a tearful apology for failing him back in his days of youth and rebellion, her son would not hear of it.

"We're past finding fault in each other, Mom. In the eyes of the Lord, his people are not ones of failure but of shortcomings that he constantly forgives. He welcomes us back into his arms with love and compassion. Let's never again talk of failure but, instead, rejoice in the love and warmth we have found with each other."

There were no J.J. sightings, however, as the calendar flipped through August and then to September, and Friday confessionals and Sunday Masses came and went. He never strayed far from the priest's mind, knowing from his long experience in the pulpit that parishioners drifted in and out, moved, or found another local church. He prayed that, wherever J.J. may be, he was at peace. If they were to meet again, Father Thomas knew, it would be, as his church's namesake, Saint Paul, penned in divinely inspired words of Scripture to the Romans. "All things work for good for those who love God."

The phone rang on his first Wednesday back home, and the call drew J.J. from a deep sleep that refused to be denied despite his best efforts to keep it at bay.

"Mr. Werth?"

He perked up quickly at the sound of the voice.

"Hiya, Bobby, how are you?"

The two had exchanged a handful of text messages since J.J. had departed Lovelock back in July, and lately the possibility was floated of the boy and his grandparents coming to Los Angeles to visit.

"I'm fine, and my grandma and grandpa are too. I was wondering…"

"Yes?"

Today the idea would take form.

"I was wondering," Bobby's excitement evident and building, "when can we come out to see you?"

"I guess anytime it works out for you guys. Why not put your grandpa or grandma on the phone and we'll talk about it?"

A fifteen-minute conversation with Lily ended with her, Chester, and Bobby scheduled for a three-day trip to Los Angeles the week after Thanksgiving.

"Can't wait!" Bobby said. "You'll take us to Disneyland?"

"And Universal Studios and Hollywood too."

After hanging up, J.J. surprised himself by actually looking forward to having guests overnight at his house. A man's home may be his castle, but you've got to lower the drawbridge every once in a while. *Who knows*, the thought entered his mind, *I might even invite Father Thomas over sometime for a bratwurst fry out.*

In the days that followed, J.J. fell back into his merry routine, climbing aboard the Disneyland Railroad, tripping to Tinseltown to people-watch and track down a sausage sandwich from a sidewalk vendor, taking in a movie, and watching the sports channels in the company of chili, potato chips, and a TV table. With no work schedule to hold him back, he branched out into new haunts as well, discovering the beauty of the Getty Center and strolling through the tranquility of the Huntington Botanical Gardens. Which brought him to a weekend and one activity that stood out above all.

The Dodgers were in town for their last home stand of the regular season and, playoffs notwithstanding, the void of the long off-season loomed like a wintry cloud. Watching Saturday's game from the confines of his living room couch tasted as palatable as that slice of blueberry pie. Determined to absorb every minute of his Chavez Ravine finale, J.J. arrived as the gates opened two hours before game time and, hot dog and beer in hand, settled in at his customary spot in the left field bleachers. The evening turned crisp, the crowd grew animated, and, in the bottom of the fourth inning, he went to stretch his legs and get a drink of water.

When he returned from the concourse, a familiar figure had joined his row in the stands. Father Thomas stood at J.J.'s approach. After exchanging heartfelt expressions of gladness at re-uniting, they nodded in recognition of more to say and much more to tell.

But that could wait for another time.

The two men sat side by side and shared in the applause of a base hit. People all around chitchatted in good humor, and somewhere a transistor radio played.

"Beautiful night for a ballgame, isn't it, my brother?" From above, four seagulls circled and alighted on the field of green.

"That it is, Father. That it is."

~

This book is a work of fiction. All names, characters, and events are products of the author's imagination. Any resemblance to actual events, places, or people living or dead is coincidental.

Made in the USA
Las Vegas, NV
03 October 2023

78505218R00193